THE LONG ROAD HOME

by
Robert Capko

A John Paxton Series Novel

Published by Class VI Publishing

THE LONG ROAD HOME

First Edition

ISBN 978-0-9895374-1-4

This book is available in ebook format from most online retailers.

ALSO BY ROBERT CAPKO
Say Goodbye

Praise for *Say Goodbye*

"Finally, a thrilling true-to-life novel about America's ultra-elite but largely unsung special operations force, the Air Force Pararescuemen."

– Matthew Bracken, former Navy SEAL and author of the *Enemies Foreign And Domestic* series.

"Great fast paced book...Seemingly realistic and accurate... I'd also recommend [Say Goodbye] to any fans of classic Tom Clancy."

– Matt D. Williams, Author of *Jak Phoenix*

"My advice...get a lot of sleep the night before you read the book, because you'll be going to bed late the day you start reading it...you will **NOT** be able to put it down!"

– Chief Master Sergeant (USAF Retired) Bill "D"

"Robert Capko has written a military novel reminiscent of Tom Clancy but more accessible–both in length and in laying out the story in a timely manner."

– Davilynn Furlow, Great Books Under $5.

"Military and National Security drama enthusiasts have found a new hero in SMSgt. John Paxton. From life and death at 50,000 feet to door busting close combat, from cloak and dagger mystery to raw human survival this book has something for everyone and you will not want to put it down."

– Chon Gann, Medical, Security,
   and Intelligence Professional

Acknowledgments

I thank my story editor, Michele Bardsley, and my copy editors Davilynn and Bill Furlow. Any mistakes remaining are purely because I was too stubborn to follow their good advice. I also thank the following, in no particular order, for their numerous and invaluable contributions to this project: Maggie Benko, Jennifer MacDonald, Andy Warren, Michael Perry, Jean Jacobs, Pat Goodwine, Cathy Jo Williams, Kristin Merrifield, Paula Cain, Matthew Bracken, CMSgt. William D'Avanzo, USAF (Ret), Caylen C. Perry, USAF (Ret), Explosive Ordnance Disposal, KC Cali, Chon Gann, Dr. Michael Brooks, Joe Helme, Rick Henson, Melody Yates, Jonathan Aponte, Mark Williamson, Nick Capko, Talitha McEachin, and Denis Bourgeois. All the things you like about this book are directly attributable to them; I am solely responsible for everything else. Finally, I cannot thank enough, the United States Military.

On a personal note, I also want to thank Deacon Connie along with the doctors, nurses and respiratory therapists who helped save my son's life. You are God's hands.

— *Robert Capko*

For my wonderful sons,
Justin, Zack, Grayson and Alex

"Never Quit!"

−Sign above the door at the Pararescue School

CHAPTER 1

HEADQUARTERS 255th RESCUE SQUADRON
BRINDISI AIRBASE, ITALY
Spring 1999

Senior Master Sergeant John Paxton climbed out
the window of Colonel Hicks's office.

The demise of the massive U.S. Air Force C-17 Globemaster
III cargo jet wasn't entirely his fault, but that meant nothing to
the security police (SP) officer standing outside the door waiting to haul him away. Then, again, there was that little problem
with McMurphy.

McMurphy!

Paxton wished he had never met that asshole.

If he hadn't, he wouldn't be facing charges of attempting
to murder McMurphy. The plane was gone. McMurphy was
missing. There wasn't anything he could do about either situation. But there *was* something he could do to clean up another

mess. But he had to first avoid arrest---thus his unusual choice of an exit.

Colonel Hicks, the commander of pararescuemen of the 255th Rescue Squadron, had left him alone in his office, even though he had just met Paxton, to give him the privacy to make just one phone call—to his wife Jill. He'd finally got to call her after being denied for so long. He finally got to say goodbye.

And now it was time to leave.

Before Paxton had opened the window, he'd grabbed the electronic device belonging to Major General Reed. It had been left on Hicks's desk. He'd shoved it back into the ratty green backpack and put the pack on his back.

Halfway out the window, Paxton looked left and right and, seeing no one, jumped down to the concrete tarmac outside the hangar that housed the 255th Rescue Squadron. He turned around to close the window. He decided against it, not wanting to make any unnecessary noise. He made his way around the backside of the metal hangar keeping his left shoulder close to the building. Time was short, so he had to move quickly.

Paxton approached a corner and stopped to peer around it. Nobody there. He went around the corner and ran the length of the hangar. Then he stopped and peered around the next corner. A dark gray Pave Hawk helicopter faced him on the tarmac. Through the cockpit windows he could clearly see the two Air Force pilots sitting at the controls. No obstacles were visible between Paxton and the helicopter.

He ran for the Pave Hawk as fast as he could. As he ran, sharp pain radiated from his wounded left knee. Sergeant Smith had done a fine job of field stitching the wound closed, but because of events over the past few days, Paxton managed to rip out all but a few of the stitches.

As soon as the Pave Hawk pilots saw the man running toward them, they did exactly what Colonel Hicks had told them to do.

They started the engine.

Paxton wore a bloody and torn Battle Dress Uniform (BDUs) with a cut and pattern unlike anything in the United States military. His uniform was bereft of any name, rank or unit identification. There was nothing on it to indicate that he was a decorated Air Force pararescueman. Indeed there was nothing on it indicating he was with any nation's armed forces, let alone the United States'.

The helicopter's rotor blades began to move. They rotated slowly at first, but continued to gain speed as Paxton closed the remaining distance.

As Paxton passed the last metal wall of the hangar and emerged into the open, he could see the rest of the tarmac. To his left was the security police officer's sedan, its blue strobes flashing. Farther to his left, near the large hangar doors, stood the police officer with his back to the helicopter. He was occupied with what appeared to be an animated conversation with both Colonel Hicks and Major General Reed. Hicks and Reed were facing Paxton but showed no indication that they saw him running like hell toward the helicopter.

Pacing back and forth in the space between Paxton's path and the police officer's back was Captain Marshall, General

Reed's aide. He was engaged in an animated conversation on his cell phone, a feat made that much more difficult by the sharp increase in noise emanating from the helicopter's engine and rotor blades. He didn't seem to notice Paxton.

Paxton picked up the pace. He was almost to the helicopter. The pilots split their attention between watching him approach, watching the group around the policeman, and watching the instruments in the cockpit. If they felt any tension, they didn't show it.

Paxton ran alongside the helicopter's port side, using its fuselage as cover. He hopped into the open sliding door and landed heavily on his bottom. He then slapped the bulkhead twice and shouted, "Let's go!"

The pilot twisted the throttle to full, and the engine whine increased exponentially. Paxton got up, turned around, and plopped into one of the seats facing forward. As he pulled on his lap belt, he looked out the open starboard door. The policeman was still talking to the officers. Paxton scanned the rest of the scene.

Movement in the backseat of the police sedan caught his attention. Someone was looking through the back window right at him. He immediately recognized the face.

Smith!

At first, Paxton didn't comprehend what he was seeing. *What the hell was Sergeant Octavious Smith doing in the back of the security police car?*

The Pave Hawk helicopter lurched forward slightly. It was taking off.

Smith needed his help.

Paxton unbuckled his lap belt as the rear of the helicopter lifted off the ground. Paxton pitched forward and almost fell out of the open door.

"No! Wait!" he shouted, even though there was no way the pilots could hear him. He reached up and pounded on the bulkhead again and then turned and leaped out of the open door.

His boots smacked onto the concrete, and he bent his knees to absorb the impact. Pain vibrated in his shins. He regained his balance and ran toward the police car.

The absurd sight of Paxton's leaping from the helicopter as it took off apparently caught General Reed's attention because he stopped speaking in mid-sentence and looked over. The security policeman turned to see what had gotten the general's attention. Paxton reached the back door of the car and yanked it open. "Smith! What the hell are you doing in here?"

The young, black pararescueman looked at Paxton, his hands zip tied behind his back. "I'm charged with insubordination in the field and assault and battery on an officer."

Paxton lifted his brows.

"They didn't like when I kicked the pistol out of Major Thompson's hand."

"This is bullshit. Look I think I can get ya out of this, but I've gotta explain what's going on."

"You know what's going on?"

The helicopter pilot in the right seat had evidently seen Paxton hop out and run to the car because he eased the copter back down. Its rotor blades were still a blur.

Paxton glanced back at the copter. The pilot had his hands open and out waving them in a gesture that politely translated to *what are you doing, idiot*?

Paxton then looked up in front of him, across the roof of the police car, and saw the security police officer walking toward him with long strides, his hand on his pistol. Reed and Hicks were trying to catch up with him.

"There's no time to explain. Come with me," Paxton said as he pulled on Smith's arm.

He shook his head. "Pax, I'm in enough trouble already."

Paxton gauged the distance between the car and the approaching policeman. "Now dammit!"

Smith looked up at Paxton. "I hope the hell you know what you're doing." He scooted to the open door, and Paxton helped his former student out.

"Let's go!" Paxton ran toward the helicopter with Smith right behind him. They were slowed by the fact that Smith's hands were tied behind his back.

Seeing the men running, the security policeman pulled his pistol from its holster. He leveled it on the men and shouted, "Halt!"

Paxton and Smith couldn't hear him over the noise of the Pave Hawk. They continued toward the open door.

Captain Marshall stepped up and blocked the police officer's view. "Don't do that, Airman."

"Get out of my way!"

"Lower the gun, Airman," Colonel Hicks demanded as he stepped beside the policeman.

The young policeman looked at Marshall and then at Hicks. His arms were still outstretched, pistol level.

"Listen to the colonel, son," General Reed said as he walked to the other side of the policeman.

The officer looked at Reed, saw the two stars on his uniform, and slowly lowered his gun.

"This never happened," Reed continued. "You will go back to your station and report to your Flight Chief that you were unable to locate either Sergeant Smith or Sergeant Paxton."

The policeman stood slack-jawed, pistol at his side.

Across the tarmac, Paxton helped Smith onto the helicopter and then climbed aboard himself. The Pave Hawk took off once again as Paxton fastened Smith's lap belt and then looked around for a medical kit. He located one and used a pair of scissors from it to cut off the tie-wraps that secured Smith's wrists. He then sat down, buckled in, and both men donned headphones to make communication possible.

"You're one crazy son-of-a-bitch, Pax."

"Don't worry. This time the stars are on my side."

"I sure hope so. I don't like breaking rocks." Smith looked out at the ground falling away. "Where the hell are we going, anyway?"

"Yugoslavia."

"*What?* We're going back?"

"Afraid so."

"Shit."

"What?"

"I should have stayed in the police car."

CHAPTER 2

On an isolated mountain road in Yugoslavia

TWO PICKUP TRUCKS THAT APPEARED TO BE HELD together by rust rolled to a stop, one in front of the other, near the wreckage in the middle of the mountain road. Armed men rode in the truck beds. Droshny, the driver of the lead truck, pulled up the parking brake, and his door squawked as he pushed it open. He unfolded himself from the front seat and stood behind the open door surveying the scene. He wore green combat fatigues and a full beard.

Several of the soldiers in the backs of the pickup trucks stood to get a better view of the carnage before them. Canted across the center of the two-lane road was the wreckage of an older-model Mercedes panel truck. Some distance behind the Mercedes was a smoldering hole. Burn marks blossomed from around the hole like a dandelion. The nose of the truck faced

Droshny. The rear axle had snapped, and the chassis rested on the asphalt. Bullet holes riddled the front windshield. The driver's body was underneath the truck's door. Droshny studied the unnatural angles of the dead man's limbs.

Droshny reached into his truck and grabbed his Benelli M1 semi-automatic shotgun. The Italian-made, matte black 12-gauge featured the recoil inertia bolt system and a synthetic butt stock with an integrated pistol grip. The extended under-barrel tubular magazine was the same length as the barrel and made it look like an over-under double-barreled shotgun. Along the butt was a side-saddle carrying extra shells. He had loaded it with slugs.

He recognized the panel truck as that of his friend, Hashim. Jashari had dispatched Hashim and his team the night before to take from the Serbian army a very valuable piece of equipment hidden at a Serbian safe house. Droshny and his soldiers had been sent by Ahmed Jashari to find out why Hashim and his team never returned.

He quickly walked to the body and confirmed his fears. The dead man was, indeed, Hashim.

His face a mask of rage, Droshny motioned for one of his fellow Kosovo Liberation Army (KLA) soldiers to join him. The soldier climbed out of the pickup truck carrying his rifle and trotted over to his leader.

"Yes, sir?"

"The Americans did this."

"What do you think happened?"

Droshny pointed at the smoky crater that represented the final resting place of what was once a van full of KLA soldiers. "Smart bomb."

The soldier looked at Hashim's bullet-riddled body. "Then it strafed with its guns?"

The leader didn't answer. Instead he walked around to the back of the enclosed panel truck. One of the two doors was slightly ajar. He opened it the rest of the way and peered inside.

The smell of blood and death enveloped the man's face. Inside the dark rear compartment was a grisly scene. The bloody bodies of two men dressed in fatigues identical to his own were propped against the front wall of the truck. The head of the dead man on the right side was flopped down on his chest as if it were no longer attached to his spine. Bullet holes were splayed at random intervals across both men's chests and joined between them puncturing the metal bulkhead that separated the cargo hold from the driver's compartment. Dark red blood covered the floor and dripped out of the back onto the asphalt.

The man slammed the door. He turned around, studying the area. He considered for a moment the large crater in the road some distance behind the Mercedes. The bomb that caused that must have been at least 500 pounds—overkill. He knew that the Americans, through NATO, were engaged in Operation Allied Force, a bombing campaign aimed at stopping Serbian aggression against the KLA and the ethnic Albanians. He couldn't grasp why an ally would kill his fellow soldiers. He cursed.

The other soldier joined him at the rear of the destroyed truck. "Why would an American plane attack our vehicles?"

"The holes are too small. They look like 9mm. American planes use at least 20mm. There are no entry holes from the outside." Droshny turned to the young soldier. "That," he said pointing at the crater, "was caused by a plane. These men," he indicated the bodies in the Mercedes, "were killed by someone inside the truck."

"What does that mean?"

"It means we need to radio Jashari right away."

• • •

Smith watched the coast of the Southern tip of Italy roll away from him. The blue-green waters of the Adriatic Sea filled his view as he sat next to Paxton in the Pave Hawk helicopter. He shook his head and turned back toward the man who had made him a Pararescue Jumper (PJ). "Lemme see if I got this right. We're going back to Yugoslavia so you can give that thing back to Jashari?"

"Yes."

"But it's not a real one?"

"Of course not."

"That's why it's got a GPS tracking device in it?" Smith said referring to the Global Positioning System.

"Yes. That's how Reed tracked me back there and sent you to pick me up."

"I get that. What I don't get is *why*?"

"Well, that's where it gets interesting." Paxton said.

"What part of this mess hasn't been 'interesting?'"

"Good point. But you don't even know the half of it. How much do you know about this conflict?"

"Just what I see on television and have been told. Basically, the Serbs are the bad guys, and the KLA are the good guys."

"Well, it's a little more complicated than that."

"I gather that."

"Quick history: the Serbian government has been accused of conducting 'ethnic cleansing' against the Muslim population of Kosovo. Thousands of civilians supposedly murdered. The KLA has been fighting the Serbs, trying to break free to have their own country."

"Good for them."

"If that were the end of the story, I probably would agree. The problem is, the KLA doesn't exactly have clean hands themselves."

"Civil wars are always nasty. But I wouldn't be sitting here with you if it weren't for ours in the good ol' USA."

"I can't argue with you there. But the KLA may cause problems for us in the long term."

"How do you mean?"

"Well, they are heavily infiltrated by jihadists associated with Osama bin Laden."

Smith cursed.

"Exactly. It's the same old 'the enemy of my enemy is my friend' crap that we fall into every time." Paxton said.

"Okay, so the KLA suck. Why give them a fake device from the Stealth fighter?"

"Because Jashari wants to sell it to the Iraqis."

"Big whoop. We getting a cut?"

"Nope."

"Then what's the point?"

"The point's what the Iraqis are exchanging for the device."

"Let me guess: oil. It's always about oil."

"Try Tabun."

"Nerve gas?"

"Yes, GA." GA was the designation for Tabun.

Smith cursed again, but preceded it with an adjective indicating the sacred nature of the defecation.

"Exactly my reaction. You see why it's so important to give Jashari the package with the tracking device?"

"So we can track the KLA to the Iraqis?"

"And the nerve gas."

"Right. But why you?"

Paxton rubbed the greasy stubble growing on his face a couple of times. It had been days since he had an opportunity to shower or shave. He wished he had thought to change into a fresh pair of underwear before he left. "Because the KLA is looking for me."

"That sounds like a good reason to send someone el–." Smith stopped mid-word, a horrible thought crossing his mind. "You didn't bring me to do this job, did you?"

"No, no! I just brought you along so I could straighten everything out. You're just along for the ride. Ultimately, You're going back to Italy."

"Like hell I am. The cops are waiting for me."

"No they won't be. You were following my orders. I'll take the heat."

"Pax, um, I think you've got enough heat coming your way as it is."

"I'll worry about that when I get back. *If* I get back. This is my last mission anyway."

"So, you are getting out."

"I was thinking about it, but after the last couple of days, don't think I'll have much choice."

Smith just shook his head.

"What?" The headphones crackled slightly with Paxton's question.

"I still don't understand why you are involved in this. Why can't they send someone else and let you get back to terrorizing poor young airmen stupid enough to want to become PJs?"

"I told you, the KLA is looking for me."

"So?"

"We want the KLA to think they are getting the real device. They took it from the Serbs, and I took it from them. If they find it with someone else, they will know something's up and it will blow the whole thing."

Smith looked out the window again. He appeared to be trying to grasp what he was hearing.

"Believe me," Paxton continued, "there is no other way. The last thing in the world I want is to go back there. I killed a couple of their friends to get away. But if I don't, that nerve gas is going to disappear and likely be used in a terrorist attack on innocent people. I can't allow that. I won't allow that."

Smith turned toward Paxton. "How are you going to get the backpack to Jashari?"

"I'm going to allow myself to be captured by the KLA."

Smith was visibly shaken by Paxton's matter-of-fact announcement. "What stupid son of a bitch came up with *that* asinine idea?"

"I did."

Smith rubbed his stubble. He had gone an equal number of days without benefit of shower or razor. "Pax, you've got a helluva lot more stripes than I do and I respect you, man, but what you're proposing is way outside the PJ job description."

Paxton smiled at the young sergeant. "We train our whole career to save lives, right?"

"Yeah, but—."

"I'll be saving a whole lot of lives if we can destroy that nerve gas."

"But…"

"These things we do…."

"So others may live," Smith said, completing the pararescue motto. Smith sat in silence. "It's a suicide mission."

"I hope to hell it's not."

"How are you going to get away once you're captured?"

"I have a plan."

• • •

Droshny finished describing the scene over the radio to Jashari.

"Everyone's dead?" Jashari asked angrily.

"Yes."

"What about the American?"

"I'm pretty sure they were the ones who dropped the bomb."

"No, I mean the American Hashim grabbed from the Serbs. There were two of them, but when Hashim got there, only one remained. Hashim had followed them from the Stealth plane crash site. Is the American dead too?"

Droshny looked around again at the dead bodies. "I don't see any Americans."

"He must have killed Hashim and the others with the machine gun."

"So the American was riding in the truck with Hashim? Why?"

"I don't know. Do you see an electronic device?" Jashari asked then he described the item in detail.

Droshny looked around. "I don't see anything like that."

"Are you sure? Check again."

Droshny put the radio down and demanded the soldiers search the wreckage. Nothing. He reported the results to Jashari.

"The American took it," Jashari said.

"Maybe it was destroyed with the van."

"No. I told Hashim to keep it close by."

Droshny looked around as if he had missed something. It was then he saw it: a faint trail of blood leading away from Hashim's truck toward the woods. A smile grew on his face as he pushed the button on the radio. "Jashari, I think I know where the American may have gone."

"Can you track him?"

"Yes."

"Well, I want that device back. And I want you to capture the American alive."

"Alive, sir?"

"Yes. Alive," Jashari replied. "I want the pleasure of killing him myself."

CHAPTER 3

"**So how did your family get involved with all** this?" Smith asked.

Paxton struggled with where to begin. "After McMurphy and I were captured by the Serbs, they interrogated us as if we were spies. I refused to answer any questions except for name, rank, date of birth and serial number."

"Standard stuff."

"Yeah, except they took my information and used it to find my family in the States. They sent in a team of assassins to kill my wife and kids—unless I talked."

"Shit, so what did you do?"

"I escaped. Well, Jashari and his KLA men helped me escape the Serbs and then I had to escape the KLA. That's when you picked me up after tracking the GPS coordinates transmitted by this device." Paxton held up the green backpack for emphasis. "I radioed my boss, Colonel Ward. He called my wife to get her and my kids out of the house. Then he took one of the other NCOs, Machette, and a shotgun and blew away the Serbs when they arrived at my house."

"In-fucking-credible."

"I'll say. Had you not picked me up when you did..." Paxton couldn't finish the sentence.

"Is your family okay?"

"They're safe."

Smith sat in silence for a moment. "What happened to Mc-Murphy?"

"I don't know. We were chained up side by side. Then a Serb named Nikolic came and took him away. I think they knew each other before this mission. Nobody knows where he is. He apparently tried to contact General Reed, but his call was cut off. I think, knowing what I know now, he was trying to warn Reed about my family."

"Do you think they will kill McMurphy?"

"Not if I can help it."

• • •

Jill Paxton stared at the bloody mess that was her foyer. The bodies of the Serbs had been removed, but there remained a hellish mop job.

"Don't worry about the mess, Jill." Colonel Ward touched her elbow. "We'll get a specialized cleanup crew to take care of it all."

Jill shook her head. A tear escaped down her cheek and she scrubbed it away. "It's not the mess. It's that *they* were here.

In my home." Anger and fear mixed. "It'll never be the same again."

"Come on. I'll drive you. We have nice temporary quarters for you. You'll feel much safer once you're on base."

Jill glared at Ward. "We can't spend the rest of our lives on base! How can I ever feel safe again?"

"It's going to be all right. It's over."

"How can you say that? He still isn't home. John's supposed to be getting out. He's supposed to retire and go to med school. I don't understand why it will take so long for him to get back home."

"It is my understanding that he has a few more things to do, and then he is coming back. We both know how John is. Once he gets set onto something, he does it. Nothing is going to stop him. Now let's go. I think you will feel better once you're safely behind the gates at Lackland."

Jill turned toward Ward. "They found us once. What makes you think they can't find us again?"

• • •

"Let me go with you," Smith said over the headset.

"I can't get you involved in this."

"Pax, I'm *already* involved. I'm drowning in it."

"I won't pull you in any deeper."

"I'm volunteering."

"This is my mess and I'll clean it up."

"The mess belongs to General Reed. Why are you sticking your neck out for that bastard?"

"I'm not doing it for him."

"Whatever damn dumb reason you're doing it, you need my help."

"You want to help? Tell me every detail about what happened after McMurphy and I left you, the C-17 flight crew, and the rest of the team."

Smith described the entire trek across the Serbian countryside. He told Paxton about using the GPS receiver McMurphy had given him to locate the hiding spot, how they waited 24 hours for Paxton and McMurphy to return, and how he struggled with the decision to leave when they failed to show.

He then went into great detail about how they happened across a Serbian Grumble anti-aircraft Surface to Air Missile (SAM) mobile launch complex. Smith was very animated telling about how he and his team, with only a handful of light weapons, took over the complex and destroyed the missiles before they could shoot down the rescue helicopters.

Paxton showed no reaction.

"Pax, you still with me?"

Paxton broke free of his troubling thoughts. "Yes, sorry."

"Man, let me go with you. You need my help."

"That's why the SEALs are coming along with me. If I need help, they will be right there tracking me. And if for any reason they lose me, this thing still has the GPS tracking device in it. So when we land to pick up the SEAL team, I'm dropping you off."

"Dammit, Pax."

"That's my final decision."

Captain Olsen's voice interrupted Smith's reply. "The *Kear-*

sarge is just ahead. Prepare for landing."

Paxton looked out the Pave Hawk's window. Below was nothing but the dark turbulent waters of the Adriatic. Then he saw it. The USS *Kearsarge* was a *Wasp*-class amphibious assault ship. Named after the sloop *Kearsarge* of Civil War fame, she looked like a small aircraft carrier from the air. Helicopters adorned her flat topside along with two AV-8 Harrier II "Jump-Jets."

"Smith, do you still have the GPS receiver that McMurphy gave you?"

"Yes. Got it right here." Smith tapped the cargo pocket of his pants.

"Listen carefully to what I need you to do."

• • •

Once onboard Paxton worked the ship-to-shore phone. Crews busied themselves refueling the Pave Hawk while Smith stood aside and watched the action.

A young seaman stuck his head in the door. "They're ready to leave, Sergeant Paxton."

"Thank you, Seaman. Uh, I need one more thing before I go."

"What's that, Sergeant?"

"I'd really appreciate it if you could hook me up with a fresh pair of underwear."

CHAPTER 4

GENERAL DRAGUSA RUGOVA OF THE SERBIAN ARMY slammed his fist on his desk. "What do you mean they're all dead? How could this happen?"

Lieutenant Colonel Nikolic winced. "I don't know how it happened, but someone discovered the place we were hiding the Americans and attacked it."

"And the prisoners?"

"We still have the one who called himself Gregori. I had moved him for further questioning before the assault. But Sergeant Paxton is gone."

"What about the anti-radar device?"

"They got the fake one that we don't care about. But we still have the real one in a safe place."

"Who did it?"

"I believe it was the KLA because there are dead KLA fighters all around. I don't know what the KLA wants with the fake device."

"I don't know either, but we must be certain no one tries to trick us again."

• • •

Paxton walked out into the sunlight on the deck of the *Kearsarge* looking for Smith. He saw him. He was having an animated conversation with one of the sailors.

"Smith!"

"Yes, Pax?" Smith jogged over to his boss.

"You're all set. You can head back to Italy, and all the charges will be dropped."

"But I don't want to go to Italy. You're gonna need me."

"I already told you, I'm taking the SEALs."

"Yeah, well, there's only two of 'em."

"What?"

"You heard me. Two. *Dos.*"

"What the hell?"

"I guess your little mission isn't as important to everyone else."

"*Shit.*"

"You need me. What if someone gets hurt?"

"No. There is no reason to risk your life for this fucked up mission. You can go back to your unit and get back to doing what you do best—rescuing people. I talked to Reed and he's clearing everything up for you."

"Reed, huh?"

"Yes."

"Since when did you start trusting him?"

CHAPTER 5

GENERAL REED LOOKED AT HIS AIDE, CAPTAIN MARSHALL. "What do you think the chances are of Paxton succeeding?"

Marshall handed Reed a drink. "I think I have a better chance of marrying a centerfold."

"That bad?"

"Well, sir, I think the KLA will shoot Paxton on sight, take the fake device and trade it to the Iraqi's for the poison gas, and there's not a damn thing we can do to stop it."

"So do you think we should call off the mission?"

"Nope." Marshall sipped his drink.

"If it's so bad, why proceed?"

"Well, the way I figure it, if by some miracle he does succeed, he saves our bacon."

"And if he fails and gets himself killed?"

"Then that's one fewer witness to testify at our courts-martial."

• • •

Paxton climbed back aboard the Pave Hawk, followed by Smith. Already seated inside were two navy SEALs decked out in full battle gear including body armor, Night Vision Goggles (NVGs) and weapons. Paxton held out his hand and introduced himself.

"I'm Petty Officer Ketterman and this here's Seaman First Class Spaulding."

"Oh, and this is Sergeant Smith." Paxton patted Smith's shoulder. "He's pestered his way onto this flight." The men buckled in and the helicopter lifted off the *Kearsarge's* deck.

"Remember Smith, you're just coming along for the ride. When the SEALs and I rope down, you're staying with the copter."

"Whatever you say, Pax."

The Pave Hawk skimmed its way over the waves toward the exact same spot it had picked up Paxton hours earlier.

"So you Zoomies need our help, huh?" Ketterman's big grin took the edge off his words.

"Just need someone to follow me around. Figured there were no better followers than a couple of Squids." Paxton grinned.

"Fuck you, Paxton." Ketterman gave Paxton a brotherly punch in the arm.

"Why'd they send only two of you?"

"That's all it takes. We're that good."

Paxton and Smith glanced at each other. "Um, the KLA is heavily armed. And there's a bunch of 'em. You plan to take out all of them, plus the Iraqi agents, and capture the nerve gas all by yourselves."

"No problem." Ketterman grinned.

Paxton sighed.

"Just kidding." Ketterman punched Paxton's arm again. "Spaulding and I are the spotters. We'll keep you in sight, and then when the time is right, we will call in the rest of the team."

"I was thinking you'd take 'em out with an air strike," Smith said.

"No good," Paxton explained. "Can't risk releasing the nerve gas. We need to capture it in its containers. Besides, it's evidence."

"Evidence of what?"

"Saddam's Weapons of Mass Destruction program. He's getting rid of the stuff as fast as he can so the U.N. weapons inspectors don't find it. We know he has them—hell he used them against the Kurds. We just don't know where he's hiding them."

"If there is a GPS transmitter in that thing, why do you need spotters? Can't it just be followed remotely?"

"Yes it can be followed remotely, just like you were able to locate me in the first place. But what it won't tell us is when the Iraqi agents show up with the gas. We need human intelligence for that."

"If we need human *intelligence*, why would they send Ketterman?" Smith ducked the best he could to avoid the anticipated punch from the SEAL.

"All kidding aside, I will feel better knowing I've got some backup hiding in the woods. I'm going in there practically naked."

"I want to go, too," insisted Smith.

"No."

"Come on, Pax. What if someone gets wounded?"

Paxton closed his eyes and shook his head.

"We don't care if he comes," Ketterman said.

"Smith, I am ordering you to not come along."

Smith looked pissed.

"Why couldn't you send us to drop the pack somewhere the KLA is sure to find it and have us follow it? Why did you have to do it personally?" Ketterman asked.

"Two reasons. First, the KLA will expect me to be protecting it with my life. I want them to believe that it is the real deal."

Paxton then was silent.

"And?"

Paxton regarded Ketterman for a moment. The others leaned in closer. "And, second, I've got some unfinished business in Serbia."

• • •

"Sergeant Droshny, we found more blood," one of the young KLA soldiers reported as he ran back from where the lead trackers were attempting to trace Paxton's route.

"Good. He couldn't have gotten too far on his own. Keep moving."

"Yes, sir!" The soldier returned to the front of the pack.

Droshny and the others hitched their weapons higher and continued their trek.

Chapter 6

THE PAVE HAWK ZIPPED OVER THE SERBIAN COUNTRYSIDE at treetop level. Tension was high. The sun was shining and the helicopter could be heard for miles. At any moment a Serbian gun position could open up and blast Paxton and his team out of the sky.

Inside, Paxton gathered up his gear. He shrugged McMurphy's ratty backpack on. Then he slung both MP-40 machine guns, one hanging on each side of his body. He had already reloaded the magazines. The World War II era weapons were heavy but effective. He had already used them to kill.

The two SEALs prepared themselves as well. Their weapons were more modern: M4 assault rifles with collapsible stocks.

Smith unstrapped his boot knife and offered it to Paxton. Clearly the security police officer had not taken the time to thoroughly search Smith. "Here, you might need this."

"No, that's yours."

"Damn right. I expect to get it back from you. Damn thing cost an arm and leg."

"Well I can't afford to replace it."

"Look, Pax. The first thing the KLA is going to do is take the guns away from you. Maybe you can hide the knife. It could be an insurance policy for you."

"Yeah, but where?"

"If you're patted down for weapons, the one place often missed is the middle of the back, between the shoulder blades."

Paxton thought about it for a moment. "I suppose it couldn't hurt."

Paxton took off the backpack and his shirt and t-shirt. Smith taped the knife to his back with medical tape and they tested his reach. He could grab the handle without much problem. He then got dressed. It was almost time to go.

• • •

Jill Paxton tried to get used to her new surroundings. The kids, John, Jr. and Megan, were resilient. They enjoyed the temporary quarters provided on Lackland Air Force Base. Then again, it was easy for them to be that way. They were completely unaware of the bloodshed that had occurred in their own home. Besides, it was only temporary. Just until the end of the conflict with Serbia. Then they could move back home. But that home would never be the same.

She was thankful. At least no hit men could get through base security and harm her or her family. It seemed impossible.

• • •

It was go time. Paxton checked his rappelling harness and clipped the line into the Air Traffic Control (ATC) device secured to the harness straps.

"Good luck, Pax." Smith's face was a mask of concern.

Paxton just nodded and handed over his headphones. The pilot maneuvered the helicopter to the precise location where they had picked Paxton up a number of hours ago and hovered. No one was shooting at that copter. So far so good. Paxton kicked the rope out of the open door and it uncurled all the way to the ground. He leaned back and began rappelling. He felt very exposed as he descended. The copter was noisy and he was sure that it was attracting lots of attention. So he sped up.

His boots hit the ground, and he yanked the rope out of the ATC. He then stepped out of the harness and tied it to the end of the rope. He gave a wave and the rope snaked back up to the copter. Paxton spun around checking his surroundings. No one was there. The Pave Hawk raised its tail and flew off to the south. They only had a few moments to get the others on the ground.

• • •

Droshny ordered his men to run toward the sound of the helicopter. It was close. The American rescuers were leading him right to the man they were seeking. He would not be allowed to escape. The man who killed his friend would pay. Droshny hitched up his shotgun and ran with his men.

• • •

Onboard the Pave Hawk, Smith stepped into the harness and secured the rope.

"I thought Sergeant Paxton told you to stay onboard."

"The helicopter is noisy...the only thing I heard him say was 'come along.'"

Ketterman smiled, gave him the thumbs up, and Smith leaned back and slid down the rope.

• • •

"Sergeant Droshny! There're the rescuers!"

Droshny broke into a clearing and saw the Pave Hawk with Smith rappelling down the long rope. Some of his men were pointing at the helicopter. Others were aiming their weapons.

Droshny's heart was pounding. The American with the device was close. And he would have a chance to take out some more Americans. They would pay.

"Shoot it down!"

The KLA soldiers opened fire with their rifles and machine guns.

• • •

Hanging beneath the Pave Hawk, Smith grabbed the rope and held on as the copter pitched around and the hail of bullets pierced its skin. He didn't know what was happening at first as the sound of the rotor masked the sound of the gunfire.

When a round snapped past his head with its supersonic

crack, understanding suddenly gripped him. Another round tugged at his shirt as it passed through his left sleeve.

Shit!

He couldn't see where the rounds were coming from, but he could sense them flying by all around him. His first thought was to scramble back up the rope and get the hell out of there. But that wasn't really an option. Paxton was down there. He wouldn't abandon his friend.

He looked up and saw Ketterman and Spaulding returning fire from the open door. Spent shell casings rained down on him. He knew he had to get on the ground pronto. The SEALs would need to follow so the copter could get out of the line of fire. Things were turning bad fast. Really bad.

Smith forced himself to ease his grip and started to slide down the rope again. Smith had to ignore his survival instinct as he descended toward the gunfire that was trying to kill him. He saw the flash in the corner of his eye. An RPG arrowed from the tree line and arced over Smith's head. Time slowed as the projectile seemed to hang for a moment before it sliced through the tail rotor boom of the Pave Hawk.

Kaboom!

The explosion shattered the boom, and the tail rotor tumbled away as Smith watched in horror.

Immediately the fuselage of the Pave Hawk began to counter-rotate because the stabilizing force of the tail rotor was gone. The rope jerked and whipped Smith around underneath the copter. He gripped with all his might, but centrifugal force and gravity jammed him down the rope.

One of the SEALs was hanging onto the door of the copter trying to not be thrown out. Smoke and flames billowed out of the shattered tail boom, tracing a crazy spiral in the sky. Bullets continued to pierce the helicopter's aluminum skin.

Suddenly the rope went slack as the copter dropped out of the sky. Smith's legs hit the top of a pine tree, and he flipped upside down. Pine needles and branches smashed into his face. He felt himself tumbling out of control. Then everything went black.

• • •

Paxton was crouched, firing toward the sound of the KLA gunfire. He had looked up when he heard the tail rotor being blown off and saw the Pave Hawk spin out of control as it spiraled down. The copter fell below the treetops, and then there was a terrible crash.

Sonsofbitches!

All Paxton could think of was Smith, the SEALs, and the crew. In rage, he emptied the magazine of the MP-40 toward the source of the RPG round. He heard shouting and cheering.

This wasn't the way things were supposed to go down. He choked on his heart. He shouldn't have allowed Smith to come on the flight. It was becoming clear that it wasn't such a good idea to come back. And he only had himself to blame.

• • •

The KLA soldiers split up. One group ran toward the wreckage of the helicopter. The other group ran toward the sound of

Paxton's gunfire. They had their orders. Capture the American on the ground alive. There was no similar order for the crew of the Pave Hawk.

• • •

Ketterman lay in a sea of pain. He was sprawled on the floor of the Pave Hawk's wreckage. He could not feel or move his legs. How many of his bones were broken he could not know. He could barely move his head. There was no movement in the cockpit. But he could hear moans of pain. He turned his head and beheld a grisly sight. Spaulding was crushed underneath the fuselage. He heard voices. The language he didn't recognize. He flitted his eyes around. He saw a rifle lying six inches from his bloodied right hand. He tried to reach for it, but his hand wouldn't move. Try as he might, he couldn't get to the rifle.

In the haze of pain, he became aware of men looking at him. Strange men. He did not recognize them. He didn't recognize the clothes they were wearing. But he did recognize the weapons they aimed at him. One man's weapon stood out. Ketterman looked back through the ghost ring sight on the black Benelli shotgun aimed straight at his face and saw a bearded man smiling. *Nice weapon*. An absurd thought for the SEAL to have as the man's finger entered the trigger guard. The man said something Ketterman didn't understand. Then Ketterman saw him squeeze the trigger, and his world went dark.

• • •

Paxton was surrounded. The KLA soldiers came out of the tree line with rifles leveled at him. He wanted to open fire with his other MP-40, but that wouldn't do anyone any good. With Smith and the SEAL team gone, there would be no one to call in the troops when the Iraqi agents showed up with the nerve gas. Of course, Paxton had no idea of how he would call in the troops. He didn't have a radio. He didn't know if they would let him anywhere near the exchange. Hell, he didn't know if they would kill him standing right there. He had to control his emotions. He had to complete the mission, as fucked up as it was. He dropped his machine gun and raised his hands in surrender.

He had unfinished business in Serbia.

Chapter 7

THE KLA SOLDIERS GRABBED PAXTON AND THREW HIM TO the ground. He could smell the moist dirt as they yanked the backpack off him. He could feel the barrel of a rifle pressing into the back of his neck. He didn't dare look as he heard them open the pack. An excited discussion occurred in a language he couldn't understand. He wondered if they were about to pull the trigger.

Thoughts of his family flashed by.

They held him there for what seemed like an eternity. He heard another group of men approach. Hands grabbed him and pulled him to his feet. Other hands patted him down. Down his sides, around his ankles and under his arms. He remembered the knife taped to his back as they patted his chest and stomach. They didn't find it.

A bearded man carrying a shotgun stepped up to Paxton's chest. He had to look up at Paxton, but he was close enough that Paxton could smell his foul breath. He spoke English. "Jashari requests your presence."

• • •

This time nobody bothered to bind Paxton's hands behind his back. They just led him at gunpoint back through the woods all the way to the road. The tableau of carnage remained just as he had left it. They prodded him into the back of the truck, and he was followed by a number of KLA soldiers. One of the soldiers carried the backpack and placed it in the front of the truck. They sat him down with his back to the cab. The other soldiers sat down and stared at Paxton, death in their eyes. The engine started and the truck lurched forward. The driver completed a three-point turn and headed back toward Jashari's headquarters.

• • •

Back in Italy, Marshall burst into General Reed's room.

"Sir, we've lost contact with Sergeant Paxton's helicopter."

Reed looked up from his newspaper.

"It's gone, sir. It disappeared from radar, and we can't contact either the SEAL team or the pilots by radio."

"What about the device?"

"According to the tracker, it's on the move."

• • •

The truck bumped along the mountainous road. Paxton wondered abstractly how many of the soldiers were hoping that a bump would cause a weapon to go off right through his heart. Sweat was pouring down his face, and his body ached. And he felt sick to his stomach about the Pave Hawk.

Smith!

He should have left Smith in the security police car back in Italy. And now Smith was dead because of him.

Hell, *he* should have stayed back in Italy and let General Reed clean up his own mess. Things had spiraled out of control.

The truck turned off the road into a dirt driveway and slid to a halt. Paxton was dragged off the back of the truck and pushed into a wooden two-story house. He hoped they would bring the device in as well. He didn't want to lose sight of it. He needed to know when the transfer with the Iraqis would occur. And, more important, it contained the tracking device that would enable him to be found.

Inside, the house it was dark. The windows had been covered so no light would escape at night—and no light could come in during the day. It smelled musty with more than a hint of sweat. Hands shoved Paxton from behind, and he tumbled to the wooden floor. He favored the knee that had the stitches in it as he made impact. He had enough agility and strength to have remained on his feet, but he allowed himself to fall because that was what they expected him to do. He wanted to appear more defeated than he truly was.

His eyes were beginning to adjust to the darkness. He took the opportunity to scan the room. A fire burned in a hearth on one wall. Only a few pieces of furniture adorned the room. He could see numerous pairs of dusty boots attached to dirty pant legs. He could also smell coffee and gun oil. There had been a lot of weapons cleaned recently in that room.

A man stood over him. "Commander Jashari, this is the man who killed Hashim and the others." He spoke in English for Paxton's benefit. "I deliver him for your disposal."

"Good work, Droshny. I look forward to disposing of him. Be it Allah's will."

• • •

Reed and Marshall studied a map of Yugoslavia. A window air conditioner hummed. Marshall had taken the coordinates from the tracking device and drawn a red X. "This is where the device stopped. It hasn't moved for several minutes," Marshall explained.

"That matches the spot Jashari was transmitting from with the satellite phone. They brought it to his headquarters."

"Do you think that is where the Iraqis are going to make the exchange?"

"Doubt it," Reed said. "Jashari wouldn't want the nerve gas brought there. Too many eyes. He will have selected a more remote location for the transaction."

"Should we send another SEAL team?"

"Have them ready, but don't send them yet. I don't want to spook the KLA and have them go underground with the device. When the device moves again and then stops for the second time, *that* is where the exchange is going to take place. Then you send them."

• • •

They had dragged Paxton to his feet and then pushed him into a chair. The soldiers wrapped a thick rope around his arms and chest securing him to the chair. This was looking worse and worse by the minute. The man who appeared to be their leader stepped up.

"Who are you?" the man demanded.

Paxton looked up. "Who the hell are you?"

"I am Jashari. Now tell me your name."

"Jashari? Why did your men shoot down the helicopter? You're supposed to be helping us." Paxton knew why, but continued to play the role.

"I'm the one asking questions here. Tell me your name."

There was no harm in telling the truth. There was a good chance that Jashari already knew who he was. They wouldn't be able to pull another stunt like the Serbs did. His family was safe behind the gates of Lackland Air Force Base. "SMSgt John Paxton of the United States Air Force."

"Why, Sergeant Paxton, did you kill Hashim and my soldiers?"

Paxton did his best to appear innocent. "I don't know what the hell you're talking about. I didn't kill anybody."

Jashari's punch smashed into Paxton's temple. "Liar!"

Paxton saw stars.

"I'm not lying! We were attacked and I escaped."

"You're a lying infidel." Jashari turned to Droshny. "Bring me the device."

Droshny crossed the room and handed him the green backpack. Jashari opened the pack and pulled out the electronic device. It was a metallic box with wires and cables hanging out of it. "What is this, Sergeant Paxton?"

Paxton considered it for a moment. "I have no idea."

Jashari's fist smashed into Paxton's face again. "Your tongue is full of untruths!"

Paxton shook his head to clear his mind. "I'm telling you the truth. I really don't know what it is."

"Then why would you be carrying it?"

Paxton knew that Jashari already knew what it was. This interrogation was clearly for punishment. Paxton strained against the ropes, but they didn't budge.

"I asked you a question!"

"All I know is that it belongs to the United States government, and it's my intention to return it to them."

Jashari grinned a coffee-stained wolf's grin. "I'm sorry to inform you that you will never have such opportunity."

• • •

Marshall checked the coordinates again. He had a strange expression on his face. "Not good."

"What's not good?" Reed asked.

"Signal's getting weaker."

"Why the hell would the signal be getting weaker?"

"I don't know. I guess the battery in the device is dying."

"You've got to be shitting me! Are you sure?"

"Yes, sir, I'm sure."

"How do you know it isn't the batteries in your receiver?"

"Those are brand new. I just changed them about an hour ago."

"How the hell could this happen?" Reed was fuming.

"No one thought it would be needed for this long. It was designed to last long enough so we could track who had the device. This is not exactly the mission it was designed for. It takes quite a bit of power to transmit to the satellite. Nobody thought about it having to last this long."

"Shit!"

• • •

Smith was right, Paxton thought, *this is a suicide mission.* He strained against the ropes again with the same result. *How am I going to get out of this?* His hands were going numb. He couldn't move his feet because they were tied to the chair as well. He was sweating all over.

Jashari was still grinning. The others were standing around watching him. There were no SEALs coming to rescue him. They were all dead. There was no one coming to rescue him. He was about to die.

"Why are you going to kill me?"

"Because you killed Hashim."

"I told you I didn't do that."

"I don't believe you. Besides, I don't want you to be able to tell the Americans that I have their electronic device. Property of the United States government, as you say."

"What are you going to do with it? It can't have any value to you."

"It has more value that you can imagine. And as for what I'm going to do with it, you will just have to watch what I do from your seat in Hell, *infidel!*"

With that Jashari pulled out a wicked knife. The blade flashed in the firelight. Paxton's heart skipped a beat.

A couple of men eased Paxton's bulk over until he was lying on his back, still tied to the chair. He fought to free himself, but the ropes were too tight. Another man stood behind a camera on a tripod video taping the scene. Jashari moved behind Paxton. Paxton was filled with rage. He could feel his blood vessels about to burst.

"Death to infidels!" Jashari shouted.

The others cheered.

"Glory be to Allah!"

Another cheer went up.

"We do this in honor of our brother Jihadist Osama bin Laden who has helped us so much."

Paxton jerked his body back and forth with all his remaining strength. *Oh my God!*

Jashari placed his boot on the side of Paxton's face, pressing it to the floor. Jashari raised his blade in triumph. Then he leaned over and placed its sharp edge against the side of Paxton's neck.

Paxton had seen videos of executions like this. Chechnyans would saw off the heads of captured Russian soldiers with a knife. It was a gruesome way to die.

"Now you die like the pig that you are."

Chapter 8

RUGOVA WAS PLEASED. HE FINALLY HAD A BUYER FOR the Stealth fighter device. The Chinese had agreed to wire a handsome sum to his Swiss bank account in exchange for the device. They had outbid the Russians by several million. He thought about going back to the Russians to see if they were willing to raise their bid. They must have wanted it badly since they had sent their man to observe it being extracted from the wreckage of the Stealth. Frankly, he was surprised they didn't just buy it on the spot.

But the Russian had to get back to his superiors. It was not their culture to allow the man on the ground to make any decisions. Even after the fall of Communism, they still had to make decisions by committee.

It was a damn good thing they discovered that the Americans were trying to pass off a fake device. Selling a fake one to the Russians, or the Chinese for that matter, would have been a good way to get himself killed.

It couldn't hurt to try to up the ante one more time with the Russians. Especially since Nikolic will be expecting a cut. Of course, Nikolic didn't have to know how much Rugova was getting. And it was beginning to look like Nikolic would get something entirely different. He lit a cigarette and picked up the phone.

• • •

A man bounded down the stairs of the old house. "Commander Jashari! You have a call on the satellite phone."

"We're right in the middle of a damn execution here," Jashari replied, his blade just opening the skin on Paxton's throat.

"I apologize about the interruption, but it can't wait, sir."

Jashari stood up. His boot was still holding Paxton's head down. "Who is it?" He held the knife in his right hand out to the side.

"It's the Iraqis. They need to talk to you. It is urgent!"

Jashari sighed. "We can't keep our customer waiting, can we?" He leaned down and said, "You are in luck. You get to live until I'm done with this call."

The energy went out of the room. They were all disappointed. The man with the video camera stopped taping and lowered his camera.

Jashari turned and headed up the stairs. Paxton lay there surrounded by jihadists, his eyes darting around, looking for a way out. He saw none.

• • •

Home Invasion Foiled, Suspects Slain

San Antonio - Two home invaders broke into a local resident's home yesterday. In a daring daylight robbery attempt, two heavily armed men entered the home of an airman stationed at Lackland Air Force Base. The gunmen were killed in an exchange of gunfire with the occupants.

A quiet suburban neighborhood was shattered when the home belonging to SMSgt John Paxton and his wife Jill became the latest statistic in the growing number of home invasions nationwide. The suspects, whose names have not been released pending notification of next of kin, were unemployed undocumented workers, according to police. The whereabouts of the homeowners and their two small children are unknown at the time of this publication.

"This is a prime example of why guns should be outlawed," said Sam Shepard, Mayor of San Antonio, "with all that shooting back and forth inside the house, an innocent person could have been hurt."

"Idiots," Jill Paxton said as she threw the newspaper down on the kitchen table of her temporary quarters. She missed her home, but she had to admit that she felt a little bit safer on base.

She ruffled the paper and took another look at the article. She sipped her coffee. A chill went through her as she recalled that day. For national security purposes, the article was somewhat less than accurate. The reporter wasn't told that it wasn't a robbery attempt. Nor was it mentioned that it was a hit ordered from Serbia in an attempt to make her husband talk. They didn't know that he had been captured in Serbia—hell, *she* didn't even know he was in Serbia.

And what was taking him so long to get back home? He said

he had one little matter to take care of and then he would come home. He wouldn't say what it was. Why couldn't he just take care of it from home? The not knowing was agonizing. Questions crisscrossed inside her head. Was she cut out to be a military wife? Where would she find the strength? How could she raise the children alone if something happened to John? Was she even cut out to be a mother? Would she ever see John again?

Chapter 9

PAXTON HEARD THE FOOTSTEPS COMING BACK DOWN THE stairs, and he struggled frantically against the ropes. His killer was coming back. The jihadists in the room resumed their positions and quieted down like actors waiting for the director to shout action! One man got behind the video camera on the tripod, and the red light came back on. Paxton was about to die at the hands of these madmen, and they were going to use the video as propaganda.

What if Jill sees the video? Oh, God, what about my kids? He couldn't let it end like this. Not this way. But what could he do? If he could get to his feet, maybe he could charge the camera and smash it. That would do no good. They would just get another. Maybe provoke them into shooting him. He'd rather die like that than to have is head sawed off as a sick Internet recruiting video.

Paxton wrenched his body back and forth, but he couldn't get enough leverage to get up. One of the jihadists saw what he was trying to do and came over and sat on him. The other jihadists laughed. Paxton's abdomen ached, but he couldn't throw the man off of him. His jaw was a vise. His vision blurred from a combination of sweat and tears. His killer reached the bottom of the stairs.

Jashari stood there and drank in the scene before him. Then he sharply shouted something Paxton couldn't understand. The man sitting on him jumped up and joined the others. Paxton heard his own heart pounding in the sudden silence.

Jashari took a few steps toward the others and shouted an order at the man with the video camera. He shut the camera off and nearly knocked it over himself as he leapt away from it. What was going on? The killer strode toward Paxton and blurted out some more words. The group of jihadists began to break up. They mumbled in low tones. Some of them left. What? Show over? Paxton strained his neck to see the expression on Jashari's face. He didn't look happy. He looked a little deflated. What had happened during his phone call from the Iraqis?

"Sergeant Paxton, you have what I think is called a 'stay of execution.'"

Paxton didn't comprehend what he heard at first.

"Get up…you pig."

"What's going on?" choked Paxton as he struggled to sit up.

"Your time to die has not yet arrived."

A wave of relief crashed over him. But his stomach was full of acid. What did Jashari have in mind for him? What the hell was going on?

"You are apparently well known to the Iraqis."

He felt the acid eat a hole in his stomach.

"Get up!" Jashari grabbed him and pulled him upright in the chair. "What did you do to them?"

Paxton's eyes stung with sweat as he tried to look at Jashari. "What did I do to who?"

"The Iraqis. What did you do to them?"

"I don't know what you are talking about." Paxton didn't recognize his own voice.

"I'm sure you know. You somehow made impression on them."

"I haven't been to Iraq in eight years. There must be some mistake." Paxton feared there was no mistake. His past was catching up to him.

"Unless there's another John Paxton, United States Air Force Pararescueman, there is no mistake."

Paxton felt empty, emotionally drained.

"Whatever it was, you sure angered them off. When they hear I holding you, they say I must turn you over to them ... alive."

"Or what?"

"Or deal was off. Can you believe that? If I don't turn you over alive, then they are going to turn around and return to Iraq with my nerve gas. *MY* nerve gas!"

Paxton knew all too well what he had done to the Iraqis during Desert Storm. He had been awarded the Air Force Cross for his actions in Iraq. His country considered him a hero. And now the Iraqis were going to extract their revenge.

And the Jihadists were going to get their nerve gas.

And the Russians or the Chinese were going to get from the Serbs the genuine device that protected the Stealth fighter and Stealth bomber from advanced radar.

Everything was going to shit, and there wasn't a damn thing he could do about it. Smith and the others were dead because he made the stupid decision to come back here. Their blood was on his hands.

"You pig!" Jashari punched him hard on the temple. "I want to kill you with my own hands, but now I have to keep you alive. My only pleasure is that the Iraqis have something very special planned for you."

• • •

An old truck pulled up to the Turkish border guards. The guards were wearing khaki uniforms and suspicious looks on their faces. Their slung rifles said they meant business. Although in the Kurdish region of Turkey, right on the boarder with Iraq, business literally meant business.

The Iraqi driver waved a guard over to the open window of the truck. He passed the guard a rather large sum of money— equivalent to six months pay. The guard looked at the money, smiled and waved the truck through the checkpoint. The Iraqis entered Turkey unfettered, and nobody inspected the deadly cargo the truck was carrying.

Chapter 10

THE JIHADISTS UNTIED PAXTON FROM THE CHAIR AND shoved him into a locked room. The lone window was covered with steel bars. He could hear activity and conversation through the solid wood door, but he couldn't understand a word they were saying.

How had things gone so wrong so quickly?

Admittedly, the plan was fraught with danger. But he was supposed to be tailed by a squad of SEALs. If things got hairy, the SEALs were supposed to swarm in and rescue him.

But there were no SEALs. Not anymore. They were all dead.

Along with the Pave Hawk pilots.

And *Smith!*

Why hadn't he left him in the security police car? Now his former student was dead.

And this time Paxton couldn't blame General Reed. Reed had not ordered him to go on this mission. The plan was his own. He had only himself to blame.

Now he sat there on the floor of the empty room. All alone.

He should have gone home when he had his chance. Home to Jill and the kids.

The fake device is in the hands of the KLA. The Iraqis were on their way with the nerve gas to exchange for the device. Paxton had no way to contact Reed and tell him when and where the exchange was taking place. If he didn't do something to stop it, *al Qaeda* was going to wind up with a large quantity of one of the most dangerous chemicals on the planet.

To top it off, Jashari planned to deliver him to the Iraqis. Only God knows what they have in store for him.

He only had one thing still going for him: *He was still alive.*

• • •

Pine and dirt. The scents filtered into his consciousness as Smith became aware of the world once again. And pain. Excruciating pain. *Where the fuck am I?* His mind reeled. He forced his eyes open.

Dirt and grass.

His vision was limited. He craned his neck and saw that he was surrounded by trees. He became vaguely aware that he was lying on the ground, his right arm trapped under him. His legs were sprawled out behind him. *What the fuck?*

His mind raced. He couldn't figure out what was going on. But he felt a sense of dread—one that reached all the way down to his soul. Every breath stabbed with pain.

It reminded him of his football days. He felt like he had been nailed by a linebacker. But this was no football field. There were no cheering fans. There was no whistle. There was no opposing team. And there was no staff of trainers to check on him. He was alone.

Smith, pull yourself together.

He forced himself up into the sitting position. His side was a furnace of pain. Surely some of his ribs were broken. *But how?*

Helicopter. Rope. It was starting to come back to him. Gunfire. He touched the sleeve of his uniform and felt the frayed tear. Explosion! The SEALs. His body whipped around on the end of a rope.

Paxton!

Shit!

Smith looked up. A thick blanket of pine trees towered above him. *I came through that.*

The branches had slowed his descent enough to save his life.

Yugoslavia. He was back.

Fuck!

It was the second time he made an inglorious arrival in this God-forsaken country.

He reached around and felt his M4 carbine. Thank God! He was still armed. He tried breathing shallowly. The pain subsided somewhat but was still there.

Where were the others? What happened to the helicopter? The sights and sounds of the tail boom being blown off flashed through his mind. Was everyone else killed? He had to find out.

• • •

"The exchange is on…what assurances can you give us that what we are buying is genuine?" The voice was distorted by the encrypting algorithms but still was understandable through the untraceable cell phone.

"You have my word," replied the American.

"Your word is not good enough! What evidence do you have that we are not getting the fake device—the risk and cost to us is very high. I must know we are getting what we bargained for."

"If you don't believe me, ask General Rugova. He had it checked out to determine which one is real."

"I do not trust the Serb either! The Serbs love the Russians. They are not our traditional ally. For all we know they are selling the real device to the Russians and pawning off the fake one to us."

"That is not what is happening. Trust me."

"Why should we trust you? Your job was to deliver the real device to us, and it has almost been lost several times."

"That is because our plan has been interfered with. But that won't happen again."

"How can you be so sure?"

The American struggled with how much he should say. "Let us just say that both of our problems are about to be taken care of."

"In what way?"

"The man who interfered with our plans is delivering the fake device to the KLA. That is how I know the fake device is not going to be sold to you."

"How can you assure me that there will be no more inter-ference?"

"Because John Paxton will soon be dead."

Chapter 11

Sᴍɪᴛʜ ᴘᴜsʜᴇᴅ ʜɪᴍsᴇʟꜰ ᴜᴘ ᴏɴᴛᴏ ʜɪs ᴇʟʙᴏᴡs. Pᴀɪɴ shot through his ribs, and it felt like he was breathing fire into his lungs. He craned his head around first to the left, then to the right. He couldn't see much—his view was obscured by the dense foliage in which he had landed. Foliage that had concealed him from the soldiers who shot down the Pave Hawk.

He couldn't hear anything but the sounds of nature. Was anyone looking for him? Were enemies lying in wait to pick him off the moment he lifted himself out of this leafy shelter? It seemed safer to just stay put. But the others on the helicopter needed his help. And God knows Paxton would need his help.

Smith braced himself for the pain, gripped his rifle in a business-like manner and pushed himself to his knees. He scanned the surroundings through the M4's optics.

Not a human in sight.

But he did see something man-made. The wreckage of the

Pave Hawk was partially visible through the foliage. It was about 300 meters away. It was upright but leaning against a large tree. Smoke billowed out of the remainder of the tail boom, but no flames were apparent.

He had to leave the relative safety of his shelter and cross the distance to the wreckage. He swept the rifle's optics around again, looking for any movement or change.

Nothing.

Was everyone gone?

Or was it a trap?

Smith kept his right hand on the grip of his weapon, finger on the outside edge of the trigger. He slowly lowered his left hand down to the ground to steady himself as he rose to his feet. He winced waiting for a fusillade of bullets to tear him in half.

Nothing.

He scoped the surroundings again from his standing position. He lifted his left foot up and over the foliage and stepped on a clear spot. He then swung his right leg over the top of the bush and placed his right boot silently next to his left.

Rifle up and ready in front of him, he ran in a crouch toward the Pave Hawk. His equipment bouncing up and down made more noise than he wanted it to.

He stopped half way and leaned against an oak. He swept 360° blinking the sweat out of his eye as it peered through the rifle's scope.

Nothing.

His heart was hammering away as he sprinted the last 150

meters to the helicopter.

He slowed and crouched lower as he got closer.

The smell of the smoke was overpowering now. Smith dreaded what he might find when he reached the copter.

Bullet holes riddled the aluminum skin, and the rotors, which were designed to fold, were bent at odd angles. The rope Smith had rappelled down was draped over the lower branches of a tree. A pool of hydraulic fluid spread from under the fuselage.

Smith's eyes darted about. If there were a trap, it would be set with the helicopter acting as a big piece of cheese. The Pave Hawk certainly looked like a hunk of Swiss.

He made his way across the remaining meters to the wreckage. The first grisly sight was Seaman First Class Spaulding's mangled body crushed under the fuselage. He had apparently fallen out at the last moment, and the Pave Hawk landed on him.

The sight was so repulsive that Smith had to force himself to approach. The thoughts of his own pain were already forgotten.

He moved to the front. The cockpit windshields were shattered, and the bloodied bodies of the pilot and co-pilot hung from their safety belts in unnatural poses. No need to check them for life.

That left only Ketterman. Smith wondered if he were inside the fuselage. He didn't want to find out, but he had no choice. The smell of death enveloped him.

He was panting as he ducked under the side of the helicopter that faced the ground. He could feel the warm aluminum with his free hand over his head. His right hand gripped the stock even tighter as he tried to transfer his tension to his rifle. The fuselage blocked the sun, but spots appeared on the ground where the light found its way all the way through the copter.

When he got to the sliding door, he was able to stand up inside the cabin. Kettermen lay on his back, arms and legs spread at different angles. His eyes were wide open as if he had just seen something surprising. But they were lifeless. His body had been torn by close-range shotgun fire. Slugs had been used.

There was no one for Smith to help. And there was no one to help Smith.

He was on his own. He didn't even know if Paxton was still alive.

He needed to see if there was any equipment or weapons he could salvage from the wreckage. Maybe there was a radio he could use.

One look at the cockpit instrument panel revealed that it had been sprayed with shotgun fire just as Ketterman's body had been. The radio was equally dead.

Smith meticulously searched the cabin. He even fought the urge to vomit as he searched the bodies for weapons, radios, or anything useful. It was clear that he was the second person to so search because anything of value was already gone.

The only thing of possible use was a medical kit. Smith grabbed that and climbed back out of the creaking wreckage. Of course, a medical kit was only useful if he found living people. Living people who weren't interested in killing him.

He sat down in the shadow of the Pave Hawk and leaned back against the hard aluminum. The thought that the wreckage could slip from its position leaning against the tree and give him the Spaulding treatment didn't seem to matter to him. He had to think.

He had no radio. He had one rifle and limited ammunition. He had no means of transportation other than his two feet. Pain throbbed, an insistent reminder he was at least alive. Two-thirds of the team were dead. He didn't know if Paxton were dead. Even if Paxton were alive, he had no idea how to find him. Not to mention that he had no idea how to find the 100 liters of nerve gas that was about to wind up in the hands of *al Qaeda*.

• • •

General Reed was still temporarily located at Brindisi Airbase. *Closer to the action.* Maps and binders littered every horizontal surface of Reed's room in the Officer Quarters. Even though he and Captain Marshall were working out of what amounted to a hotel room, he appreciated that it was actually nicer and roomier than his Pentagon office. It certainly was in a beautiful location in the southern portion of Italy.

The room also had a well-stocked wet bar that he and Marshall made the most of. Every day, their rooms were cleaned and a steward restocked the general's favorites.

The men were enjoying glasses of expensive scotch when the phone rang.

Marshall answered it.

"General, it is Colonel Ward," said Marshall, covering the mouthpiece of the phone. Ward was the commander of the

Pararescue training group that employed Paxton.

Reed blew air through pursed lips and shook his head.

"I'm sorry, Colonel. The general is not available at the moment. Is there something I can help you with?"

Reed watched Marshall as he listened to Paxton's commander.

"I'm sorry. He isn't available either at the moment."

The sound of Ward's voice leaked out from the handset held tightly to Marshall's ear.

"I can't say when he will be available."

Marshall winced.

"I don't know the answer to that. I'll have either General Reed or Senior Master Sergeant Paxton call you back as soon as either one is available." The captain hung up.

"What the hell does he want now?"

"He wants to know when Paxton is coming home."

Reed scoffed and took another sip of his drink. "If Ward only knew that Paxton was back in Yugoslavia, he would know the appropriate question is not *when* is Paxton coming home but *is* he coming home?."

"I think we both know the answer to that one, sir."

• • •

The two Iraqi men bounced around in the cab of the truck as they drove down a stretch that seemed more pothole than road. The larger Iraqi was in the passenger seat of the truck and was on his cell phone with Jashari. Jashari was using his satellite phone provided by the Americans. Ironically, since the Iraqi's native language was Arabic and Jashari's native language was Serbo-Croat---more commonly known as Serbian---the only language they had in common was English.

"Do you still have the individual in custody?"

"Yes, we do."

The truck continued to bump its way down the dusty Turkish road.

"Good. We will go dark for a little while until we cross the border into your country." The Iraqi knew that traversing Bulgaria would be much more difficult than their trip through Turkey. Bulgaria was in the process of becoming a European Union nation, and thus things were much more above-board than they were in the past when it was a Soviet satellite.

To transport the deadly cargo across Bulgaria, the Iraqis would require some help. That help had already been arranged.

• • •

Chapter 12

SMITH SAT NEXT TO THE PAVE HAWK WRECKAGE contemplating his next move. It wasn't a good idea to stick around the crash site. The KLA might return looking for treasures. Besides, he needed to see if he could help Paxton somehow. He had insisted on coming along to help his friend and mentor. Now it was time to deliver that help.

The only problem was, he had no idea where Paxton was.

Or if Paxton was even alive.

Sitting here was pointless and dangerous. But he felt horrible just leaving the bodies. Those men had loved ones. They deserved better than to be just left there, rotting in the wreckage.

He had no way to contact anyone to come get them.

He couldn't take them with him.

Burying them would take too long.

He had to hope that someone had noticed that they were down, and rescue was on its way.

There wasn't time to wait for them. He had to get moving.

If he was ever able to get in touch with American forces, he wanted to be able to tell them where to find the bodies. McMurphy's GPS unit. Smith still had it. He had never given it up to the SEALs like Paxton had told him to.

He pulled it out and turned it on. The small screen blinked to life, and it began searching for a satellite signal. The hour-glass spun and spun to no avail. Smith lifted the device higher, as if he were making an offering to God. He squinted at the screen.

The offering worked. The signal connected, and the small screen blinked and then rendered a series of lines representing terrain and numbers representing coordinates…coordinates accurate to within a few meters.

Smith touched the button with his thumb to tag his location. Future reference.

If need be, he could lead others back to this location to recover the bodies.

If he survived.

Smith then turned to the next order of business: *find Paxton*. He lowered the GPS unit and stared at it.

It was starting to come back to him. On board the Pave Hawk when Paxton learned that Smith still had the GPS unit from McMurphy, he had given Smith very specific instructions. Smith had obeyed all of Paxton's orders but one.

General Reed had reluctantly given him two sets of GPS coordinates, and Smith had entered them into the memory of the unit. The memory already had two sets of coordinates, one previously provided by Reed, and the second marked by Smith himself. And now a fifth location had been added: the Pave Hawk wreckage.

Since Paxton wasn't onboard the Pave Hawk, that left four locations to search for him.

Smith hitched up his weapon, stretched his arm above him with the unit to capture the weak signal, and began moving to the first of the possible locations.

Smith hoped to hell Paxton wasn't there.

• • •

Where Paxton was, he sat on the floor. There was nothing to do other than pace the floor of his small cell or run through everything in his head.

He had already done the latter repeatedly, but pacing wasn't going to accomplish anything.

The first contact he had with this fiasco was when General Reed burst into his office back at the Pararescue Schoolhouse at Lackland. He had never seen or heard of Reed before. But he had two stars on his shoulder-bars, and Paxton's commander, Colonel Ward, was with him. So however crazy the words coming out of Reed's mouth were, they were couched in legitimacy.

Reed had interrupted Paxton's day and told him that a Stealth fighter had been shot down over Serbia. The Stealth had been part of numerous sorties being flown in support of Operation Allied Force. The Serbs had been accused of various atrocities, including ethnic cleansing, against the minority Muslim population. The Muslims, however, didn't have clean hands—the

Kosovo Liberation Army, also known as the KLA, had been accused of bombings of civilian targets and police stations.

The United States, through NATO, chose sides and threatened to bomb Serbia if certain demands were not met. Deadlines passed, and the bombs began to fall.

Somehow, the Serbs managed to shoot down the Stealth. "Lucky shot," according to Reed.

Having been a PJ for most of his career, Paxton was used to being sent in when a plane goes down. Rescue the pilot behind enemy lines.

But Reed's request was odd for three reasons.

First, Reed wasn't in Paxton's chain of command. He had come from the Pentagon. Rescues are coordinated out of Scott Air Force Base in Illinois, not the Pentagon. And they don't send a two-star general to make the request in person. Orders are radioed, and a rescue team is dispatched. Sort of like when the fire department gets a 9-1-1 call.

The second anomaly was that Paxton was no longer an active PJ. He was an instructor training airmen to become PJs. He was located at the Medina Annex to Lackland AFB outside of San Antonio, Texas. It would make no sense for PJs to be sent from Texas to Yugoslavia to rescue a pilot—it was simply too far away. There were pararescuemen located in Italy who were perfectly capable of rescuing a pilot.

Which brought him to the strangest thing of all. Reed didn't want Paxton to rescue the pilot. In fact, he prohibited it at first. And he ordered Paxton to lie to his team. He was told to convince them it was a bona fide rescue mission.

Reed demanded that Paxton locate the Stealth wreckage, collect it up using a bulldozer and a dump truck, and return the wreckage to the States.

National Security.

To prevent secrets from getting into the wrong hands.

It seemed to Paxton that a 500-pound bomb on the wreckage could accomplish the same thing, with a lot lower risk.

Paxton learned, after it was too late, that returning the wreckage to the States wasn't really what Reed had in mind.

Enter McMurphy. Reed's mystery man.

Reed injected McMurphy into the mission without Colonel Ward's knowledge. Who was McMurphy? Paxton still wasn't sure. All he knew was that he wasn't a PJ. He wasn't even military. And McMurphy had his own secret mission to complete.

Apparently, the Chinese were well on their way to developing a radar system that would defeat ordinary Stealth technology. To combat the Chinese system, the Stealth fighter and bombers were retrofitted with specialized electronics packages.

Chinese agents had been working to get their hands on the package so they could find a way to counter it. A counter-counter measure, if you will.

This was General Reed's department. Head of advanced technologies, he conceived of a plan. Rudimentary at first and then growing into a fiasco.

The simple concept was to make a fake "black box" and pass it off to the Chinese. They would spend years analyzing it and working to defeat it while the Stealths could continue to fly with the real black boxes.

But Reed said there was some sort of information leak. Apparently, the Chinese had learned of the scheme and knew a fake device was being developed. Two American CIA officers lost their lives because of the leaks.

So the circle of knowledge collapsed inward, and a new plan was hatched. Reed would sit back and in the event a Stealth ever went down, he knew the Chinese, and probably the Russians, would swarm it in the hope of getting their hands on the genuine box carried by the aircraft.

McMurphy was the government's man in Yugoslavia, and he was called back to Washington for training on how to locate and switch the real box in the wreckage for a fake one outfitted with a GPS tracking unit.

Reed told Paxton that the Stealth had been shot down before McMurphy was ready. So Paxton and a team of PJs were to be sent in as cover to insert McMurphy and allow him to make the switch. Secrecy was the key. No more leaks.

McMurphy told Paxton that Paxton had been chosen because he had taken two years of Russian. Knowledge of the Russian language was necessary since their cover was to act as freelance Russian advisors.

The Serbs planned to sell the box to the Chinese but they figured out that they were being scammed and captured McMurphy and Paxton. The Serbs sent a team of assassins who would kill Paxton's family unless he answered the Serb's questions. McMurphy was taken away. Paxton was broken out of captivity by members of the KLA.

Members of *al Qaeda* more accurately.

Unbeknownst to the KLA, they had the fake box, and the Serbs had the genuine one.

Paxton killed three of the *al Qaeda* and escaped, only to learn that they were planning to trade the box for nerve gas.

Hence Paxton found himself in this position.

And the Iraqi's wanted him—no doubt to torture and kill him for his activities during the Gulf war. Actions that won him the Air Force Cross. Actions that to this day remain classified.

He had no idea how he was going to stop the jihadists from getting the nerve gas. He had no idea where McMurphy was or if he was even still alive. Nor did he have any idea of how he was going to escape with his life.

At least this time he didn't have to worry about his family.

• • •

Jill pushed the cart through the Lackland AFB commissary. Megan rode in the seat by the handlebars. John, Jr. was hugging the front. She went up and down the aisles, periodically grabbing an item off the shelf and placing it in the cart without really looking at it. She wore a plain white t-shirt and blue jeans.

She was thankful that she could do all her shopping on base. She still didn't feel safe venturing "out there." She probably wouldn't feel safe until John returned home.

Whenever that was.

How could Colonel Ward have sent him on that mission?

Rescue the pilot of the Stealth fighter!

He was an instructor.

The mission was done. John had called her from Italy.

He had made it back safely. What was the holdup?

Why wasn't he on the next fight home?

A wheel wiggled as she went down another aisle.

She and the kids were more than ready for him to return home and for their lives to return to normal.

She decided she would call Colonel Ward.

John wouldn't be happy about that.

Well, she wasn't happy that John hadn't called to let her know what was going on.

If he didn't want her calling his boss for an update, maybe he should pick up the damn phone!

"What's wrong, Mommy?" the voice squeaked from the front of the cart.

"Nothing, hon. I'm just tired." She needed to keep her emotions in check in front of the kids. They were so perceptive.

She would confront John's boss. What would it matter? John was getting out soon anyway.

• • •

Smith moved from cover to cover through the green labyrinth. The GPS receiver showed the way—but he had to adjust where he was pointing it from time to time to maintain the signal. He didn't particularly like having to divide his attention between the receiver and scanning the surroundings for deadly threats, but he didn't see where he had much choice.

The air was crisp with smell of spring blooms. He could hear the babble of water. He was getting close. He crouched even lower, his finger on the edge of the trigger.

Smith peered into a clearing by a mountain stream. It was the very same spot he had picked up Paxton hours ago. The same spot where they dropped Paxton off just a short while ago.

But there was no sign of Paxton. The ground was disturbed, but nobody remained. No good guys, no bad guys.

That was somewhat of a relief for Smith. If Paxton were still there, it would have been because he was dead. So he either left on his own, or he was taken somewhere. That meant Smith would have to try the next spot. Each succeeding location, unfortunately, was increasingly dangerous.

• • •

The terrain was difficult and all uphill. The only positive thing about it was that the GPS signal grew stronger. Smith no longer had to mimic the Statute of Liberty just to find out where he was and where he was going.

For now, the GPS unit was superfluous because he was retracing the path of the KLA soldiers, and they had cleared the way through the brush with reckless abandon.

He was becoming more comfortable with the fact that he was all alone in enemy territory with only his rifle for protection. It wasn't bravery so much as it was just an acceptance. No need to waste energy worrying. Fear can be exhausting, and exhaustion can get you killed.

So he came to terms with the fact that he could be killed at any moment and moved on.

As a result, he was able to move more quickly.

He was still cautious, but it was caution mixed with determination.

Despite the cool weather, he was sweating quite profusely. His uniform stuck to him, and he figured if the enemy didn't see him, they could certainly smell him.

From time to time, he grabbed a tree trunk to pull himself up the hill. The scrapes on his palms were starting to bleed. He ignored that and pressed on. Paxton needed him.

He slipped and landed on some sharp rocks. He hung onto the GPS unit and protected it from any potentially damaging impact. It was his only link to his former instructor. It was more important than his elbow or shoulder that took the brunt of the impact. Nonetheless, he cursed.

Smith slowly climbed to his feet, repositioned his rifle and continued upward. He crested a particularly steep hill, and then the ground flattened out. What he saw made him duck for cover.

In front of him sat a Mercedes panel truck on a mountain road. The rear axle had been broken off, and the chassis rested on the asphalt. The truck was filthy and rusty. And it wasn't going anywhere—at least without assistance.

Smith peered through the scope of his M4. He scrutinized the surroundings. He didn't see anyone. Behind the truck was a smoldering crater. The road was completely gone. On the other side of the road, the ground sloped down and then formed a line…a break before the mountains in the distance. Probably a cliff or at least a steep drop-off. There was no guardrail. He listened for a short while and came to the conclusion that no one was around.

Smith moved out from cover and walked over to the vehicle. He found three bodies. Two in the back of the truck and one lying on the road next to an open driver's-side door.

Just as Paxton had left them.

Just as Paxton had described to him.

He didn't waste anytime searching the vehicle or the corpses. Anything of use would already be gone.

He looked around. To the left of the road, there was no guardrail. Just a relatively steep, gravelly slope that ended in a sheer drop off the edge of a cliff. No help there.

He examined the screen of the GPS unit and squinted down the road in the direction the truck had been headed. He realized that he was out of breath from his trek. He looked back down at the screen and did some mental calculations.

He was going to need a vehicle.

It was too damn far to walk to Jashari's headquarters.

• • •

"Lay down on your stomach and put your hands under you." The command was muffled though the thick door.

Paxton did what he was told.

A heavy latch clacked and the door swung open.

"Don't look!"

Paxton looked and then turned away.

He could hear something slide on the floor and then the door was pulled shut and locked again.

He turned his head and saw a tray with a small bowl and coffee cup on it.

He sat up and then moved over to the tray.

The coffee looked dark. The bowl was filled with a thin white liquid. A small crust of bread was next to it.

Paxton had no idea what it was, but he was hungry so he grabbed the plastic spoon provided and brought the bowl near his lips so he wouldn't waste any. The soup was cold.

So was the coffee.

He rapidly consumed them both along with the stale bread.

Paxton had no clue what kind of soup it was, but he didn't care. He at least had something in his stomach.

Last time he was sent to this God-forsaken country, he had been ordered to do so and he was prevented from calling Jill to say goodbye.

This time he wasn't ordered—he volunteered.

This time he wasn't prevented from talking to his wife. He had privacy and could tell her anything he wanted to. But he chose not to tell her he was going back to Yugoslavia. He just said he had something to take care of before he came home.

He didn't want to worry her. He wanted to maintain mission security. There was no time to give an explanation. There were a lot of reasons he could give to try to rationalize. Was it that he just couldn't bring himself to tell her? Was it easier to just do it and ask for forgiveness later?

Like the old days...only in those days there was no one to ask for forgiveness.

Just random beauties who had no choice but to put up with

his job—his lifestyle.

But Jill was different. The first woman to really make him think twice. The first woman to cause him to put on the brakes. There was just something about her.

It wasn't just her beauty—-her long muscular legs, that smile that made his heart melt. PJs had their pick of beautiful women.

He remembered a quip from one of his instructors when he went through the PJ Indoc course as a young airman. *In the beginning, God created man…but woman remained unsatisfied, so God created the PJ.*

That's exactly what it was like with the other women in his past.

And, frankly, it got a little boring.

Jill wasn't impressed with him like the other women. She didn't chase him like the others would.

She saw him as more of a work-in-progress.

She thought he had a lot of unfulfilled potential.

Imagine that, her thinking that he, a skilled and decorated pararescueman, wasn't fulfilling his potential. He had saved dozens of lives. He had risked it all countless times. What more could be asked of him?

But she was right.

She thought he should settle down and start a family.

She saw it before he did, but he was ready. It would be nearly impossible to raise a family and keep up the crazy pace of his career. It was time to take a step back. Paxton couldn't bring himself to give it up completely. So a compromise was reached: He would apply to become a PJ instructor. Much greater stability, but he could keep one foot literally "in the pool."

He excelled. He had never thought of himself as a teacher before, but he found that he loved taking his knowledge and experience and transferring it to a whole new generation. Teaching young airmen how to stay alive and to save other lives empowered him. It was like multiplying his effectiveness. Plus he got to be a gatekeeper. He was on the front lines of making sure the quality of his beloved PJs remained stellar.

Jill also encouraged him to return to night school so he could have a career after the Air Force. He was reluctant at first, but again she was right. Once he got back into the swing of school, he found that he loved learning. He excelled at that too.

Then his tour of duty as an instructor was almost up. He was going to have to make a decision: Either return to being an active PJ or leave the service. Rock and hard place.

Colonel Ward saved him from that choice. He asked him to extend his tour of duty as an instructor and to take over the Indoc School replacing the retiring Non-commissioned Officer In Charge (NCOIC). By then they already had one child, and he needed the job. Plus he needed time to finish his Bachelor's degree. So Jill agreed to allow him to take the position. The understanding was that he would retire from that position and never return to a Rescue Squadron.

Things were pretty sweet. Another child came along. Two children and a loving wife. A job that he loved and that his wife tolerated.

Then in walked General Reed. Everything changed.

It would be easy to blame the general. But that was a cop

out. It was Paxton's choice to come back here. That was probably the chief reason he didn't tell Jill he was going on another mission. Yes, things were really bad at the moment. His life was definitely on the line. When you boiled it all down, however, there was one inescapable conclusion:

He really missed this shit.

• • •

From his concealed position, Smith watched through his riflescope as a truck approached. He counted at least four men. Each of them appeared to have a rifle or submachine gun. Not the best choice for him. The vehicle slowed down as it reached the destroyed truck in the road. It then turned off onto the shoulder passing between Smith and the wreckage. It barely slowed down—as if this were an everyday occurrence. It probably was. Fortunately, the men were busy looking at carnage and thus didn't see the American hiding off to the side of the road.

The truck continued on its way, and it was once again quiet.

Smith continued to wait for his opportunity. He considered starting to walk, but the wreckage would provide a natural choke point for him to make his move. So he sat and waited.

His plan was simple. Wait for a vehicle to slow or come to a stop because of the wreckage. He would then spring from cover and order the driver out by gunpoint.

A carjacking.

If it were a military vehicle, he would let it pass. Too risky. He didn't expect resistance from the driver of a civilian vehicle.

Sure, the driver would be upset at losing his car. But Smith was quite confident that a close look at his M4 assault rifle would be sufficient to change the mind of the most recalcitrant victim.

He had no plans to kill the driver. Just take the car and leave him standing by the side of the road. He had no interest in killing anyone. He didn't know what side they might be on, and most likely they were innocent bystanders in this conflict.

Besides, he didn't want to waste any precious ammunition.

In fact, he felt a little bad about it. But he needed wheels. He had to save Pax.

Smith wondered absentmindedly if his carjack victim would likely have car insurance.

He didn't have to wait long for the payoff. An orange VW Golf came around the bend and approached the wreckage. Smith tensed. Through magnification he could see there were two occupants. Males. No visible sign of weapons.

The car was coming fast, and the driver evidently wasn't paying attention because he had to brake hard to avoid plowing into the destroyed truck. The tires locked up and white smoke billowed out. The driver and the passenger appeared momentarily shaken.

That was Smith's opportunity.

He dashed out from cover, sighting down the rifle barrel. The smell of burnt rubber lingered.

"Get out of the car!" Smith shouted.

The occupants appeared stunned to see the airman pointing the rifle at them as he moved beside the driver's door. "Out now!" Smith waved the barrel of the rifle to the right a couple times to indicate what he wanted them to do.

For an instant, the driver looked like he was going to open the door. Then the driver jammed the car in reverse and stomped on the gas pedal. The front fender swept toward Smith, front wheels chomped at his left shin as he leaped backward as if he were avoiding a linebacker.

Shit!

The bumper tagged Smith's boot as it was up in the air and spun him clockwise. He almost lost the rifle as he flailed to keep his balance.

If it weren't for all those years of football, he would have wound up right on his ass. As it was, his left shoulder faced the Golf as it screeched to a halt. Its rear tires had almost dropped off the pavement onto the gravel.

The car was now perpendicular to the normal flow of traffic, its rear toward the far side drop-off. Smith saw the driver reach for the gearshift.

Son of a bitch; they are getting away!

At any point Smith could bring his rifle to bear and start blasting away. The passenger was ducking down the best he could to avoid having his head blown off. He seemed to have a problem with the fact that the driver's maneuver brought the passenger to the position closest to the American.

But shooting would do Smith no good. He didn't want to kill or injure the occupants. And he certainly didn't want to disable the vehicle. One disabled vehicle was already blocking the road.

He had to act fast or he might lose his only chance at getting a vehicle. If they got away, surely they would tell someone about the crazy man in the American uniform trying to jack vehicles. The roads would swarm with police and military. But what could he do?

The driver grabbed the gearshift knob and jammed it forward. He popped the clutch, and the Volkswagen lurched forward and stalled.

Evidently, in his haste the driver had shifted into third gear instead of first.

This was Smith's chance. Now or never.

In full panic, the driver tried to start the car without fully depressing the clutch, and the starter whined as the car jumped forward and stopped again.

Smith was too far from the car. He needed to close the distance. To do that he needed to buy some time.

He lined up his rifle.

He considered just firing over the hood, like a warning shot.

But that might only make them move faster.

He needed to break their concentration. He wanted to make them both duck down.

The passenger was still trying to fold himself onto the floor. The driver had moved the gearshift to neutral and was reaching for the ignition.

Smith pulled the trigger. One shot. Straight through the passenger's window, over his back and out the driver's side rear window. Glass sprayed all over both occupants—which was the point.

The driver recoiled and covered his face by crossing his forearms.

Smith covered the distance to the passenger door in a flash. He reversed the rifle as he ran and jammed the butt through the shattered window with both hands striking the driver's forearms with enough force to bounce his head against the window.

No more Mr. Nice guy.

Smith then turned his attention to the passenger. He reached in and pulled the door latch. He yanked the door open and grabbed the cowering man with this left hand. His right held his rifle out at a safe distance as he dragged the passenger onto the pavement.

For whatever reason, the passenger chose that moment to start fighting back. Instead of just falling to the ground in submission, he wrapped his arms around Smith's legs and drove forward in an attempt to tackle.

Bad move.

Smith drove the rifle down onto the back of the passenger's head. Adrenaline had taken over, and he struck with more force than he had intended. After the sick sound of the impact, the man collapsed and remained motionless.

Smith was stunned for a moment by what he had just done. He snapped out of it when he realized the driver was again trying to start the car.

Smith dropped his rifle and lunged through the open door. He chopped the driver's hand off the ignition with the knife-edge of his right hand and simultaneously shoved his head against the window with the palm of his left.

It was an awkward position. Smith's legs protruded out the open door behind him, and he really couldn't get any leverage as he lay on his belly across the passenger seat. He could feel the shards of glass poke into his midsection and upper legs. His ribs were on fire.

The driver connected with a hammer fist to the top of Smith's helmet. He was full of fight.

It was at that moment that Smith realized he felt another sensation—the car was rolling. The driver must have put it in neutral to start the engine, and now the slope of the road was pulling the car backward toward the edge of the steep cliff.

Shit shit shit!

The driver managed to get his hands around Smith's neck and was squeezing with all his might. Smith pushed harder against the driver's face, smooshing it against the window. The young airman started to see stars as he tried to bring his right arm into the fight, but the damn steering wheel was in the way. He couldn't swing with any force. Plus the driver's knees were braced against the steering wheel, so he couldn't get past them.

One of the tires bumped over the rifle as the car continued to roll backward.

Smith had to get the driver to stop choking him, or he was going to pass out. He blindly felt around the driver's face and pushed his thumb into his eye socket like he was pushing a button.

The driver let go of Smith's throat and grabbed Smith's fingers with both hands attempting to pry them off his face. Smith pushed harder feeling the eyeball deform under the pressure. The driver desperately swung his legs between the steering wheel and the gearshift and kneed Smith's midsection.

The car's rear tires dropped off the pavement onto the dirt

shoulder. Smith tried to wrap his right arm around the driver's legs to stop the kicking, but it was pinned under the legs. The man screamed in a combination of panic and pain.

The front wheels dropped off the pavement and the car continued to roll.

"Stop kicking me and hit the fucking brake!"

The man either didn't understand or, in his panic, didn't even hear.

Smith had no idea how far before they rolled over the edge. The car jacking had turned into a fight for his life.

Survival instinct took over. The man was pulling with all his might to remove Smith's left hand from his face. Smith stopped fighting him—just for an instant. The driver was able to wrench Smith's arm away from his eye and back over the airman's head. Coiled like a spring, Smith punched down toward the man's face, but the man wouldn't let go. At that same instant, Smith sprung with his knees, letting the force propel him further into the car. The man twisted away, forcing Smith's arm to miss his face to the upper left, over his shoulder. Smith's punch struck the car door, completely harmless—except to Smith who felt the impact jolt his wrist.

The car gained speed as the tires crunched over the gravel.

Smith hitched up and slapped his hand along the inside of the door. Realizing what Smith was doing, the man frantically tried to pull the American's hand away from the door handle. Smith was completely blind, his head buried under the man's legs. The smell of sweat, dust, and fear filled the air.

The situation clarified for the man, and he tried to swing his legs back down to hit the brake, but now he couldn't get them back between Smith and the dashboard. He simultaneously tried to wrench Smith's hand away, and the end result was that he writhed and floundered, incapable of achieving either goal.

Smith fought against the man's arms as he tried to find the door latch. Any moment he expected to pitch over the lip of the cliff.

The emergency brake!

Smith curled his right arm around and fished it between the seat and the gearshift. He found the handle for the brake. He tried to force it up, but his own chest was in the way. He was lying across the space between the seats unable to move the brake at all. He twisted to make room for it to swing up, but the man, in his panic, forced him back down.

The left rear of the car sunk lower, and the terrain turned the steering wheel.

Smith frantically slapped at the door.

Where's the damn handle?

The steering wheel spun back the other way as if it were controlled by some invisible hand.

Time was running out.

The man bit Smith's forearm, but Smith no longer felt any pain. He was a machine.

His fingers brushed the metal of the door latch. *There it is!* He shoved up closer and grabbed at the latch again. The man shrieked. Smith yanked.

Nothing.

The door stayed closed. Locked.

The front of the car was visibly higher than the rear as it gained backward momentum down the hill.

Smith burrowed higher with all his might and located the thumb lock just above the door latch. He ticked it out and jerked the handle again.

The driver howled as the door against which he was leaning gave way. He pitched backward headfirst. Smith shoved the man's legs up and off of him as the man's head struck the gravel. The driver did a backward summersault out of the car, and the open door struck his backside spinning him around, landing him face up with legs away from the car.

Smith caught a glimpse of the cliff looming less than two yards from rear wheels as he grabbed the steering wheel and dove down below the dashboard. He reached for the brake pedal as he felt the left front wheel bump up and down abruptly. He stabbed the pedal with his hand and the car slid to a halt.

Holding the brake down, he arched up and pulled the emergency brake lever till it ground tight. He gingerly let off the brake pedal slightly. The car didn't move. The emergency brake was holding. He let off the brake completely and unfolded himself until he was sitting up in the passenger seat. He could see the road above him through billows of dust.

The driver!

No time to rest. The man would surely be on his feet and attacking Smith in an instant. Smith grabbed the door jamb and pulled himself to his feet. He ran around the front of the car and was greeted by a gruesome sight.

The driver lay there on his back, arms splayed. The man's

head and neck had been run over by the left front tire. He wasn't going to attack anyone ever again.

He looked past the man's body to see another unsettling sight. The Golf's rear tires were less than a foot from the edge of the cliff. Smith walked over to get a better look.

Jagged rocks and trees lay at least two hundred feet below. They would have never survived going over the cliff. A shiver passed through his body. He shook it off and climbed into the driver's seat.

Soon someone else might come along and discover him.

It was time to get the hell out of here.

Smith put both hands on the wheel and looked up the hill that lay in front of him. He then glanced in the rearview mirror and saw nothing but the distant landscape far below.

He wondered what the hell he was going to do. He now had a vehicle. The problem was, however, he'd never learned to drive a stick shift.

Chapter 13

THE IRAQIS PULLED UP TO THE GUARDHOUSE ON THE Bulgarian border. The Bulgarian guard walked up to the driver-side window. His sidearm protruded from his hip at a jaunty angle. The driver cranked the dusty window down and spoke one word—the name of a former Bulgarian Secret policeman.

The former Soviet Bloc nation was no longer a puppet, but its early attempts at democracy did not result in any improvement of the standard of living. Thus, former members of the secret police still wielded tremendous power, and many of them formed crime syndicates.

As a result, with the pressure brought by the crime syndicate combined with some generous bribes, the Iraqis were allowed to enter the country without further inspection. The 100 liters of Tabun remained securely concealed in the back of the truck.

The next border crossing would bring them into Serbia.

• • •

Smith dropped his helmet and gathered his rifle from the road and the medical bag from the bushes where he had hidden before the car came along. He jogged to the man lying on the road, the former passenger. Blood oozed from the back of his head where Smith had smashed him with the butt of his rifle. He carefully rolled him over onto his back and pushed his fingers into the side of his throat. There was a faint pulse. Then he put his ear above the man's mouth and nose and watched as his chest rose and fell unsteadily.

The good news was the man was still alive.

The bad news was the man was still alive.

Smith was relieved that he had not inadvertently killed him. But that posed a problem. If the man were dead, Smith could just drag his body, and that of his buddy, into the woods and drive off. It would be quite some time before anyone discovered what had happened and would come looking for the car. As it was, he now had a dilemma.

The safest thing for him to do would be to drag the man into the woods anyway. But then he would surely die before he was discovered. To say the man needed medical treatment would be an understatement. Smith had no means to call in a rescue helicopter to just whisk him away to a military hospital. His conscience told him he should stay with the man and render aid until someone came along who could get him to a hospital. But to do that would mean Smith would be captured or killed. He wouldn't be much help to Paxton if that happened.

He decided he would stabilize the man, leave him in the road where a passerby would discover him and, he hoped, call an ambulance in time. Smith would pray that the man remained unconscious long enough for Smith to get far enough away. He didn't need the authorities looking for the vehicle.

Smith turned the man on his left side—the recovery position. He made sure he had a clear airway and he quickly bandaged the back of his head to stem the bleeding. He pulled a thin Mylar blanket from the medical kit and used it to keep the man comfortable and to help prevent shock, and then he gathered the rest of his gear and headed down the steep slope to the car.

Smith considered shoving the dead man's body over the cliff, but that would be pointless and cruel. With the other man still alive in the road, someone was sure to find out what had happened. Instead, Smith grabbed the man under the arms and dragged him back so he would be out of the way. He had to move quickly…someone could come along at any moment.

He tossed his gear, helmet, and rifle into the car and considered the situation.

The principle of how a standard transmission worked was not a mystery to Smith. Clutch, gears, shift before the redline. He had just never actually done it before. While he was confident he would be able to do it once he was on relatively flat ground, the car's current location proved to be a particularly sticky predicament.

The nose of the car was headed up the steep hill, and the rear tires were uncomfortably close to the drop-off. Not the best conditions to learn to drive a stick shift.

He knew that he had to depress the clutch to put the car in

gear, but once he did that it would surely roll backward. How the hell was he supposed to get it in first gear before it rolled off the cliff?

He needed more room.

What the hell, the Golf wasn't that big of a car. He would push it up the hill a little ways to give him some breathing room. Hell, if he got the momentum going, maybe he could push it all the way up onto the relatively level road. He could then finesse the clutch without having to worry about the car rolling.

Smith positioned himself behind the open driver's door. He tested several hand holds and settled on one with this left hand on the door frame at the height of the dashboard and the right one on the top of the steering wheel so he could keep it going straight up the hill. He bent his legs ready to explode with power. He braced himself and then reached down with his right hand for the parking brake. He practiced the quick movement in his head. He would release the brake and then grab the wheel and push the car up the hill.

1...2...3

He released the brake and shoved with all his might as he grabbed the wheel. He felt the entire weight of the car push back. Smith heaved, but the car rolled backward, the door jamb pressing on his neck and shoulder.

No!

He was losing it. The car seemed as if it were going to push him backward right over the cliff. The wide-open door would sweep him up if he tried to escape. He didn't look back at the edge of the cliff, but he felt its presence.

Smith strained with every ounce of strength. His right boot felt like it was about the slip. The car creaked, and gravel popped under the tires. The steering wheel bent back under the force and felt as if it were about to pop off its stem. Smith switched handholds from the wheel to the dashboard to the left of the wheel. He grunted with the effort.

The car stopped rolling.

He envisioned a football field, his opponents with a goal-line stand. The quarterback hands him the ball, and he explodes through the defenders for a touchdown.

The car rolled ever so slightly. But this time it rolled up, away from the edge.

His abdomen and legs were burning from effort, and his ribs felt like they had knives in them, but he had turned the tide. The car was moving slowly up the hill. He started to gain momentum. One foot in front of the other. Step by step. Sweat poured down his face, obscuring his view. His thighs shook with strain. But he wasn't going to stop. Now that this train was moving, he was going to push it all the way up the hill. He was putting all the weight on the balls of his feet so he could maintain his balance. He found that the built-in caster caused the front wheels to track pretty straight, so he didn't have to worry about steadying the steering wheel.

One yard, two yards, five yards. Soon he would make a first down.

His heart felt like it was going to explode. His breathing was labored. It was as if there weren't enough oxygen in the air.

He was going to do it. It seemed he might actually be able to push the car up to the road. He had to keep going though. He felt like he was running out of steam.

Not now. Keep going. Keep moving. Never quit!

He couldn't tell how far he had yet to go as the sweat burned his eyes. He tuned out everything except the sheer determination to put one foot in front of the other.

His next blind step landed on a sandy rock and his foot slipped out from under him.

He landed on his knees and all forward progress ceased.

Shit. Shit. Shit.

The Volkswagen Golf began rolling back toward the cliff. Smith couldn't get any purchase, and the car pushed him along on his knees.

The car gained speed. He considered for a moment trying to get away from the death trap, but there was no way. He couldn't get enough leverage to push himself free past the driver's door that was sweeping him up like a bowling pin.

He frantically tried to dig his feet in, but all he managed to do was create two ruts as his soles bulldozed back down the path he had just climbed.

Any moment he would be carried over the edge. His mind reeled trying to find a way to save his own life.

In a last effort to save himself, he dropped his hand from the dashboard to the floorboard. He flailed around with his right hand until he located the brake pedal. With the last of his energy he pulled himself with his left hand and jammed down on the pedal with his right. The wheels locked up and the car slid to a halt.

Smith remained frozen there, surrounded by dust.

He tentatively pulled himself onto his knees, never letting off the pressure on the pedal. He then let go of the door jamb with his left hand and placed that one on the pedal next to his right. He reached up with his right, located the parking brake and yanked it tight.

Slowly he released the pressure on the brake pedal. The car didn't move.

He carefully let go of the parking brake lever as he sat on the ground next to the driver's seat, his back against the open door. He wiped the dirt and sweat from his eyes.

The first sight was of his bloody and gashed knees. All the material of his uniform around his knees had been shredded.

The next sight was of the open air. Openness past the sheer edge of the cliff. The edge was only a few feet from the soles of his boots. He looked over at the rear tire. It was a mere six inches from the edge of the cliff. Six inches from death.

Smith's heart was pounding. He was utterly exhausted and having difficulty catching his breath. Every muscle in his body ached.

He still needed transportation. But he couldn't wait for another vehicle to come along. The risk was too high. His chances of pulling off another ambush were nil. With the other man in the road, if a military transport came along, there would be no chance to obtain a vehicle.

As much as he hated this fucking orange Golf, he was going to have to go with it.

But he wasn't going to be able to push the car up the hill. That effort had nearly killed him.

No. There was only one way.

If he was going to get the car up the hill, he would have to drive it.

• • •

"Bad news, sir."

"I don't think I can handle anymore. What is it now, Marshall?" Reed looked as if he had aged ten years since the start of the operation.

"The tracker is completely dead, sir. I'm not picking up anything."

"Wonderful…so if they move the device, we won't have anyway to know where."

"'Fraid so, General."

Reed closed his eyes and shook his head.

"Shit. So there is no way for us to know when and where the exchange is going to take place."

Marshall didn't answer.

Reed slammed his fist on the table. "We're fucked!"

"Sir, I know it seems hopeless…."

"No seeming about it…it *is* hopeless." Reed looked up at Marshall to add emphasis. "The KLA is going to be able to make the exchange, and we won't be able to stop it. *Al Qaeda* is going to wind up with the nerve gas, and God knows how many people they are going to kill with that shit. The Iraqis will wind up with the fake device. And you know what? When it is discovered to be fake, and the shit hits the fan about the GA, the trail is going to lead one place. You know where?"

Marshall was silent.

"Right to you and me. Son of a bitch!"

"I don't think…"

"You kidding me? I guarantee it. When the Iraqis figure out they have been duped, they will be out for revenge. We just handed them an ace. When people start dying from GA, the investigation will lead back to Iraq and that is when they will play their card. They will be more than happy to point out that we helped the KLA trade for the shit and it's all going to land on our heads."

Marshall let the general blow off his steam.

Reed planted his forehead in his hand.

"Sir, there is another way."

Reed turned toward Marshall without lifting his head. "Just what the hell are you talking about?"

"Well, we can still stop the transaction and sever our connections."

"How the hell we going to do that? You just told me we can't track the device anymore."

"True, we can't track where it is going. But we know where it is right now."

"What are you suggesting, Marshall?"

"Send in a plane and bomb the device."

Reed sat up. "The device is sitting at the headquarters of an ally. Do you realize what you are suggesting?"

"Jashari isn't much of an ally, is he, sir? You just told me how he intends to kill countless numbers of civilians with nerve gas."

"The people in Washington still consider him an ally."

"Because they don't know what he is up to."

Reed furrowed his brow. "You know how much trouble we are going to have for bombing a KLA headquarters?"

"More or less than if thousands of innocent civilians are gassed?"

"Shit."

"We can chalk it up to a targeting error. Just another friendly fire incident. Happens all the time."

"But if it's looked into?"

"We have the translations from the satellite phone. We point out that we learned that Jashari was a bad guy, and he was eliminated. Hell, you'd be doing a good thing. Right or wrong?"

"It would be a good thing. In the long run…But what about the GA?"

"Well, Jashari would be dead and the device destroyed. So the Iraqis wouldn't have a trading partner. They'd be stuck with it. Let the nerve gas be the U.N. Weapons Inspectors' problem. Let them find it."

"They can't seem to find anything."

"There you go. It's not your fault the U.N. is incompetent and couldn't find it in the first place. They should have destroyed it right after the Gulf War."

"I suppose you are right."

"I know I am. The beautiful thing is the bomb will destroy the fake device, thus severing all ties back to us."

"I don't know about that. So wait a minute...we are right back to where we were after we picked up Paxton. We had the fake device in our hands and the KLA wouldn't have had anything to trade for the GA. We wouldn't be in a position where we have to bomb an ally. What the hell?"

"Well, sir, sending Paxton back wasn't my idea."

"How *do* we explain Paxton leaving here and heading back to Yugoslavia?"

"That's obvious. He was escaping. He was under arrest for the destruction of the C-17 and he escaped."

"Why the hell would he escape back to Yugoslavia?"

"Revenge. He knew he was going to prison, so he would rather get revenge against those who sent the assassins to kill his family."

"You're forgetting one thing, he didn't get to Yugoslavia by himself. He went in an Air Force helicopter—one that was shot down."

"And who gave the order that the copter take him there?"

A smile crossed Reed's face. "That would be Colonel Hicks."

"Exactly, sir."

"What about the SEALs? I gave them their orders."

"Yes, sir. You ordered them to search for the nerve gas—which you learned about in the satellite intercepts."

"I don't know about this. The Serbs still have the real device, and they are going to be able to make the transfer."

"Which would have happened anyway. At least we tried to stop it."

"We did try."

"This still works out better, anyway. If Paxton had not gone back, he could still cause problems for us. The way I see it, Paxton, Smith and McMurphy would have been key witnesses against us. It is a relief that they are gone."

Reed glowered at Marshall. "That's awfully cold, Captain."

"Sir, I know it sounds that way, but your conscience is clear… you didn't send Paxton back. He volunteered. You told him you were washing your hands of it. Besides, he is the reason the mission failed. If it weren't for him, I really think McMurphy could have pulled it off."

"I suppose you are right."

"I know I'm right. If Paxton were still alive, he could cause a whole lot of trouble."

• • •

Paxton sat with his back leaning against the wall of the concrete room that was his prison. It was good news/bad news time.

The good news was he was still alive. His family was safe and he didn't have to worry about them so long as they remained on base. The fake device contained a GPS tracking device, so General Reed knew where he was. And the Iraqis wanted him, so that would ensure he was brought to the site of the exchange.

The bad news was his team was dead. The Iraqis wanted him. And even if he lived to see the exchange, he had absolutely no way to contact U.S. forces to have the nerve gas seized.

He had to figure out a way to contact them.

Satellite phone. General Reed had said they had supplied a satellite phone to Jashari, and they were intercepting its transmissions. That was how they found out about the exchange in the first place.

That would be perfect for contacting Reed. He just had to figure a way to get it away from Jashari. No doubt he would bring it along to the exchange point so they could stay in touch with the Iraqis.

So all he had to do was get access to it just long enough to call in help.

Since Jashari likely wouldn't just offer him the phone, he was left with two options: force or fraud.

The nature of the exchange dictated that the number of people involved would be kept to a minimum. Jashari wouldn't want to bring too many along so he could keep it secret. And the Iraqis would be traveling light. It would be easier to get a few men across the border than an army. So the numbers said Paxton had a chance.

But fraud might be a better option. He could plead for one final call to his family. It didn't matter who he actually called. Reed would be listening in. He just would give the signal and in no time the SEALs would swarm in.

Paxton closed his eyes and began rehearsing what he was going to say to Jashari.

• • •

Smith took a deep breath and exhaled through pursed lips as he held the steering wheel. He turned the rearview mirror away—it wasn't a comforting sight. He pulled his left foot in, and the door swung closed on its own. The air inside smelled stale.

He looked down at his nemesis. The knob had an "R" on the far left forward position. To the right of that were the numbers one through four laid out in the shape of an "H." In the far right forward position was the number five.

I can do this.

He grabbed the knob and shook it back and forth. Neutral.

He tested the clutch pedal. It depressed with ease. He practiced a few shifts, first, second, third while depressing the clutch. It seemed easy enough in theory.

The trick was going to be to avoid rolling backward off the cliff when he depressed the clutch with the emergency brake off.

No more time for practice. It was time to go.

Smith screwed his eyes shut, said a brief prayer and then he reached for the ignition key.

The engine fired up on the first try. The steering wheel blurred with vibration. He blipped the throttle and pressed the clutch to the floor. He pushed the gearshift forward into what he hoped was first gear.

Why the hell did they have to put reverse right next to first?

He pushed the brake pedal as far down as it would go and he released the emergency brake. The car stood still.

Smith eased off the clutch and the brake pedal equally. The car lurched forward and the engine strangled to a halt. He jammed the brake pedal, but the car wasn't going anywhere.

More gas.

He engaged the clutch and restarted the engine.

Sweat flowed down his face.

He eased off the clutch and the brake and then stabbed his foot toward the gas pedal, but it was too late. The car had already bucked forward and died.

I need to give it gas and brake at the same time.

Smith peered at his boots. There wasn't much room between the pedals. He turned his right foot in and laid it across the brake and the gas.

He jammed the clutch down and fired up the engine.

He applied pressure to the gas pedal and eased the brake pedal up. The engine revved and the car started rolling backward. He popped off the clutch and the car lurched forward as he mashed the accelerator to the floor.

This time the engine didn't die.

It whirred as the Golf climbed the hill. Slowly at first. But it gained speed.

Smith bounced around in the seat as the wheels found every rut. He remained focused. He was driving!

Further and further away from the edge of the cliff, the little car powered up the hill toward the road. He was going to make it.

The tires bumped over the lip of the asphalt, and the first sight Smith saw right in front of him was the man he had left lying in the road in the recovery position. He jerked the wheel to the left to avoid running him over. That sudden turn brought him face-to-face with a large Ford SUV that was barreling down the road toward him.

The driver of the SUV locked his brakes, and Smith veered

to the right. He wasn't fast enough. The left front bumper of the SUV smacked into the left rear quarter panel of the Golf. Smith's car spun to the left and bounced off the left rear door of the SUV. Both vehicles rolled to a halt.

Smith was stunned. There was silence. The engine had died again.

Smith looked at the vehicle that had just hit him. It was filled with large men and they all seemed to have rifles. All four doors of the Ford opened, and boots hit the pavement as the men climbed out.

Chapter 14

JASHARI GAVE HIS INSTRUCTIONS TO AHMED, ONE OF HIS
trusted aides. He then sent the man out to meet the Iraqis as
they crossed the border. His aide would be able to lead them
to the location he had chosen for the exchange. Of course it
would be easier to call the Iraqis and give them the location
using the satellite phone. But he didn't want to do it like that.

Someone might be listening.

• • •

Captain Avila sat and took notes during the pre-flight brief-
ing. The lieutenant colonel turned to him and handed him a
sheet of paper.

"New targeting information, Captain. A General Reed
out of the Pentagon has received information that part of the
downed Stealth fighter is being stored at that location, and we
need you to take it out. Those are the GPS coordinates."

"Yes, sir."

• • •

Smith saw the armed men pour out of the Ford as he twisted the key in the ignition. The Golf lurched forward as it was still in first gear. Smith jammed the clutch and the gas to the floor and tried again. He saw figures in the corner of his eye reaching for the door handle. The men pounded on the outside of his car, Smith was nearly surrounded.

The engine fired to life, and he popped the clutch. He never let off the gas. The drive wheel shrieked as it spun; smoke billowed out of the wheel well. The Golf slid sideways slightly, pushing some of the men, and then the tires found traction. Smith was slammed back in the seat as the little car accelerated away from the men, leaving smoldering rubber in its wake.

Smith dared a peek in the rearview mirror and saw the men jumping back into the SUV that was already moving. The engine howled and the needle approached the redline. Smith knew it was time to shift.

He grabbed the stick and jammed the clutch to the floor. The needle jumped past the redline, and he lifted off the gas for fear of blowing the engine. Smith pulled the stick out of first and back into what he hoped was second. He divided his attention between the winding road in front of him and the SUV growing larger in the rearview mirror. Simultaneously, he lifted his left foot and jammed his right down. The revs died at first and then built once again, and the car accelerated.

To the right of the road was a wall of rock, and to the left the drop-off continued. Yugoslavia evidently did not believe in the concept of guardrails. The good news was the road sloped downhill, and the little car was gaining speed the whole way.

The engine howled again as Smith completed a series of S curves. Time to shift to third gear.

Smith repeated the process, this time pushing the stick forward and to the right.

He was thrown into the steering wheel as the acceleration disappeared. He floored the accelerator, but the engine struggled. *Shit! Fifth gear!*

The SUV continued to accelerate toward Smith.

Smith corrected his mistake and selected third gear, and the Golf jumped ahead.

He was using the entire road, and he prayed that no one would come around one of the blind bends. He glanced in the mirror and saw that the SUV was getting slightly smaller.

Fourth gear.

Smith slid the car around the curves, tires squealing for mercy.

The next bend was followed almost immediately by a hairpin to the right. Smith stomped on the brake pedal and turned the wheel to full lock to the right. The Golf slid through the turn like a drift racer. Smith had to dial in some major corrections to point the car straight again.

He successfully downshifted and accelerated on down the hill.

In the mirror he saw the truck slide through the turn, leaning so far it seemed it would roll over. But it stayed upright, and

Smith could see the driver fighting with the steering wheel. Then it shot forward like a locomotive.

They were still coming for him. Smith hammered it.

He heard a sharp crack to his left.

A bullet had whizzed by at supersonic speed.

Shit!

He couldn't outrun those. He glanced into the mirror. The SUV was closing the gap. Flashes confirmed that they continued to shoot at him.

He had no idea where he was going. He didn't have time to fish the GPS unit out, but he knew he was headed generally in the direction of Jashari's headquarters. Toward Paxton, he hoped.

But he had to lose the killers in the Ford. He had the advantage in cornering, but they had a huge advantage in horsepower, allowing them to catch up with him in the straights. His speedometer indicated he was going more than 170 kilometers per hour—well over a hundred miles per hour.

They definitely had the advantage in firepower.

Smith had his hands full, so he wasn't able to return fire.

It wasn't going to be easy to lose them in their own neighborhood.

Smith had the pedal to the floor, and yet the SUV filled all of his mirrors. They were nearly on top of him.

Smith swerved to avoid an oncoming car.

The windshield shattered in front of Smith as a bullet passed clear through. He ducked instinctively.

It was just a matter of time before they hit something vital—

like Smith's body. He looked around frantically for a way to lose them. The rock wall had receded but there were no side roads— just the occasional dirt driveway. He peeked at the rearview mirror just it time to see it shatter as a bullet ripped it off its mounts.

Way too close for comfort.

Time for drastic action. He grabbed the stick shift and stomped on the clutch.

Chapter 15

TIMING WAS THE KEY. SMITH FELT THE POWER EVAPORATE as he engaged the Golf's clutch, but it wasn't apparent to the driver of the SUV who was still accelerating. Smith jerked up the emergency brake and dialed the wheel hard to the right. Because the emergency brake doesn't illuminate the brake lights, it took an extra second for the SUV driver to realize what was happening.

The Golf skidded sideways and overshot the dirt driveway Smith was aiming for. Centrifugal force threw Smith hard against the driver's door. The Golf leaned hard to the left. Smith downshifted and snaked the Golf back onto the dirt road, accelerating with a sandy rooster tail.

The sudden turn caught the SUV driver by surprise, and he made the mistake of trying to follow Smith's car. He locked up the brakes and cranked the wheel full lock to the right. The Ford's tires howled and produced great plumes of white smoke. The turn was too sharp for the tall SUV's suspension. The right side tires lifted off the road and the vehicle rolled completely over and kept tumbling until it landed on its left side. The truck scraped to a halt. The men who had been leaning out shooting were strewn onto the road, sliding down the rough asphalt.

Smith saw the crash out of the corner of his left eye and slid his car to a halt.

Shaken, he leaned against the steering wheel and caught his breath. This time he remembered to depress the clutch, so the engine remained running. Time was short. He had to get out of there.

Smith fished the GPS receiver out and examined the screen. He would have to pass right by the wrecked SUV to head toward Jashari's headquarters. He grabbed his M4 rifle and put it on the dashboard, pointing straight out the shattered windshield. He took a deep breath, then turned the car around and drove toward the road.

He stopped as he reached the pavement. He looked both ways. No one was coming. He switched off the rifle's safety and drove onto the road.

Smith accelerated and zipped past the mangled hulk of the SUV.

• • •

"Jill, I understand your concerns, but I assure you that John is safe." Ward switched the phone from his left ear to his right. "You spoke to him yourself."

"When can I talk to him again?"

"I can't say for sure. They aren't even letting me talk to him right now."

"And why not?"

Ward blew air through pursed lips. "I suppose he is being debriefed. Lots of high-level secret stuff. He is probably locked in some room working on paperwork."

"Then how do you know he is safe?"

"He is on a NATO airbase in Italy. He is as safe there as he would be in the United States—heck, *safer* than some parts of the States."

"Why should I believe you? You lied to me. You said he went TDY."

"Well…in a way he did. He had left for a temporary duty…."

"To rescue a pilot! He *deployed*. Why couldn't you just say that?"

"I'm so sorry, Jill. I was under strict orders to not tell you or anyone else where he was."

"Why? And how do I know you aren't still under orders to not tell me things now?"

"I'm not." Ward cringed as he said it.

"And how the hell did his going to rescue a pilot result in the Serbs sending killers to *my house*?"

Ward wasn't sure how much he was allowed to say. He knew there was a whole lot he couldn't say. "Look, Jill. It was a very sensitive mission. I'm sure you will feel much better once you see John."

"Well, I'm tired of waiting."

An idea popped into Ward's head. "Jill, I'll tell you what. I have an idea that might speed things up. Let me make a few phone calls, and then I promise I'll call you back with more information. Just sit tight and stop worrying. John is perfectly safe."

• • •

The F-16's afterburners blazed as the fighter jet took off from Aviano Air Base, Italy. Slung under its wings were two 500 pound, GPS-guided, high explosive bombs. Programmed into their guidance systems were the precise coordinates of Jashari's headquarters.

Chapter 16

SMITH DROVE AS FAST AS HE DARED. HE DIDN'T WANT people to get a good look at him—he wasn't sure how common black people were in Serbia. Yet he didn't want to drive so fast as to draw the attention of the police. He couldn't afford any more distractions from his mission.

The GPS receiver lay on the passenger seat of the beat up Golf, and he periodically looked down at it to check his progress. He was getting close. He needed to start looking for a place to ditch the car. He wanted to approach Jashari's headquarters on foot for maximum concealment.

He could almost feel Paxton's presence. He was getting close.

There seemed to be more and more armed men walking down the road. And they all seemed to have their heads on a swivel as they checked Smith out as he drove by. The hair on the back of his neck was standing up.

GPS indicated that he was within a half a kilometer of the

headquarters. Smith turned off the road. He drove down a dirt trail that led back into the woods. When he felt he was sufficiently out of sight he turned off the trail and stopped. He killed the engine and sat there in silence for a moment.

Turning back was not an option.

Smith grabbed his GPS receiver, his medical bag, and his rifle. He didn't bother with his helmet. Then he opened the door and climbed out.

• • •

Helicopters from the 255th Rescue Squadron launched from Brindisi Air Base. They turned and headed for the last known coordinates of their brethren helicopter pilots. The spot that Smith had already vacated.

• • •

Smith carefully worked his way over the terrain. He had his rifle at the ready. His catlike footsteps covered the ground quickly. He checked his GPS receiver. The headquarters was only two hundred meters away now. He needed to keep aware of possible sentries hidden in the woods. He saw what appeared to be a large house when he crested the next hill. He moved behind a tree. He peered around the trunk through his riflescope. He saw men with rifles patrolling outside the building. There were several upper-floor balconies manned by armed soldiers. Chances were good that he had located Jashari's headquarters.

The windows all seemed to be covered by iron bars. Several trucks and vans were parked outside.

Smith scanned the balconies more carefully. One of the upper floors sported a mesh dish. Satellite phone?

He had to figure out whether Paxton was there. And if he were, he had to figure out a way in. And, of course, a way back out.

He switched off his GPS receiver. He didn't need it now, but he might need it later, and he had no way to recharge the battery. Best to conserve.

He resumed surveying the scene in front of him, his trained eyes looking for a way to breach security. He needed a way to create a distraction. He eyed the vehicles again. Maybe he could figure a way to blow one of them up. Then he could sneak in during the resulting confusion.

Or, maybe he could set fire to the woods. Men would run out to put it out before it reached the building. That would be easier than getting past the guards to the vehicles, but the problem with that plan was that the burning woods would cut him off from the Golf. It was never good to block your escape route.

Maybe he could find a way to set fire to the house itself. Then everyone would evacuate. But what if they didn't bring Paxton? What if they left him inside to burn? He would then have to go into a burning building to rescue him. Not the best plan.

He was sweating again. There had to be a way to get inside. Paxton's presence was stronger than ever. He felt it in his spine.

Then he felt something else with his spine—the cold barrel of a shotgun.

"Do not move—do not even breathe." The English was broken and heavily accented. But the message was crystal clear.

"Drop your weapon."

Smith cursed bitterly to himself and let his M4 rifle drop to the ground.

Chapter 17

SMITH STUMBLED IN THE FRONT DOOR, PRODDED BY THE shotgun in his back. Everyone turned to see him. It took a moment for his eyes to adjust to the relative darkness. One man stepped forward.

"What is this?"

"I caught him outside, Commander Jashari. He was aiming his rifle at the building." Smith hadn't even gotten a chance to turn to see what his captor looked like. Under the circumstances, it seemed a good idea to follow the command to keep his eyes forward.

Jashari stepped uncomfortably close to Smith and looked him over from head to foot. "Good work, Droshny."

"What do you want me to do with him?" Droshny jabbed Smith with the Benelli shotgun again as if to add emphasis.

Jashari stared into Smith's eyes. Smith stared back. He could smell coffee on Jashari's breath.

"Put him with the other. I don't have time to deal with him now."

Jashari returned to the maps he had been studying, and Droshny pushed Smith toward a hallway. Smith got the distinct impression that they had conducted that conversation purely for his benefit. Well, he had been looking for a way into Jashari's headquarters. He was definitely in.

They continued down the hallway until they reached a door with a bar and a lock on it. "Don't move."

Smith heard keys and then, without any relief from the pressure the gun barrel was exerting on him, Droshny reached out and unlocked the pad lock.

Smith could feel Droshny's breath on his ear as he spoke. "I'm looking forward to killing you."

Smith didn't say anything.

"Now open the door."

Smith lifted the bar and turned the doorknob.

• • •

Paxton was sitting across from the door with his back against the wall. He looked up as the door swung open and a man shoved Smith inside. Smith almost fell, but he caught himself. The door slammed behind him. The mechanical sound of the bar dropping and a padlock being fastened could be heard through the thick steel door.

Their eyes met, and recognition was immediate.

"Am I looking at the ghost of Octavious Smith?"

"Not a ghost yet." Smith had his hands on his thighs, as if

he were catching his breath. Then he straightened up. "John Paxton. How the hell are you?"

Paxton smiled wryly. "Livin' the dream."

"I hear ya."

"Have a seat. Make yourself comfortable."

"Yeah, thanks." Smith lowered himself to the floor. He leaned his back against the wall to Paxton's left.

The room was lit better than the room Jashari was in, mostly because of the sunlight streaming in through the barred window. Stale sweat hung in the air.

"I thought you went down with the Pave Hawk."

"I did...sorta." Smith looked at Paxton. "I was hanging on the rope rappelling down."

"The others?"

"Dead. After the crash, Jashari's goons shot the survivors."

"Son of a bitch."

Both men sat there in silence.

Finally, Smith turned to Paxton. "I completed two of my three objectives."

"Which were?"

"One: to get inside here. Two: to find you. The last one, us escaping alive, will take a little doing."

"That last one is going to have to wait."

"Wait? What the hell do you mean? Why would we wait?"

"We have a mission to complete."

Smith reached over and knocked gently on Paxton's head with his knuckles. "Knock, knock...are you in there, Pax? Didn't you hear me say the others were dead? How the hell are we going to complete the mission?"

"I have a plan."

"Sheeeet. I see where your plans land us."

"I'm serious."

"I am too. Just what is your plan?"

"No. The walls may have ears."

"Gotcha."

Both men sat in silence again.

Smith looked at Paxton again. "How can I help if I don't know what the plan is?"

Paxton didn't say anything.

Smith contemplated his feet. Both men had torn pants with bloody knees.

After a bit, Paxton spoke. "You know, my cable company sucks."

"I hear ya. Mine too."

Paxton looked at Smith to make sure he had his full attention. "I'm *serious*. I don't get the programs I want. I'm going to switch. Soon. You know what I mean?"

"Yeah, five hundred channels and nothin' to watch."

"I'm jealous," Paxton continued. "This place I've been staying lately...you know, they get all the programs they want. But they don't have cable...."

"No cable? What do they have? Sat...."

Paxton slapped Smith in the chest, cutting him off. His eyes communicated *shut up*.

Smith was confused for a moment, and then he realized what Paxton was doing. "Oh, I see."

"You follow me?" Paxton emphasized each word.

"Like a baby duck."

"Good. Like I was saying. I'm going to switch soon. Like as soon as I get a chance after I get out of here."

"Will they let you out of your contract?"

"I may have to break my contract. Maybe you can help me with that."

"Absolutely."

"Anyway, after I hook up my new service, I'm going to pull an E.T."

Smith contemplated the movie reference. "Gotcha."

Paxton was quiet for a moment, considering what to say next.

"You like that song, 'Kiss from a Rose'?"

"Yeah, it's a good song," Smith agreed.

"One of my favorites. I want to see those guys in concert."

"I think it's just one guy…His name is….."

Smith cut himself off before Paxton had to smack him again.

"As I was saying. I really want to see those guys soon. I wonder when they are coming to town."

"Me too."

"Maybe after I pull an E.T. we can order some tickets and see them together."

"I'm all for it, of course."

"But I want to see Georgia first."

"Who is she?"

"The state. Georgia. I want to see it like a postman would."

Smith thought about it for a moment, and then remembered the postal abbreviation for the state. "Gotcha. Maybe we can see the band when we see Georgia."

"I like the way you think, Octavious."

"I just hope it's worth it. The price has been awfully high."

"Believe me…it is going to be worth it."

• • •

Jashari stepped up next to a man wearing headphones sitting at a table covered with electronic equipment. The man had one headphone covering one ear, but the other was above his other ear. "Have we learned anything?"

"No. They are just talking about television and bands they want to see in concert, Commander Jashari."

"Wishful thinking on their part. They aren't going to live to see either of those things ever again."

Chapter 18

THE MAN ANSWERED THE PHONE ON THE THIRD RING. "Major Right." He was wearing a crisp long-sleeve uniform. His knit tie was held tightly to his light blue shirt by a silver clip adorned with the Air Force symbol. A steaming cup of coffee rested on a ceramic coaster within easy reach.

"Jason, how the hell are you?"

"Colonel Ward! I'm doing better than I deserve. How 'bout yourself?"

"I'm busier than a one-legged man in a butt-kicking contest."

"I hear ya."

"How is that slice?"

"It's the only thing consistent about my game." Right took a loud sip of coffee. "We should hit the links again sometime soon."

"Would love to. I could use the stress reliever."

Right laughed. "What stress? You run a training squadron.

It's not like you're operational or anything."

Ward scoffed. "You'd be surprised. Like you've got room to talk. You're over at MPF where the only planes you fly are paper ones." The Military Personnel Flight (MPF) was the Air Force's latest configuration of a base-level human resources department.

Right chuckled. "Yeah, but our paper airplanes are better than the Russians.'"

"Russians? We don't have to worry about them anymore. They're our friends now—don't cha know. Now the Chinese... They are the ones we have to worry about."

"Not worried about them. They can't even get my takeout order right."

Ward laughed.

Right slurped his coffee again. "So to what do I owe the pleasure?"

"Jason, I've got a situation. I was wondering if you could do me a favor."

"You mean you're wondering if I could do you *another* favor."

"I think I did the last favor for you, if I recall correctly."

"Yeah, but you owe me so many more."

"Well add this one to the list. I wanted to see if you could cut some 'invitational orders' for some dependents of one of my instructors."

"Why? Is your man injured?"

"Well...not exactly. Other than some minor scrapes and bruises."

"I'd love to help you, Colonel, but what is the justification?"

Ward hesitated. Then he sighed. "Jason, you know about that home invasion? The one where one of my instructor's homes was attacked?"

"Oh yeah. I read about that in the paper. Scary stuff."

"Very scary. Well, that instructor is TDY, so he isn't around to comfort his family. They are real spooked, as you can imagine."

"Of course."

"I thought it might help the situation. You know…take their mind off of it. It's an unusual situation."

"I'll say."

"Jason, these are good people."

"I'll see what I can do, Colonel."

"Thank you."

"But you're going to owe me big time."

• • •

"So, Smith, where are you from anyway?"

Smith looked over at Paxton, trying to determine if he was still talking in code.

"I'm just asking."

Smith looked at that wall straight across from him. "Chicago."

"The windy city."

"Yep. Where you from?"

"Central Florida. Near Orlando."

"Mickey's playground."

Paxton smiled. "Yeah."

"You play any sports in high school?"

Paxton stared off into the distance. "When I wasn't surfing, I played football."

"Me too."

"They have surfing in Chicago?"

"No…football. What position?"

"Tight end. You?"

"Wingback."

Paxton looked at Smith with a furrowed brow. "Like the chair?"

"No. Like as in a fullback in the wing formation. I lined up outside the end."

"We didn't have them. Must be a Chicago thing."

"Yeah, I guess so."

Both men were silent. Muffled voices could be heard through the door from time to time. The air was heavy. The sunlight in the room would dim periodically as a cloud passed by.

"So, Pax, what do you think are the chances of us surviving this?"

Paxton sucked his lips in between his teeth. "That is the wrong question."

"It is? What's the *right* question, then?"

"The question you should be asking is 'What can I do to make sure the mission gets accomplished?'"

Smith stared at Paxton.

Paxton continued. "Your question focuses on factors outside of yourself. What are the chances….like it's a roll of the dice. Things outside of your control. Things that might happen *to* you. Have an action focus. Look inside yourself. The only thing in the world you have control over. What should you be doing to ensure success?"

"Easier said than done. Cooped up in this cell, all I can do is think about things that might happen to me."

"Stop thinking in terms of things happening to you. I prefer to think of me happening to things."

"Pax, you're somethin' else."

"Try it. You might find that you will feel a whole lot less helpless."

Smith sniffed sharply.

"I'm telling you…"

"Ok, Pax. I'll try it. What action can I be taking now to ensure the success of this mission?"

Before Paxton could answer, the sound of the door being unlocked made them turn their heads. The door swung open and a short man with spiky black hair and a full beard stepped in. He cradled a nasty-looking shotgun in his hands. He pointed it at both of them alternately. "You two get up."

Smith recognized the voice as that of Droshny. Now he knew what he looked like.

"Up! Up!"

Paxton and Smith pushed themselves to their feet. Paxton brushed his hands off.

"What now?" Paxton asked.

A second man appeared in the doorway. "Turn around."

Smith and Paxton turned their backs to the men. The second man tied both of their hands behind their backs. He cinched the rope extra tight.

"Come."

"Where are we going?" Paxton asked.

"Commander Jashari is ready for both of you. Now move!"

Paxton and Smith glanced at each other. Then Paxton led the way out of the cell, followed by Smith, the other man, and Droshny and his shotgun.

Chapter 19

PAXTON AND SMITH WERE LED BACK INTO THE MAIN ROOM. Jashari was standing there smiling, wicked knife in his hand. More disconcerting was that the video camera was set up again. The cameraman was there making adjustments. In front of the camera was a blank wall—a backdrop. Crowded behind the camera were men with MP-40 machine guns. They looked like they were ready for the show to begin.

Paxton glanced at the scene and then at Jashari. "What's going on? I thought you were taking me to the Iraqis."

"Shut up!"

"They aren't going to be happy."

Jashari reached up and pressed the point of the knife against Paxton's throat. "I said shut up!"

Paxton shut up.

Smith stepped up next to Paxton. The two men stood shoulder to shoulder. Droshny covered them both with his nasty shotgun.

The room smelled like a locker room with a fireplace. Flecks of dust floated in the air.

Jashari spoke again. "I want to remind you that you are both pigs. Barnyard animals. You will be slaughtered like swine. Infidels. And your country will be given a choice…." Jashari paused. "Convert or die!" He nicked Paxton's throat for emphasis.

Paxton could feel warm liquid drip down inside the collar of his shirt. He swallowed hard.

Paxton looked at Smith out of the corner of his eye without moving his head. The young sergeant's eyes were saucers.

"We will soon be in possession of poison gas. If America does not convert to Islam, if it does not follow Sharia law, then we will use the poison gas. We will release it in schools and in shopping malls. We will pour it into your drinking supply.

"I can just see it now," Jashari continued. "Little children. First they will have runny noses and teary eyes. Then they will be coughing, drooling, and sweating. Then their little chests will tighten. They won't be able to breathe. Their muscles will twitch and contract until they die convulsing on the ground. America, The Great Satan, will give in the first time this happens. It will be the only way to save their precious offspring.

"The two of you, however, made a choice. When you joined the military of The Great Satan. Military that occupies holy land. Yes, you made a choice. You chose to *die*."

Jashari swiveled and pressed the knife against Smith's throat. Smith's eyes grew impossibly bigger.

Paxton's eyes searched the room. There were at least fifteen men with weapons. He tested the knot in the rope holding his wrists together behind his back. It held fast. His plan was going to shit and it was going fast. Sweat dripped into his right eye. His heart was thundering. He saw Smith's chest rising and falling rapidly.

Jashari turned back to Paxton. The knife returned to Paxton's throat. Jashari's smile grew. He spoke again. "You, Sergeant Paxton, get in front of camera."

Paxton glanced over at Smith. Smith was gritting his teeth.

Droshny shoved Paxton with the barrel of his Benelli. "Commander Jashari said front of camera."

Paxton moved. He stepped in front of the camera and stood there. He counted at least ten guns pointing at him. He saw the forlorn look on Smith's face. The cameraman crouched down and peered through the viewfinder.

Jashari stepped up behind Paxton, knife by his side. The red light on the video camera lit. Jashari raised the knife.

• • •

Chapter 20

THE F-16 VIPER JET FIGHTER FLOWN BY CAPTAIN AVILA PLUS one flown by his wingman split off from the other three Vipers as they crossed into Serbian airspace. They headed south carrying enough destructive power to obliterate the intended target.

"See y'all on the flipside." He radioed.

"Good luck and happy hunting."

"No hunting about it…it will be like shooting fish in a barrel."

• • •

Jashari sliced down with the blade. With a minimum of sawing it cut cleanly through the sinewy strands that held Paxton's hands behind his back.

Newly freed, Paxton brought his hands up in front of him.

"Hands down."

Paxton lowered his hands to his sides.

"Camera off."

The red light went dark.

Jashari produced a folded piece of paper from his pocket. He unfolded it and handed it to Paxton. Paxton looked down at the handwritten note.

"This is message for America. You read it. On camera."

Paxton studied the words.

They read:

> *America is evil.*
> *Americans are barn animals.*
> *America must bow down to Allah.*
> *America has an evil past.*
> *Americans must hail all that is good.*
> *Or it will be a dark day.*

"I can't read this." Paxton said.

"You read or your friend dies now." Droshny pressed his shotgun against Smith's head. Droshny was about the same height as Smith, but Smith had about twenty more pounds of muscle.

Paxton shook his head. "No, you don't understand. I *can't* read this. The handwriting sucks."

Jashari looked over Paxton's shoulder at the note. He then pushed it up toward Paxton. "You read."

Paxton put the note near his face and squinted. Then he shook his head again. "I'm telling you this is too hard to read. Who wrote this?"

"I wrote it." Jashari said.

"You need a penmanship class."

Smith's eyes were wide once again.

"Read or friend dies." Droshny raised the butt of the shotgun higher, as if that would make the shot any more lethal than it already was.

"Pax, just read the damn thing," Smith said.

"I can't make it out. What does it say, Josh?" Paxton offered the note to Jashari.

"My name is Jashari."

"Whatever. Just read it to me."

Jashari read it to Paxton.

Paxton nodded. "OK. I got it." He tapped his temple with his index finger.

"Now read it."

"Look, Josh. I still can't read it. But I get the gist. I know what you want. I'm just going to put it in my own words."

Smith closed his eyes and shook his head. He looked like he wanted to crawl away.

"You must deliver message."

"Oh I get it. America bad. Change our ways. You want me to denounce my country. I don't want to do that, but I'll do it so you don't blow my friend's head off."

"Then do it. Now."

Jashari stepped back out of the frame. The red light came back on.

Paxton took a deep breath and then cleared his throat.

He began. "My name is SMSgt John Paxton. I am a para-rescueman with the United States Air Force. I am currently the NCOIC of the Indoctrination School for the 37th Training Squadron, Lackland Air Force Base, Texas."

Smith's chin rested on his chest. He couldn't bear to watch

Paxton humiliate himself.

"I have a message for all of America." Paxton continued. "America is *baaad*." He shifted his weight from one foot to the other. "America is definitely bad. In fact, they are the baddest.

"And Americans…well, when I think of America I think of a big stable. A stable filled with asses. Asses that are bad. That is my opinion of America. It is a stable full of bad asses."

Smith lifted his head slightly. He raised one eyebrow.

"And America's day is coming. When that day comes, I think everyone in America needs to *get down*. Men, women, children…young and old alike. I say we all *get down*. In fact, you shouldn't wait. You should *get down* tonight."

Smith peeked at Jashari. He looked very pleased.

"Just look at ourselves. If you want to know what kind of nation we are, just look at our history. When people think of America, they should remember the *Redskins*, the *Braves*, the *Seminoles* in Tallahassee, and let's never forget the *Indians* from Cleveland."

Smith raised his head the rest of the way and looked right at Paxton. Paxton was waving his arms like a preacher.

"We have become a *Savage Garden*. And I think each and every soccer mom out there should be in her *Van*… in her *Van Halen* all that is good. If we don't, it will be a *Black Sabbath*."

Jashari was nodding yes. The corners of Smith's mouth twitched.

"Everything I say here is true. It is my firm belief. And I say it voluntarily. I must say our host here, Jashari, has treated us very well. He has treated us like a President treats an intern.

Good night."

Jashari clapped and the red light went off. The other men in the room followed Jashari's lead and clapped as well. "Excellent work!"

"Thank you."

"Now over there next to your friend."

Paxton stepped next to Smith. Smith just stared at Paxton. Paxton winked ever so slightly. Smith shook his head.

"Sergeant Paxton," said Jashari.

"Yes?"

"Put your hands behind your back."

Chapter 21

THEY CINCHED THE KNOT EVEN TIGHTER BEHIND PAXTON'S back. He and Smith stood there waiting for what would happen next.

"You," Jashari pointed to the cameraman. "Upload the video to the website. You." He pointed at another man, "Bring my satellite phone."

Paxton and Smith glanced at each other.

The cameraman removed the camera from the tripod and carried it upstairs. The other man followed.

Jashari barked some more orders in an unintelligible language, and the room became a sea of activity. Men scurried about the room, packing bags, loading ammunition. Others left through the front door. Jashari stood there supervising it all. And Droshny stood behind them with his ever-present shotgun.

Paxton watched all of the activity.

The man came down the stairs carrying a box with a receiver and a folded up antenna. Jashari's satellite phone. Smith and Paxton followed the device with their eyes as the man carried it over to his commander.

"Put it on the table. Get the rest of my things and then load them in the van." The man did as he was told.

Jashari addressed Paxton, "It is time to go. Our Iraqi friends have crossed the border. They can't wait to see you again."

"The feeling is mutual."

Jashari turned to Droshny. "Take those two out and put them in the van."

Droshny jammed the barrel into Paxton's back and he started walking. He and Smith walked out the door into the bright sunlight. They stood on the porch and squinted. Their faces felt warm.

"Van."

They saw a white van parked near one of the outbuildings. They walked down the stairs and crossed over to the vehicle. Droshny pulled on the door handle, but it was locked.

He turned and said something to Jashari who was following him. He was wearing the ratty green backpack. Jashari produced keys from his pocket.

"Pax, you're a nut." Smith whispered.

Paxton shrugged.

"Treated like interns? You shouldn't talk about our Commander-in-Chief like that."

"It seemed like the right thing to say."

Jashari unlocked the van. Paxton and Smith watched the

other man step out of the door carrying a black backpack and the satellite phone. As the man reached the top of the stairs, there was a dual high-pitched shriek punctuated by two nearly simultaneous explosions. The explosions burst the walls of the building, and a fireball leapt outward on all sides, rolling toward the van. The shockwave struck Paxton, sweeping him off his feet, and the world went dark.

Chapter 22

"**Jill, I have good news.**" **Ward had reached her on** the phone at her temporary quarters.

"I could definitely use some."

"I've arranged it so you can see John very soon."

"Really? When is he coming home?"

"He's not…at least not yet."

"What do you mean?"

"I've arranged for you and the kids to fly over to Italy and see John there."

Jill was silent.

"I thought you would be excited."

"I would love to do that, but I can't afford to fly to Italy."

"No, no. I've arranged for you to take a military hop. It won't cost you."

"Really? Oh my God. That is fantastic!"

Ward smiled. "Usually dependants have to fly with the military member, but I had a buddy of mine cut some invitational orders that allow you and the kids to fly unaccompanied."

"I just don't know. I'm scared. We have already been attacked once…to travel so far…be in a strange town…."

"Not to worry…you will fly from a military base on a military plane to another military base. You will be just as safe there as you are here. Besides, I'm sure you will feel better when you see John."

"Yes. Yes I will."

"What is even better is the type of aircraft you will be on."

"What do you mean?"

"Well, usually military hops consist of cargo planes…not the most comfortable…but my buddy came through a found a flight on a C-137."

"What is that?"

"The military version of the Boeing 707. It will be like flying on a commercial airliner. You have one stop at Rhein Main Air Base in Germany, but then you will be flying right to Brindisi, Italy."

"Colonel Ward, I don't know how to thank you."

"No thanks necessary. I feel terrible for what you and your family have been put through. It just makes me feel good getting all of you back together. I know how much you love him."

"To pieces!"

• • •

Marshall hung up the phone. "Good news, General."

"What is it?" Reed asked.

"We have confirmation that Jashari's headquarters was successfully struck. Initial bomb damage assessment indicates that the building was completely destroyed. No way anything or anyone survived."

"Is there any way to confirm if the device was destroyed?"

Marshall's face twisted. "No sir. If the locator beacon was working we could check to see if it was still transmitting, but the batteries were dead."

"We don't know for sure."

"No, sir. But we dropped a thousand pounds of high explosive with pinpoint accuracy right on it."

Reed was silent.

"What is it, sir?"

"Marshall, sometimes I wonder whether the advice you give me is any good."

"Sir?"

"I keep following your suggestions, and yet I can't shake the feeling that the mess just keeps getting bigger."

Chapter 23

THE SHARP PAIN IN PAXTON'S SIDE LET HIM KNOW HE WAS still alive. So it was safe to open his eyes. The only sound he could hear was the blood pumping through his ears. It felt as if all the hair had been singed off his face. Paxton quickly saw the source of the pain in his side. He was lying across Smith's bony knees. He lifted himself up on his arms.

Smith stirred and moaned, but the moan sounded muffled.

Paxton looked around and saw Droshny crawling toward his shotgun. For a fleeting instant Paxton wondered if he could beat him to it. But the man reached out and grabbed the stock before Paxton could make a move.

Over to his left, what was left of Jashari's headquarters was engulfed in flames. Thick black smoke rolled up toward the heavens. There was no sign of the man who had been carrying the satellite phone. Everything sounded as if Paxton had pillows over his ears.

He wasn't sure what had happened. But he could guess. The shriek right before the explosion was probably a couple of bombs traveling close to the speed of sound. He never heard the plane that had dropped them. It was too high and moving too fast. It had to be a NATO plane—the American's had already established air dominance. No Serb aircraft could fly without being quickly shot down.

What the fuck?

Why would we bomb Jashari's headquarters?

"Get up!"

Paxton looked up. It was Jashari yelling at him. He seemed unfazed by the destruction of his headquarters. He still had the green backpack that presumably contained the fake device. Droshny poked him with the shotgun. Paxton got on his hands and knees and then lifted himself to his feet. Smith did the same. Evidently the van shielded the four of them from the brunt of the explosion. Although what they got sure packed a wallop.

"Get in. The Iraqis have crossed the border and it is time to go meet them. They won't wait."

The exchange was still on.

But along with the satellite phone, Paxton's plans had just gone up in flames.

• • •

"John, Mommy's got a surprise for you."

The little boy looked up with wide eyes. "What?"

"You, your sister and I are going to fly in an airplane."

"Willy?"

"Yes, really."

"I never flewed in a plane."

"I know, honey."

"I'm scared."

"It's going to be just fine, honey. You will like it."

"Megan, we fly in plane." The boy pointed at the ceiling, his thumb off to the side. He was squinting with one eye.

Megan paid no attention.

"That's not the best part of the surprise. Guess what."

"What, Mommy?"

"When we get done with our plane ride, guess who you will see?"

"Daddy!"

Jill gave her son a big hug. "That's right, Daddy. He will be waiting for us when we get off the plane."

"I can't wait, Mommy."

A tear formed in the corner of her eye. "Me either, sweetie. Me either."

• • •

Paxton and Smith were trundled into the back of the van and the doors slammed. There were no rear seats. They sat on the floor, hands tied behind them. Not even the courtesy of a seatbelt was provided. Jashari climbed into the passenger seat. Droshny got into the driver's seat. There was a wire mesh barrier between the passenger compartment and the cargo hold. Jashari's machine gun and Droshny's shotgun lay on the floor between the jihadists. Jashari pulled out Smith's GPS receiver and discussed the route with his driver.

Droshny started the engine, and they drove off.

Paxton and Smith bounced around in silence for well over an hour. From Paxton's position, it was impossible to tell where they were going. He could feel them speed up and slow down, curve left and right and go up and down hills. Not once did they encounter a checkpoint. He could see sky and trees pass by the windows above.

Smith looked stoic. Paxton wished he had never pulled him out of the police car. The SEALs and the Pave Hawk pilots were dead because of his plan. He better stop the transfer of the nerve gas lest those deaths be in vain. And if Jashari got hold of the GA, many, many more innocent people were going to die. He had to think of something—and fast.

The van made a left turn and slowed. It rolled to a stop and Jashari and Droshny got out. They took their weapons, and they slammed the doors. Paxton heard voices outside. Then the back doors opened.

Sunlight washed in around Droshny. He indicated with his shotgun that Paxton and Smith should get out.

Paxton got out first. Smith followed. They stood there surveying the scene. Parked about thirty meters away was a rusty truck. Jashari was talking to two dark-skinned men wearing blue jeans and tan long-sleeved shirts. Those men each had pistols in holsters on their waists. The Iraqis.

Another man in green fatigues stood near a motorcycle. He had a pistol. Evidently he was the man Jashari sent to lead the Iraqis to the exchange site.

The ground was dark soil. Trees surrounded them. But it wasn't like a forest. The trees were arranged in rows. They all seemed to be between ten and fifteen meters tall. Their trunks were wide, in some cases several meters wide, twisted and gnarled. They were mature olive trees. They appeared to be in the middle of an olive orchard. Off in the distance were two buildings. One a large metal shed. The other looked like a wooden barn. No one else was around.

The sun beat down, but there was a cool breeze. Under different circumstances, it would be a nice day.

Droshny prodded them and Paxton and Smith walked toward the Iraqis. Jashari was pointing at the airmen. One of the Iraqis stepped up to them.

"Which of you is Paxton?"

"I am."

The Iraqi stepped in front of Paxton and looked him over. He had a wolfish grin. "There is a man in Baghdad who has been waiting almost ten years to see you again."

"I look forward to catching up with him."

"Don't be so cocky, Sergeant Paxton. He will be just as satisfied if I bring your corpse."

"I'd probably smell better if you bring me alive."

"Makes no difference to me." He jammed the muzzle of his pistol up under Paxton's chin to add emphasis.

Paxton was silent.

After a moment of tension, the Iraqi lowered his pistol and stepped back. He looked over at Droshny. "Untie them."

Paxton and Smith looked at each other, puzzled.

• • •

Chapter 24

PAXTON AND SMITH QUICKLY LEARNED WHY THEY WERE being untied. They were being put to work. Since the men Jashari planned to bring were killed in the air strike, the grunt work of moving the GA from the Iraqi truck to Jashari's van fell on the Americans.

The nerve gas was contained in two plastic 55-gallon drums. They were black with a skull and crossbones spray-painted in white on their sides. Nothing else indicated what was inside.

The Iraqis were kind enough to supply a hand truck to help with the effort. The American's were not given a choice in the matter. Paxton and Smith strained as they lowered metal drums down from the truck. It took both of them. Evidently, it was in liquid form because they could hear it sloshing around inside. Needless to say they were extremely careful. Paxton hoped the caps were properly tightened. One drop of the stuff and they were dead.

Neither man spoke as they worked. They worked together as a team nonetheless. Paxton's mind raced. Time was running out. With the Iraqis and Jashari's men pointing weapons at them, there didn't seem to be an opportunity to turn the tables.

They wheeled the first barrel over to the van. It took all their strength to lift the barrel into the back. Both men were soaked through with sweat.

Paxton gazed around as he dragged the empty hand truck back to the Iraqi vehicle. They were outnumbered five to two. And the bad guys had guns.

There was no way to call for help. Even if they could call, help was a long way off.

It was humiliating to have to help with the nerve gas. Paxton wanted no part of the capricious death of innocents that it represented.

Smith didn't say a word. He didn't have to. His eyes said it all. What the fuck are we going to do?

The second drum was wheeled over to the van and loaded. So much for stopping the transfer. All that was left was for Jashari and Droshny to drive off.

Paxton noticed that the Iraqis now had the green backpack. Maybe Reed was following the transmitter, and help would arrive at any moment.

Paxton knew that was wishful thinking, but it was a glimmer of hope that helped him move forward.

Jashari's man who had been standing next to the motorcycle walked up to Paxton carrying a pistol. Droshny walked up to Smith. "Hands on head." Paxton and Smith did as they were told.

The Iraqis leaned against their truck, satisfied. Paxton and Smith were standing in the vast space between the vehicles. The motorcycle was parked in front of the van. Jashari addressed the Americans. "Sergeant Paxton, it is time for you to begin your journey to Iraq. Ahmed, walk him to our guests."

Ahmed pressed the pistol into Paxton's side and began walking toward the truck.

"For you," Jashari said to Smith. "Unfortunately, your journey has ended."

Paxton stopped and turned toward Smith. Droshny had his shotgun lined up with Smith's head. The young sergeant stood motionless with his hands on top of his head.

"The Iraqis have no need for you Sergeant Smith. And, unfortunately for you, your usefulness to me has run out."

All eyes were on Smith.

Paxton's hands moved slightly down to the back of his head, as if he were lounging in a hammock.

Smith stood there stoically. Paxton tried to read Droshny's face, but Smith was blocking his view.

The shotgun was unmistakable.

"My only regret," Jashari continued, "is that we don't have the video camera to record your head coming off."

Paxton's fingers inched downward and touched the back of his neck.

"Droshny....kill him."

Droshny braced the butt of the shotgun on his shoulder and his finger moved into the trigger guard.

Chapter 25

SMITH TENSED ALL HIS MUSCLES AS HE STOOD THERE, HANDS on his head. He was gritting his teeth waiting for the bloody end. Ahmed stood absentmindedly holding his pistol to Paxton's head, waiting for the show.

"Does anyone have last thoughts for the man who is about to die?" Droshny asked. He was clearly savoring the moment.

"Yeah," Paxton shouted. "Smith, do what the Cubs do every year they reach the playoffs."

Smith looked quizzically at Paxton. Then understanding bloomed on his face.

"Do it *NOW!*" Paxton shouted as he reached down inside the collar of his shirt and grabbed the handle of the knife Smith had taped there back on their flight over. He yanked up and out, the tape sharply tearing off his back.

Smith collapsed like a sack of potatoes—just as Paxton had commanded. Smith batted the barrel of Droshny's shotgun up and away as he went down. The shotgun blasted harmlessly above where Smith's head used to be.

The tape was still stuck to the knife as Paxton sliced through Ahmed's throat. Ahmed's hands shot to his own neck to capture the blood jetting out of the severed arteries.

The recoil and Smith's swat had caused the shotgun to rise in Droshny's hands, but he quickly recovered and swept it down toward Smith.

Paxton reached out and grabbed the pistol and twisted it out of Ahmed's hand. The man didn't put up much of a fight because he was losing consciousness as the blood drained out of his brain. Paxton gained control of the pistol as Ahmed dropped to the ground. Paxton punched the pistol out toward Droshny and squeezed the trigger twice.

Blood erupted from two places on Droshny's body. The sure shot to the center of mass and the second just above his left eye, instantaneously shutting off brain function. Droshny and his shotgun fell to the ground at the same time.

The other men were stunned. But the Iraqis recovered quickly. They brought their pistols up and began shooting toward Paxton. Paxton was already diving to his right. Bullets whizzed by and struck all around him.

Blam!

The shotgun rang out. Paxton swung his aim toward the sound. Smith was on the ground taking aim with Droshny's shotgun. He turned the same direction Smith was shooting to see one Iraqi running around the back of the truck, firing wildly in Smith's direction. The other Iraqi was firing in Paxton's general direction as he climbed into the truck's driver's seat. He had the green backpack on.

Blam!

One Iraqi stopped firing at Smith and fell to the ground. Three down, two to go.

The flat staccato of an MP-40 machine gun filled the air. Jashari was firing from around the front of the van.

Paxton fired back. Jashari recoiled into hiding as the bullets struck the front quarter panel of the van.

Paxton crawled to his left until he was even with the back of the van. He had the knife in his left hand and the pistol in his right.

The Iraqi started the truck's engine.

"Pax, he's getting away!" Smith shouted.

The van's engine started as well.

"Let the truck go. Stop the van. It's got the nerve gas!" Paxton shouted.

Smith had to turn 180 degrees to bring the shotgun to bear on the van. Paxton got up and sprinted to the left of the van, and catching a glimpse of Jashari in the driver's seat, he squeezed off a couple rounds.

Instinctively, Jashari floored it to avoid Paxton's shots. The van plowed into the motorcycle and its front wheels bumped up and over it.

Blam!

Paxton could hear the shotgun, muffled somewhat by the van. The van dipped extra low on the front right side as it crunched over the motorcycle. Smith had apparently taken out the right front tire.

Another burst from the MP-40 sticking out of the driver's window caused Paxton to duck behind one of the trees. Jashari gunned the accelerator, dragging the cycle underneath.

Blam!

The van's engine coughed and sputtered. Then it died. Smith had struck something vital.

"Pax I'm out!" Smith was out of ammunition.

The sound of the truck spinning its wheels in the dirt was punctuated by the sound of the Iraqi firing a rifle.

Smith screamed, and then Paxton heard a muffled thud.

"Smith! You okay?"

Smith didn't respond.

"Shit!" Paxton shouted.

Jashari fired at Paxton again. Paxton ducked to the left side of the tree. The wide trunk blocked his view of the van. He switched hands, knife now in his right and gun in his left. He yanked the remaining pieces of sweaty medical tape off the bloody knife. He reached out around the left side of the tree with the pistol and let go with a few blind shots.

The Iraqi truck sped away.

Paxton could hear the van door open. Then another blast from the machine gun. Paxton could hear the disconcerting sound of the nine-millimeter rounds burying themselves deep into the other side of the broad tree trunk.

Paxton poked the pistol out again and peered around the tree. He lined it up and squeezed the trigger as another hail of bullets struck the tree. Paxton recoiled. He pressed against the sharp bark as tightly as possible.

Shit! He missed. Jashari's firing continued, and it was getting closer.

Paxton looked down at the pistol. The slide was locked back—a clear indication that he was out of ammunition.

Paxton leaned his back against the tree, trying to catch his breath. He could hear the approach of Jashari's boots as he ran toward Paxton.

Chapter 26

PAXTON'S EYES SWEPT HIS SURROUNDINGS. THE NEXT TREE was too far away to reach before Jashari arrived. And he would have to turn his back to the approaching jihadist in order to run.

He scanned the ground for something he could use for a weapon.

Nothing.

All he had was a knife with a sticky handle and an empty pistol.

Not a favorable match up against Jashari's German-made machine pistol that fired at a cyclic rate of 500 rounds per minute.

Jashari had gone silent. All Paxton could hear was the approach of running boots.

Maybe Smith can help.

"Smith!" Paxton shouted.

Paxton heard a groan. Smith was still alive but was clearly in pain.

Shit, I just made him a target.

Jashari's boots slowed as he got closer to the tree. Paxton looked up at the olive buds hanging from the branches. He gripped the knife tighter.

Paxton could hear Jashari slapping in another magazine and yanking the bolt back, cocking the machine gun. Paxton wished he had another magazine full of rounds to slap into his gun.

"Pax, I'm bleeding real bad," Smith shouted.

"I'll be right there, Smith."

"If you are talking about meeting him in Hell, then yes you two will be meeting there shortly," Jashari said as he stepped around the far side of the tree. His machine pistol was leveled rock-steady on Paxton.

• • •

"Help Mommy pack," Jill said as she handed a folded shirt to John, Jr. He took it and dropped it into the suitcase.

"No, hon. Make it neat." She flattened the shirt. "We want to look nice for Daddy."

"Daddy won't care. He loves me no matter what…he told me so."

Jill scrubbed the little boy's head. "That's right, sweetie. He loves you no matter what. But, one way we can show him our love for him is to look our best."

"Aw, okay, Mommy."

Jill hugged him to her chest.

"Mommy?"

"Yes, baby?"

"Why hasn't Daddy called?"

Jill squeezed her eyes shut. A small tear leaked out.

"I don't know, honey. But I'm sure he has a good reason."

Chapter 27

THE LOOK OF SATISFACTION ON JASHARI'S FACE WAS absolute. Paxton instinctively raised his hands in surrender. The blade still had residue where the pieces of white medical tape were stuck to the knife. Jashari was too far away for Paxton to attack. Jashari saw the slide locked back on the pistol in Paxton's left hand, tilted his head back and laughed.

That was Paxton's opening.

Throwing a knife is an exciting carnival skill. Audiences gasp as the blade buries itself into the board next to the gorgeous assistant. But throwing a knife as a weapon was generally not a good idea. First, you're giving up your weapon and throwing it to your enemy. Second, Paxton knew from experience that unless you have the distance and the release almost exactly right, it will strike flat or on its handle, at which point your opponent bends down, picks up your knife, and thanks you for the gift. Third, it had been many years since Paxton had thrown a knife—and that was for fun. A barroom bet—one that he had lost.

But Paxton had no other choice. Jashari was standing too far away to just stab.

So throw is what Paxton did. He threw the knife with all his might. He stepped forward and followed through like he was Greg Maddux hurling a fastball. He let the handle slip from his grasp without imparting any spin. The blade flew through the air like a dart without any rotation.

Jashari's laugh ended abruptly, punctuated by the staccato of the MP-40.

Paxton ducked, but the firing was wildly in the air. Jashari was gasping and grabbing at the handle of the blade sticking out of the center of his throat. Right where one would cut for a tracheostomy.

Jashari's eyes were filled with fear and pain. Paxton ran right at him, just in case he lost another bet. He crashed into Jashari's body and smashed it to the turf as if he were a linebacker. The two men landed hard on the ground, Paxton on top. Paxton began pummeling Jashari with his elbows and fists.

Jashari tried to swing the machine pistol around to aim, but Paxton was right on top of him, making it difficult to maneuver the slung weapon into position. Jashari reached for the handle of the knife sticking out of his gushing throat.

Jashari fired off a few more wild rounds as Paxton took his fist and pounded the knife further into the jihadist's throat. Paxton drove the blade down until it penetrated and severed Jashari's spinal cord.

Jashari's arms dropped as he lost all control of his body.

Paxton continued his barrage until he realized Jashari was no longer fighting back.

Dead men don't put up much of a fight.

Paxton got up and grabbed the MP-40. He had to struggle with the sling to get it off Jashari's body. He had to help Smith.

Paxton ran past the olive tree. He then dashed over around the van and found Smith lying in a pool of blood.

Chapter 28

PAXTON RAN TO SMITH. SMITH BLED FROM HIS RIGHT BICEP and was holding his head. "You okay?"

"This hurts like hell."

"Your head or arm?"

"Both!"

"I see you were shot in the arm, but what happened to your head?"

"I don't know, I woke up and my head hurt, and my arm is in agony."

Paxton examined Smith. "Looks like you got knocked down when you were shot and hit your head on this rock." Paxton held the rock out for Smith to see.

"Great luck, huh?"

"Well," Paxton said, "it's better than getting shot in the head and bumping your arm on a rock."

"True that."

"Here, try to stop the bleeding while I see what I can scrounge up."

Paxton ran to the van and found a small first aid kit. He then ran back to the olive tree and retrieved the knife from Jashari's body. He wiped the blood on Jashari's shirt. Not exactly a sterile procedure.

He returned to Smith and used the knife to cut the sleeve of Smith's uniform away from the bleeding wound.

"Man, I worked hard to earn those stripes," Smith said as he watched Paxton slice through the part of his sleeve holding his rank.

Paxton examined the wound. It was a through and through—in one side of the arm, passing through the muscle tissue, missing the bone, and out the other side. Painful but not permanently damaging.

Paxton dug into the medical kit and pulled out bandages and cotton. He cleaned the wound, packed it and bandaged it to stop the bleeding. He helped Smith take off his over shirt. He then fitted a sling he found in the kit on Smith's arm to immobilize it and prevent a resumption of bleeding.

He helped Smith to his feet. "Good as new," Paxton said.

"I beg to differ."

Satisfied that Smith was stabilized, Paxton looked around. No one was within sight. He retrieved Smith's GPS receiver from the van and examined the screen. They were a long way from help. He searched the van for anything he could use to communicate with the outside world but found nothing.

"What's up?" Smith asked.

"I'm trying to figure out what to do with the GA."

"What do you mean?"

"Well, I can't very well just leave nerve gas sitting in the back of the van, free for the taking."

"Blow the shit up."

"You kidding me? That would make a toxic cloud for miles."

"So what are we going to do? I'm not moving that shit again."

"Well, the van is shot—literally— so we can't drive it out of here. I need to make it safe."

"How do you propose to do that?"

"I've got an idea...but it all depends."

"Depends on what?" Smith winced in pain.

Paxton stared off at the buildings in the distance. "It all depends on what I find in those buildings."

Chapter 29

PAXTON AND SMITH WALKED TO THE CORRUGATED STEEL building. A padlock secured the hasp on the door. Paxton looked around and came back with a length of metal. He shimmied it between the hasp and the door. He forced it with a grunt. The screws pulled out halfway. He grunted again and the hasp ripped from the door. Paxton yanked the door and walked inside. Smith followed.

Wooden shelves were on the far wall. Cans, bottles, and other containers filled the shelves with no apparent organization. Everything was covered with a thick coat of dust. Paxton crossed to the shelves and examined the containers.

"You mind telling me what you are looking for?" Smith asked as he sneezed.

Paxton would take a container off the shelf, hold it up in the shaft of light coming through the open doorway, shake his head and replace it. He'd take another off the shelf, and repeat the process.

"Hello?"

Paxton was becoming less careful about how he replaced the containers. He was muttering to himself.

Then his face lit up. "Here it is."

"Here what is?"

"See this container?" Paxton held up a plastic bottle with a yellow label and a twist off top. "Find as many of these as you can."

Smith stepped closer to the shelves. "Ok...but what the hell is it?"

"Sodium hydroxide."

• • •

Jill Paxton finished packing the kids' clothes. She sat on the bed and took a breather. Finally a moment to relax. John, Jr. and Megan were taking a nap. She would love to take a nap too, but she had so much to do to prepare for her trip. She had to pack her clothes and everything she would need for the trip. Stroller, car seat, the list was so long. She wished John were there to help...she felt like she was always doing everything by herself.

She knew he was just doing his job, but the damn job always came first.

• • •

"What is all this sodium hydroxide for?" Smith asked.

"It is otherwise known as lye," Paxton answered. "We are on

an olive orchard. The farmers use it to cure their olives."

"Thank you Sergeant Less-Than-Helpful. I mean what are *we* going to use it for?"

"To neutralize the nerve gas."

"How the hell we going to do that?"

"We mix it into the GA, and it causes a chemical reaction that renders it relatively harmless," Paxton explained.

"Pax, you hosing me?"

"No, it is an accepted practice. I learned it when I took the chemical weapons course at the Edgewood Arsenal at the Aberdeen Proving Grounds."

"I mean how are we going to mix the two without getting ourselves killed?"

Paxton paused for a moment, looked at Smith and said, "That, my friend, will be the tricky part. Keep looking for all the sodium hydroxide you can find. I'll be right back."

Chapter 30

Sᴍɪᴛʜ ᴘɪᴄᴋᴇᴅ ᴛʜʀᴏᴜɢʜ ᴀʟʟ ᴛʜᴇ ᴄᴏɴᴛᴀɪɴᴇʀꜱ ᴏɴ ᴛʜᴇ shelves. Pain shot through his slung arm every time he would reach and pull one out. He segregated the lye just as Paxton had asked. He turned when Paxton pushed a wheelbarrow through the door.

Tied to the top of the wheelbarrow with heavy twine was a metal container about three feet tall, four feet long and two feet wide. It had rounded ends and straight sides, like an elongated oval. The bottom was flat and the top was open. It was filled with tools.

"What the hell is that?"

"A stock tank. Farm animals drink out of it."

"Where did you get that?"

"The barn next door." Paxton was covered in sweat. He also had taken off his over shirt and was wearing only his brown T-shirt.

"So are the animals going to dehydrate now?"

"There are just a half-dozen horses in there and a second tank. This one was already empty. I topped off the other one."

"How nice of you."

"Come on. Help me load all this stuff into the tank."

• • •

The person in front of Jill finished his business, so Jill stepped up to the counter. Megan and John, Jr. were sitting in a double stroller. The female airman behind the counter asked if she could help her.

"I need to see Major Jason Right."

"Who shall I say is here to see him?"

"Jill Paxton."

The airman got up. She was wearing a short-sleeved light blue shirt and tab tie. Her dark blue skirt was neatly pressed. She headed across the office. Soon she returned with the major.

He was tall and thin and had a sheaf of papers in his hand. "Mrs. Paxton." He held his hand out and Jill shook it. "It is a pleasure to meet you."

"Thank you, Major."

Right spread the papers out on the counter. "Here is the AF Form 937." The form had "Request and Authorization for Dependant Travel" printed at the top. "This will allow you and your children to travel on military aircraft even though you are not accompanied by your sponsor."

Jill examined the paper.

"You need this, your immunization records, and your passport, and you will be all set to go."

"Will I be flying directly there?"

"No, there is a short layover at Rhein Main Air Base in Germany. Then you will fly directly to Brindisi Air Base."

A disappointed look crossed her face.

"Ma'am, just so you know, you are getting top-of-the line treatment. Normally, you wouldn't be allowed to fly military, and even if you were, you would be on an uncomfortable cargo plane. You're going to be on a nice comfy passenger jet."

"What are you saying?"

Right sighed. "I guess what I'm trying to say is, Colonel Ward must think highly of Sergeant Paxton for him to go to all this trouble for you."

"Of course he did. My husband has gone to a lot of trouble for Colonel Ward."

• • •

Paxton and Smith arrived back at the van. Paxton lowered the wheelbarrow and shook out his arms. He reached into the stock tank and pulled out a roll of duct tape. He held the tape out to Smith.

"Take anything useful out of the van and then tape up the door seams and windows." Smith took the roll and went to work.

Then Paxton opened the rear door and examined the containers. The top of each of the barrels had a six-inch threaded plastic cap sticking up about an inch. It was located near the edge of the top. The caps had vertical ridges spaced around them to aid grip.

Paxton wrapped medical tape five times around the cap, counter-clockwise. He then lay the heavy twine that had secured the tank to the wheelbarrow on the cap under the tape and continued to wrap it around about ten more times. He worked carefully and slowly. A small drop of the substance on his skin would be deadly. He would have preferred to don the heavy gloves, but he needed too much manual dexterity for this part of the operation.

He repeated the process with the second barrel. He guided the two strands of twine out the back door of the van like two fuses.

He arranged the stock tank in the middle of the cargo hold and used the hand truck to place the barrels on opposite sides. Then he put on the heavy gloves and opened a container of lye. He poured the powder into the stock tank until the bottom was evenly covered.

"Smith, how we doing?"

"All done, Pax."

"Excellent. Be ready to tape the back door."

Paxton donned a painter's mask and grabbed the first barrel cap. The moment of truth had arrived. He knew the gloves and mask would provide little or no protection if the liquid splashed or if he inhaled any vapors. He held his breath and twisted until he broke the initial resistance and stopped. He did the same with the other cap. Then he shoved the top of the first barrel as hard as he could. He estimated that the barrel weighed over four hundred fifty pounds. It was impossible to continue to hold his breath. In fact, he was breathing quite heavily with the effort.

He put his legs into it and the bottom lifted off the ground. He shoved again and the barrel tipped over upside down into the stock tank. He quickly did the same with the second barrel. Next he worked quickly to fill the tank with the rest of the lye. It seemed to take forever to pour out of the container. Finally, he dropped the last empty container and dashed out into the sunlight.

Once Paxton was clear, Smith slammed the door and started taping.

The men looked at each other. Paxton nodded slowly and Smith nodded quickly. Paxton tugged on the two strands of twine. They held fast.

He pulled harder, wrapping the twine around his hand. Inside the van the caps started to move. The caps rotated until the GA gushed out into the powdered lye. The lye bubbled and white smoke could be seen through the windows.

The entire inside of the van was filled with smoke. Smith and Paxton stepped back and held their breaths, hoping none of the gas would escape.

Inside the van, the GA bubbled and steamed in the stock tank until both barrels were empty. Paxton and Smith waited until the reaction subsided. None of the GA escaped.

"That should do it," Paxton finally said.

"Hot damn, Pax. Can we go home now?"

Paxton shook his head. "'Fraid not."

"Why the hell not? Jashari is dead. We destroyed the nerve gas. What more is there to do?"

Paxton looked at Smith. He almost couldn't believe what he was about to say, but say it he did. "We have to rescue Mc-Murphy."

Chapter 31

"**Son of a bitch, Paxton. Now I know you are hosing** me."

"I'm serious."

"That man is nothing but trouble. He messed up the Cue Ball rescue."

Paxton shook his head. "You have it completely backward. We were never supposed to rescue Cue Ball. Another team was tasked to rescue the Stealth pilot. *We* messed up McMurphy's mission—more accurately *I* messed it up."

"I thought for sure you would want to head home to your family."

"I do. We're just going to take the long road home."

"Still, Pax."

"Still nothing. We don't leave a man in danger. You pestered your way onto this mission. I'm going to rescue him—you can either come along and help or find your own way back home."

"Damn, that's cold."

Paxton stared at his former student. "What's it going to be?"

"No question, Pax. I'm coming with you."

"Good. We have to move fast."

"How are we going to do it? We don't even know were he is."

"First things first. Come with me."

• • •

Nikolic burst into the room. "General Rugova, I have bad news."

"What is it now, Nikolic?"

"It's Delevic and Labus, sir." Nikolic referred to the two secret policemen Rugova had sent to kill Paxton's family.

Rugova's eyes narrowed. "What about them?"

"Reports are they're dead, sir."

"Dead? Dammit. Did they at least kill Paxton's wife and children before they died?"

"I don't know, sir."

The general's face turned purple. "How the hell did that happen?"

"We don't know all the details, but newspaper reports say they were shot inside the house."

Rugova looked out the window and shook his head. "Impossible. They were professionals. How many Albanians did they kill? They were experts on bursting into homes and causing terror. They were unstoppable. They were the best!"

"Rifles behind every blade of grass?"

"Ridiculous! Besides, Yamamoto never actually said that. They must have been tipped off."

The room suddenly felt warmer, and Nikolic's knees felt a little weak. "That's impossible, sir."

"Are you sure that the prisoners never had a chance to contact anyone?"

Nikolic swallowed. "I'm sure. They have been separated and had no access to communication equipment."

"How can you be so sure, Nikolic?" Rugova stepped in front of Nikolic.

Nikolic's voice sounded weaker. "Grigori has been in my custody," Nikolic said, referring to the fake name McMurphy had been using in Serbia, "and I assure you that he has not had any access."

Rugova's eyes narrowed more. "You fool."

"Sir?"

"Paxton was rescued by the KLA. Obviously he sent a warning through them."

Nikolic stopped holding his breath. The tension left his body as quickly as it arrived. "Yes, sir. How foolish of me. You are correct."

Rugova walked back to his desk. "Of course, I am right."

A shiver went through Nikolic's body.

"The prisoner is no longer of use to us. Kill him."

"Sir?"

"You heard me."

"I think we should interrogate Grigori further. See what he knows...."

"I'm not interested in what you think. He has become a liability. I'm ordering you to kill him."

"Yes, sir."

• • •

The smell of manure and hay was overwhelming. Smith looked around the small barn and saw stalls lining the walls. He sneezed twice. Paxton was already hard at work pulling equipment off the walls.

"And just why are we here?" Smith asked.

"Transportation," Paxton answered as he yanked a saddle down.

"What, we going back to the Wild West?"

"Too far to walk. And the vehicles are obviously trashed."

"I don't know about this." Smith watched as Paxton pulled a second saddle down.

"Got a better idea?"

"I like walking. I'm good with walking."

"Yeah, well I'm not. Too slow. McMurphy's life depends on speed."

Smith shook his head as Paxton led one of the horses out of his stall. He was broad, muscular, and tall. "Why don't we just commandeer a car?"

"Too risky," Paxton said. "I want to stay off the roads. Too many checkpoints. Driving long distances in a stolen car isn't the best idea."

"Oh, yeah? What about stolen horses? In the Wild West horse thievery got you the rope."

"Doubt these will be reported stolen. The owners are long gone. I'm guessing they were run off by the ethnic cleansing." Paxton threw a saddle blanket on the first horse. He then hefted the saddle onto the horse and stooped down to buckle the straps.

"How can you be so sure?" Smith couldn't take his eyes off the horse.

"I'm not. It's just that these beauties were out of oats, and the water was low. No one seems to be taking care of them."

"You're guessing."

"Yes, Smith, I'm guessing." He led the second horse out of the stall.

"What if you're wrong."

Paxton stopped as he was throwing the saddle. "What's the matter, Octavious? You afraid of horses?"

"Uh-no. I've...I've just never ridden one before."

"Damn it, man...you have had a sheltered life."

Smith shook his head quickly. "No. Not sheltered. Man, I grew up in the mean streets of Chicago...we didn't have a lot of horses there to ride."

Paxton finished saddling the horses. "Come on. You can do it. You're a PJ."

The horse snorted at Smith. "You sure I can't just walk beside you?"

"It's easy. I'll show you." Paxton walked the first horse outside. It wasn't a good idea to mount a horse inside in case it reared up and smashed you into the ceiling. Smith hesitated, and then followed. Paxton brought the horse beside Smith.

"Grab the horn with your good hand, put your left foot in the stirrup, and pull yourself up."

"I don't know about this." Smith did as he was told and heaved himself up, but couldn't get himself all the way onto the horse's back.

"Wait," Paxton said. He dashed back inside and came out with a small stool. "Here, step up on this."

Smith stepped up and heaved himself up with his one good arm onto the horse's back. He leaned all the way forward, pressing his chest against the mane.

"Sit up straight." The horse danced as Paxton handed the reins to Smith.

Smith slowly rose until he was sitting up. His back was still bent forward slightly.

"See. Easy, breezy."

"Yeah, breezy." Smith fought to steady himself with his one good hand.

Paxton brought the larger horse out of the barn and pulled himself up on it with ease. Paxton then proceeded to give Smith a brief lesson on controlling a horse. Smith was a quick study.

"Now what?" Smith asked.

Paxton turned his horse toward the open barn door. "Now let's ride back to the van and collect as much equipment and weapons as we can find. I have a feeling we're going to need them. Yah!" Paxton coaxed his horse forward and rode out toward the abandoned vehicles.

• • •

Chapter 32

PAXTON AND SMITH GATHERED THE WEAPONS LYING ON the ground. They also grabbed the GPS receiver that Jashari had taken from Smith. Paxton helped Smith steady himself on the horse. Smith had an MP-40 machine gun slung next to the medical sling holding his arm up. His hand poked from the end of the sling and gripped the firearm.

Paxton climbed onto his horse, Droshny's Benelli shotgun slung on his back. He had found more slugs to load into the magazine. He looked at the small screen on the GPS receiver and touched several buttons.

"So, what did you call the coordinates for the first point I asked you to get?" Paxton asked.

"Point A."

Paxton nodded. "Makes sense." He fiddled with the buttons some more. "Here it is." He looked up, as if to get his bearing, and pointed. "Head west, young man."

"Easy as that? You know were McMurphy is?"

"No…but I know who does. Let's go."

• • •

Smith rode beside Paxton as they covered a significant distance. Paxton checked the GPS from time to time and adjusted their course north. They avoided the roads. As a result, they saw surprisingly few people. The ones they saw simply waved at them and continued about their business. Paxton knew from his experience riding horses in his younger days that horses could dehydrate easily. They had to make sure the horses were well watered.

Shadows were lengthening. They found a sheltered spot and stopped to rest the horses. The men needed a little rest, too. "I'll take the first watch," Paxton said.

Smith didn't argue. He was too tired.

They tied up the horses, and Smith found a relatively soft spot on the ground and nestled himself under a Mylar blanket from the medical kit.

Paxton sat down and leaned his back against a tree. The Benelli lay across his lap, loaded and ready to go. Every minute that passed, Paxton wondered whether they would make it in time. He figured he would let Smith get some rest, and then they would move on.

• • •

Both men were up before dawn. They saddled up, and Paxton checked the GPS receiver for the correct bearing.

The horses handled the rough terrain with ease. Smith was becoming more comfortable in the saddle.

And yet the hours dragged on.

"I still don't understand how we are going to find McMurphy in such a vast place," Smith said.

"Finding McMurphy won't be as hard as getting him out of here. We may encounter some resistance."

"No shit."

The countryside was truly beautiful. Under different circumstances, it would be a wonderful place to take his family to visit.

Paxton looked at Smith. Smith was beginning to look like an old pro on horseback. He could still remember the first time he met Conehead Smith. It was a tradition for the PJ instructors to refer to the trainees as Coneheads or Cones for short. The reference came from an old Saturday Night Live skit. The Air Force had constantly tried to end the practice, deeming it too demeaning. But the students craved it. It was a badge of honor to go through the very same things their predecessors had. No conehead wanted to ever be told that the instructors had gone easy on them. So the practice continued without official sanction.

Smith had come a long way. He always had determination and athletic skill. But now he had confidence that came from training, and combat experience.

After a while, Smith and Paxton came to a road and Paxton turned the horse and continued alongside it. Smith followed. Paxton arrived at a dirt road that veered off the main road into the trees. He examined the GPS unit. Satisfied, he turned and headed down the dirt road.

The horses' hoofs splashed through the ruts. Smith saw tire tracks and many footprints in the dark mud. He looked around nervously. No one else was around.

The forest thinned out as the men rounded a curve. Ahead of them was open pastureland with rolling hills. To the left, the woods were still dark and dense. To the right of the road was a wooden fence holding back grazing cattle.

Paxton pulled on the reigns and stopped. Smith rode up next to him.

Parked ahead to the right was a lone car. Directly in front of them was a huge pit. The grass all around it was scorched. Debris was scattered, but none of the pieces was larger than a foot across.

"What the hell is this?" Smith asked.

Paxton scanned the tableau in front of him. "Point A."

Chapter 33

PAXTON LOOKED AT THE CHARRED GROUND IN FRONT OF him. "This is what's left of the Stealth fighter's wreckage."

"Yeah, well, looks like someone blew it up," Smith said.

"Doesn't matter. We didn't come for the Stealth."

"What the hell did we come here for then? All I see is that piece of shit Yugo over there." Smith pointed.

"That, my friend, is exactly what we came for."

"You gotta be shittin' me."

"I assure you I am not."

"What the hell…how did you even know it was there?"

"McMurphy and I left it… I took a chance that it would still be there, and I was right."

"You took a chance …Pax, did you have a 'Plan B?'"

"Yeah, but you wouldn't want to know what it was," Paxton replied.

"I'm not that thrilled with 'Plan A.'"

"We can't exactly ride horses into Belgrade. It might raise a few eyebrows. Come on." Paxton guided his horse to the car.

It was rusty and covered with mud.

"What a piece of crap," Smith said as he rode up beside Paxton.

"Did you know they build Yugos close to here?" Paxton said as he dismounted.

"Can we drop it at the factory doorstep and get a refund?"

Paxton jerked open the driver's door. He climbed in and looked around. He opened the glove box and the ashtray. He lowered both visors. "Shit."

"What?"

"No keys. McMurphy had them."

"No Triple-A." He shrugged.

"Smith, I get the distinct impression that you are not on board."

"We're risking our lives to save that asshole McMurphy."

"That asshole is an American intelligence officer. Besides, if anyone's going to kill him, I want it to be me. Now go hot wire the car."

Smith jerked his head up. "Aw now, Paxton. What? You think I know how to hot wire a car just because I'm *black*?"

Paxton snorted. He got out of the car to make room for Smith. "That you happen to be black has nothing to do with it. I think you know how to hot wire a car because you're from *Chicago*."

• • •

"I'd like to speak to General Reed." Ward's voice was distorted by the distance over the phone lines.

"I'm afraid he isn't here at the moment," Marshall replied.

"Shoot. Well, perhaps you can help me, Captain. Hell, you're the one Reed is going to have make all the arrangements anyway."

"What arrangements?"

"Paxton's family. They are taking a hop to Brindisi, and I was hoping you could use the general's influence to set them up with the finest quarters."

"Sergeant Paxton's family is flying *here*?"

"Yes. I know you have him busy, but he can't work twenty-four hours a day. I thought it would be a good idea for his family to be there…for a little R&R after the mission."

Marshall was silent.

"Captain…it is the least we can do under the circumstances."

"It's not a good idea for them to be coming here right now."

"Captain, your boss pulled him away from his family and didn't even give him the opportunity to say goodbye. Then your mission caused his family to be attacked in their own home. I don't think it is an unreasonable request that he get to see his family when he is off duty."

"Like I said, Colonel…he is busy right now."

"I know Paxton much better than you. If you want to get the best out of Paxton, it is in your best interest that he gets to spend time with his family. That way he gets to see with his own eyes that his family is safe."

Marshall furrowed his brow. He felt a little panicked. He

wasn't sure what to do. He certainly didn't want the colonel to know Paxton had returned to Serbia. His mind quickly processed the situation. The colonel might be right. It might be in his best interest that Paxton's family be here when Paxton returned…if he returned. Marshall nodded to himself.

"I can't guarantee that they will get to see him…at least not right away. But I'd be happy to make the arrangements."

"Wonderful! I knew you would understand."

Marshall pulled a pad in front of him and clicked his pen. "I will, of course, need detailed information about the family and their flight. And, Colonel? I will take care of them myself."

Chapter 34

PAXTON LOADED THE WEAPONS AND SUPPLIES INTO THE Yugo's hatchback as Smith worked under the dash. The engine fired up and spewed acrid smoke into Paxton's face.

Paxton coughed as he walked the horses away from the crash site. He let them go and watched as they ran off toward the meadow. *Have a good life, beautiful creatures.*

Smith got out and crossed over to the passenger seat. Paxton climbed behind the wheel, put the car in gear, turned the Yugo around, and headed toward the main road. A trail of billowing white smoke followed them. He turned right on the pavement and pointed the car toward Belgrade.

• • •

Jill Paxton buckled John, Jr.'s seatbelt and checked the belt on Megan's car seat. She was too small to sit in the plane's seat without it. She had one arm wrapped around the neck of a teddy bear dressed in camouflage—a gift from her daddy. God help Jill if she forgot the bear at home. Jill then buckled her own seatbelt, her heart beating rapidly in anticipation of take off.

An Air Force steward passed through the cabin in a last-minute safety check. Soon they were rolling down the runway. Jill closed her eyes and said a prayer to keep her family safe on this trip.

• • •

"Pax, you sure you know where you are going?"

"Yes, Smith, I know where I'm going."

"You've passed that same building three times."

Paxton ignored him as he turned down another road.

"'Cause it looks like to me, you don't know where you are going."

"Smith."

"Yes."

"Shut up."

Smith shut up.

Paxton tried to replicate the left and right turns he remembered McMurphy making. If he had known it was going to be important, he would have paid more attention. When he was riding with McMurphy, he was focused on practicing his non-existent Russian language skills. "It's around here somewhere," he said, mostly to himself. He was leaning forward, scanning his surroundings.

His eyes lit up and he downshifted. White smoke billowed

from the back of the Yugo. He turned down a boulevard and sped up.

He maneuvered the Yugo into a crowded parking lot. In the center of the parking lot was a wooden building with a slanted roof and neon signs. Centered over the front door was sign shaped like an oversized beer mug overflowing with foam.

"A bar? We're going to a bar?"

"Yes, Octavious, it is a bar, but *we're* not going to it…I am… your job will be to sit here and wait in the car."

"What the hell?"

"I don't know how this is going to go down. If things turn bad, you need to just get the hell out of here. You can drive a stick shift, can't you?"

"I'm self-taught."

"Good." Paxton disconnected the wires, shutting the engine off and climbed out. He left the shotgun in the car. Outside the bar were several empty tables. Paxton yanked the door and went inside.

The smell of smoke assaulted him. As his eyes adjusted to the darkness, he saw a long bar filled with drinkers across from the door. Heads turned toward him. He stood there for a moment. People lost interest and returned to their drinks and conversations.

The place was pretty much just as he remembered it when McMurphy brought him here. This was going to be tricky since Paxton didn't speak Serbian. He crossed the room and squeezed between a man wearing an orange and white striped t-shirt and a man in a tweed jacket. He leaned over the bar top and motioned for the bartender to come over.

The older man walked over and said something unintelligible to Paxton. Paxton smiled disarmingly. Serbia was crawling with Russian advisors so, just like he had practiced with McMurphy, he said in Russian, "Good afternoon, my name is Ivan."

The bartender scowled and shook his head.

A failure to communicate—just like Paxton had hoped.

Paxton switched to speaking with a heavy Russian accent. "English? Speak English?"

The bartender nodded. *Bingo.*

The man in the orange and white striped t-shirt turned his head slightly, suddenly interested in what was going on.

Paxton continued as if he were struggling with the English language. "I'm looking for man—Lieutenant Colonel Nikolic of Serbian Army. You know him?"

"Maybe. Who wants to know?" The bartender was speaking better English than Paxton was at the moment.

The man in the orange shirt sipped his drink slowly.

"Ivan. He knows me. Can you get message to him?"

The bartender absentmindedly toweled off a glass. "If I were to know Colonel Nikolic, what message would you want me to give him?"

"Ivan needs to see him right away."

The bartender considered him for moment. Then he said, "I'll see what I can do."

Paxton nodded and continued to lean with his elbows on the bar. On the wall over the bartender's head was a photo of Serbian president Slobodan Milosevic, war criminal.

The bartender stepped away and picked up a telephone and spoke for a few moments. He then returned and placed an odd shaped glass in front of Paxton. It reminded him of a small vase with a picture of a flag on it. The bartender opened a clear bottle and poured a shot.

"Colonel Nikolic says for you to wait here. He is on his way. He said you are to drink on his tab."

"Danka." Paxton lifted the odd-looking glass to his nose and sniffed. It smelled fruity. "What is this?"

"Slivovitz."

Paxton raised an eyebrow then shrugged his shoulders. Not wanting to appear unappreciative, he raised the glass and emptied it with one gulp.

Big mistake. It tasted like dirt that someone had soaked in rubbing alcohol. There might have been a plum essence, but he wasn't sure. His tongue and throat were burning too badly to tell. He placed the glass in front of him as he fought the urge to vomit.

Before he could refuse, the bartender had refilled his glass. Paxton was blowing through pursed lips, and he felt the back of his mouth water.

"Drink," ordered the bartender.

Paxton complied. His stomach was in full revolt. It was in knots in part because of the awful tasting plum brandy, but mostly because the last time he had seen Nikolic he was leading McMurphy away at gunpoint.

• • •

Chapter 35

509ᵗʰ Bomb Wing
Whiteman Air Force Base, Missouri

THE NORTHROP GRUMMAN B-2 SPIRIT IS BETTER KNOWN
as the Stealth bomber. The bat-shaped flying wing bomber is
much larger than the F-117 Nighthawk Stealth fighter that was
shot down over Serbia. For example, the Spirit has a wingspan
of 172 feet compared to the 43-foot wingspan of the Nighthawk. It is better armed as well. While the Nighthawk carries two 500-pound bombs, the Spirit can carry eighty. These
capabilities come with a significant cost, however. Each Spirit
purchased for the Air Force cost the taxpayers close to $1 bil-
lion. More if you include research and development costs. Line
up five of them, and you have pretty much the cost to construct
the *U.S.S. Ronald Reagan* aircraft carrier. The result is a strategic bomber that can slip through most modern air defenses
undetected.

The infrastructure required for the Spirit is substantial. The nation's entire fleet is stationed at Whiteman AFB in Missouri. It is there that the specialized climate-controlled hangars house the bombers and protect the classified "low observable" stealthy skins. As a result, all missions, no matter where on the planet the target sits, start in Missouri and return to Missouri. The Spirit refuels in mid-air as necessary. The crew of two has enough room in the cabin to nap, use the bathroom, or cook a hot meal during the long flight.

The Kosovo operation was the first use of the Spirit in combat, and so far its performance had been flawless. The burden of continued flawless performance lay on the shoulders of the crews of the two Spirits that taxied to the end of Whiteman's runway. Last minute checks were performed, the engines were powered up, and they accelerated. The noses pitched up, and both Spirits climbed into the sky, each carrying a full load of 500-pound Joint Direct Attack Munition (JDAM) bombs, plus some other surprises, and headed toward Belgrade.

• • •

Paxton banged the shot glass on the bar, his face twisted in displeasure. He leaned on his elbows.

The man with the orange striped shirt was watching him. "What's the matter? You don't appreciate Slivovitz?" The man spoke English.

He looks like a prisoner dressed in a shirt like that.

Paxton rotated his chin to this right shoulder and continued with the Russian accent. "It isn't Russian vodka."

"Russian vodka is shit."

"Hmmm." Paxton said as he turned away from the man.

The man bumped him. "You hear me? Russian vodka is shit." He was slurring his 's.'

"I hear you." Paxton tried to ignore the man.

The bartender poured another shot before Paxton could wave him off.

The man poked Paxton's shoulder. "Drink the Slivovitz. Maybe you grow some balls."

Paxton continued to ignore him.

"Hey…you listening to me?"

Paxton turned his back completely to him.

"Don't turn your back on me!"

Paxton decided it was time to find a new place to stand. He took a step. A hand grabbed his shoulder and spun him around.

"Don't you leave when I'm talking to you."

"What do you want?"

"I don't think you're a Russian."

"Then you're stupid."

"I think you're an American spy."

"Why would I meet with a lieutenant colonel in the Serbian Army if I'm a spy?"

Paxton started to leave and the man blocked his way. The man leaned in close as he spoke. "I have an American expression for you." The man was spraying Paxton with spit as he talked. He grabbed Paxton's shirt with his meaty hands. "I am going to open a can of whoop ass on you." The man cocked his scarred fist back and swung with all his might.

Paxton stabbed his palm out and blocked the man's bicep before the man's fist could make contact with Paxton's face. The man stood like a photo of a boxer snapped mid-punch.

Paxton leaned in close and dropped the Russian accent. "You better have brought more than one can."

• • •

Smith fidgeted in the car. He fixated on the neon signs in the large window in front of him. The window was tinted so he could not see in past the neon tubing. His machine gun lay across his lap. He lowered his window to let the stale air out.

He wondered how Paxton was faring. How long should he wait before he defied Paxton's orders and go check on him? He felt so exposed sitting out in the parking lot. He wanted to duck down every time a car drove by. His arm and ribs still throbbed with pain.

Suddenly the plate glass window in front of the car smashed, and a man in an orange and white striped shirt tumbled onto the sidewalk.

• • •

The man's friends headed toward Paxton. The bartender, seeing the brawl erupt, grabbed the phone and quickly punched the numbers. He watched the patrons pummel Paxton. Paxton fought back.

"You better hurry…my customers are going to kill your man.

And they are destroying my bar! I'm hanging up and calling the police."

The bartender ducked as a glass tumbler whipped past him and smashed on the wall.

Angry men surrounded Paxton. They were screaming and shouting. The Serbs evidently were not happy with what he had done to their orange-shirted, drunk friend.

Paxton brought his fists up to protect his face as he turned on the balls of his feet, waiting for the next attack. He looked for an exit, but they were all blocked.

One loudmouth stepped toward Paxton. He had his fists out, like he was driving a truck, leaving his vital areas completely exposed. Paxton never gave him a chance. Quick jab to the man's throat, then Paxton smashed his elbow into his nose. As the man pitched forward, Paxton drove his knee into his gut.

The man collapsed to the floor.

The crowd was silent for a moment. Then they started screaming even louder.

Whenever one would be brash enough to charge forward, Paxton would put him down. There was no fair fight about it. No sparring. When someone attacked, Paxton would use well-practiced Muay Thai strikes to break one of the attacker's bones, and the person would drop.

The bartender picked the phone up again and dialed the police.

• • •

Chapter 36

"THIS IS COLONEL WARD."

The voice on the phone said, "Colonel, this is Major Turner with the Defense Intelligence Agency."

"What can I do for you, Major?"

"Do you have a SMSgt John Paxton in your unit?"

Ward sat up. "Yes. He is the Commandant of the Pararescue Schoolhouse. Why?"

"Well, something very interestin' came to our attention and we wanted to verify it with ya."

"What is it?"

"A new video's popped up on a Jihadist website, and you might find it interesting. You have a computer handy?"

"Right here." Ward wiped the pad with the mouse to wake up his screen.

"Take a look at this website and tell me what you think." The man on the phone read the URL web address. Ward typed it into the address bar of his browser.

A blank screen popped up with a triangle in the middle indicating it was a video. Ward moved the mouse and clicked to start the video. John Paxton's face appeared on Ward's screen.

"My name is SMSgt John Paxton. I am a pararescueman with the United States Air Force." The sound was tinny. The jihadists had successfully uploaded the video to the Internet before the American bombs struck Jashari's headquarters.

"Holy crap! That's him!"

• • •

Smith's palms sweated as he gripped the MP-40 machine pistol. Thoughts cascaded through his mind.

Pax needs my help.

He ordered me to stay put.

Something's not right.

Maybe the man crashing through the window had nothing to do with Paxton.

Yeah, right.

Smith's body rocked physically toward the car door and back away from it based upon the thought of the moment.

Even if I go in there, what am I supposed to do? Shoot up the entire place?

Smith was certain he didn't have enough ammunition to do that.

Maybe I can surprise them and shoot enough of the key people that Paxton could get away.

It would be a suicide mission on Smith's part. But he was prepared for that. There was no way he was going to let Paxton go down alone.

Smith braced himself and reached across his body with his good arm and opened the car door.

Chapter 37

THE MEN WERE GETTING SMARTER IN THEIR ATTACKS AND started to overwhelm Paxton with sheer numbers. One man jumped on Paxton's back and Paxton drove backward slamming him into the bar at kidney level. Three men swarmed in, piling on to pin Paxton to the bar.

People were throwing objects including mugs and bar stools. They were hitting Paxton's attackers as much as they were hitting Paxton.

Paxton used brute strength to pry a man away, but for each one he successfully removed another immediately replaced him.

His head was buzzing from the pummeling he was receiving. He knew there was a danger of losing consciousness. He could smell and taste blood. He didn't have the chance to check, but he was pretty sure it was his own.

The bartender was screaming for them to take the fight outside and to stop tearing up his bar.

Several of the larger men who evidently cared more about having a place to drink than beating up the stranger grabbed the fighters, including Paxton. They dragged the human clump toward the door. They pounded away with their fists to encourage compliance, not particularly caring who they were hitting.

The bartender pushed from behind but stopped immediately when one of the errant blows struck him in the forehead. He stood there stunned for a moment, holding his head.

Momentum built as the mass of flailing arms, legs and bodies reached the front door. The whole group crashed through the door without the courtesy of opening it first, and they piled out into the sunlight next the Yugo.

• • •

Smith was in the process of pushing the car door open with his injured shoulder when he saw the crowd of combatants burst out to the parking lot. They were so close that one man lost his balance and bounced off the front fender on the driver's side.

Smith recognized Paxton in the center of the group. His arms were restrained.

Some of the men were backed up to the Yugo's driver-side door. Luckily, Smith was on the passenger side, so he was able to swing his door open.

The good news was they had essentially brought Paxton to him.

The bad news was it was going to be very difficult to shoot into that crowd with a machine gun and not hit his friend.

As Smith climbed out of the car, his mind raced with possibilities of how to attack the throng.

What happened next made such planning superfluous.

A black sedan skidded to a halt immediately in front of the rowdy crowd. A man in a sharp military uniform jumped out from behind the wheel and raised a pistol.

A single shot rang out.

Everyone froze. The sound of the gunshot reverberated in the stunned silence.

The military man lowered the aim of the pistol from the sky and leveled it on the crowd. He shouted an order in Serbian.

The men instantly released Paxton.

He shouted another order and Paxton was shoved toward the sedan.

He then grabbed Paxton and shoved him in the sedan on the passenger side. He shouted one more order, climbed behind the wheel, and sped off.

Smith heard the wail of sirens in the distance. The crowd reacted by dispersing. Some of them hopped into cars and drove off. A few others ran. A tiny group shrugged their shoulders and returned to the bar.

Smith stood there in stunned silence.

What the hell had just happened?

• • •

Chapter 38

THE SIRENS GREW LOUDER. SMITH SNAPPED BACK INTO action. He wasn't about to lose Paxton again. And he certainly didn't want to be hanging around when the cops arrived. He darted around to the driver's side, yanked the door open and hopped in. His slung machine gun bounced off the steering wheel and smacked him in the chest. He slammed the door shut and looked at the controls as if for the first time.

Another damn stick shift!

He shook his head. Then he leaned down, touched the two live wires together to complete the circuit to the starter. Once it turned over and started, he twisted the ignition wires together.

Oily smoke wafted though the cracked window molding.

He had to hurry. He had to catch up with the sedan carrying Paxton before it drove out of sight.

At least this wasn't going to be his first time driving a stick shift.

It was, however, going to be his first time driving a stick shift with his right arm in a sling.

• • •

Inside the sedan, Nikolic's eyes darted from Paxton to the road and back. As Nikolic drove, he pointed the pistol at Paxton. Paxton noted that it was a Soviet-made Makarov.

"SMSgt John Paxton." The Serb spoke English. "You have some nerve contacting me."

"You call it nerve, Lieutenant Colonel Nikolic. Others might have another name for it," Paxton replied.

The car bumped over rough spots in the road.

"Do you know I could have you killed? Don't you understand that I could just kill you myself?" Nikolic raised the pistol slightly for emphasis.

"I'm well aware of that."

"And yet you come back here and ask for me?"

"Calculated risk."

Nikolic nodded. He watched the road.

A thought flashed through Nikolic's mind, and he turned to Paxton. "Your family?"

"Safe."

Nikolic breathed out.

"Have you come, Sergeant Paxton, to kill me for the attempt on your family's lives?"

"No."

"Why should I believe you?"

"If it was my intent to kill you, I would have already killed you. Just as if it was your intent to kill me, you would have already done so."

"Ah. The fact that we are both still alive is evidence we both have other intentions?"

"That is one way of putting it."

"So the great John Paxton is going soft?"

"Hardly. The two goons sent after my family are in a morgue in San Antonio. If I ever get the chance to meet up with your boss General Rugova, I will put him in a morgue, too."

"There are many people who feel that way about him."

"And you? How do you feel about him?"

A wry smile crossed Nikolic's face. "The world would be a better place if Rugova were in a morgue."

"So why don't you do the honorable thing and kill him yourself?"

"You do not understand how things work in Serbia, Sergeant." Nikolic smiled sardonically and shook his head. "If you haven't come back to kill me, then why did you come back to Belgrade?"

Paxton calculated some more risks in his head.

Nikolic looked over at Paxton. "Tell me, Sergeant Paxton, I want to know what brings you back."

Now it was Paxton's turn to smile wryly. Then he gave his one word answer.

"McMurphy."

• • •

Chapter 39

THE YUGO VIBRATED IN NEUTRAL. SMITH DEPRESSED THE clutch and the brake as he reached across his body for the stick shift with his left hand. He had to reach over the MP-40's sling. The machine pistol pressed into his chest as its barrel was stopped by the steering wheel, and its stock was trapped under his sling. Wedged as it was, it prevented him from turning as far as he wanted. Smith had to twist, raising his bad shoulder up as he reached down with the good arm to the shift knob. His fingertips touched it and flicked it into reverse.

The Yugo bucked backward as he released the clutch. The friction point surprised him, as it was completely different from the Golf. He immediately engaged the clutch again as the car rolled back through its own smoke.

Smith was grateful that he hadn't stalled the car.

Smith could not see any police cars, but the sirens sounded like they were just around the corner. He wondered if they would stop him before he could wrestle the Yugo out of the parking lot.

Sharp pain shot through his arm as he twisted to shift the car into first gear— At least, what he had hoped was first gear.

The Yugo lurched forward again, and Smith performed some fancy footwork attempting to find the right balance between clutch and gas.

He erred on the side of too much gas. The Yugo spun its tiny wheels as it bounced over the curb onto the street.

Smith looked down the road and could barely see the sedan carrying Paxton away. The Yugo's engine screamed as it redlined. He felt sharp pain as he twisted to shift into second.

He was disconcerted to find that it was impossible to hang onto the steering wheel with his right hand as he did his twist-shift maneuver. As a result, the Yugo swerved slightly as he shifted.

Right in front of Smith, a police car slid around the corner in a wild left turn. Smith had to grab the wheel and recover lest the swerve carry him into it.

Their eyes met as the policemen passed by him headed toward the bar. Smith floored the Yugo.

The engine was winding out, but acceleration was very disheartening.

Twist, shift, swerve. Third gear.

Plumes of smoke trailed Smith.

Ahead, the sedan turned right and disappeared from sight.

Smith glanced in the rearview mirror. Two more police cars made the same left turn toward the bar. A fourth one approached the same intersection, slowed, and turned right.

Smith twisted, shifted and swerved into fourth gear.

He looked again and saw through the dissipating smoke the last police car growing in his mirror.

• • •

Nikolic looked at Paxton. "By McMurphy, I assume you mean Grigori."

"One in the same…but then, you already knew that." Paxton replied.

Nikolic's gaze returned to the road as he nodded in understanding. "What makes you say I knew that?"

"Because you were McMurphy's asset here in Serbia."

"Meaning?"

"You are working for him. You set up this whole deal for him. You got General Rugova revved up, and you handed him over on a silver platter to McMurphy." Paxton wished he was as confident in that statement as he made it sound.

Nikolic's face reddened, and he raised the pistol ever so slightly. "What you are accusing me of, Sergeant Paxton, is treason."

Paxton did his best to appear completely relaxed. "No treason. You were not selling out your country. At worst, you were selling out your boss. You know what a bad person Rugova is… you know he is evil and greedy. You used that to your advantage."

"How do you figure I was selling out Rugova? He stands to make a substantial amount of money on this deal."

"Because after the Chinese figure out that they have been sold a fake device, they will come after Rugova and likely kill him. You will be doing your country a favor…and no one would ever know you were in on it. Brilliant."

"You give me too much credit, Sergeant Paxton."

"It is true, isn't it?"

"You tell me."

"Of course it is. Only now the Chinese get the real device… so that screws it up for you and for us."

"Rugova wasn't supposed to find the fake one."

"The capture of McMurphy and myself wasn't part of your plan."

"No."

"That is when Rugova discovered the real device and figured out that he had been tricked."

Nikolic nodded.

"So now the heat is on you. Rugova is wondering why you had a fake device delivered to him. You are under suspicion."

Nikolic didn't say anything.

"What I cannot figure out," Paxton continued, "is what was in it for you. You took a huge risk, with no evident personal gain."

Nikolic remained silent.

"Tell me, Colonel Nikolic. Why?"

• • •

High over the Atlantic, Jill Paxton brushed the hair back from her sleeping son's eyes. She glanced beyond her son at the passing clouds and then looked at her daughter, sleeping in her car seat to her left, the camouflaged teddy bear clutched in her tiny arms. The air-pressure differential in her ears made everything sound muffled yet at the same time louder.

She pushed the button on the armrest and leaned the seat back. She took a few deep breaths, trying to relax.

Why do I feel this way?

Jill tried to shake it off.

I'm sure it is just nerves.

She closed her eyes. It didn't help.

Sleep eluded her. It wasn't the cabin noises that disturbed her. Nor was it the harmonic hum of the engines.

The more she tried to block out the external stimulus, the more pronounced the deep feeling grew.

I should be ecstatic.

She could hear the cabin steward talking to one of the other passengers. It sounded like a mumble to her.

I should be looking forward to this trip.

She kept her eyes closed. The drink cart rattled by in the aisle.

I'm getting to see John, finally.

The wait was over.

It was as if she could feel every step of the digestion process in her abdomen.

What the Hell was up with John? He should have called.

She shook her head.

He knows how I worry.

How could he be so inconsiderate?

She took another deep breath.

The "job" has suddenly become more important than talking to his wife and children?

How hard would it be to call? Just for a few minutes?

Her headshake slowed and became more deliberate.

What if we had an emergency?

I thought John had changed. Guess not.

She opened her eyes and gazed at the Air Force symbol on the headrest of the seat in front of her.

Aim High? More like Same Lie.

She reached out and flicked the insignia. She quickly looked at her freshly chipped nail.

Stop it, Jill! People are being really nice to you putting together this trip.

She had never been to Italy before.

Why am I not happy and excited? What is wrong with me?

She opened her eyes wider. There would be no sleep for her.

Jill reached out to both sides and pulled her children closer. The side of the car seat was a barrier between Megan and her. The little ones stirred, but then went back to sleep.

Jill stared straight ahead.

She tried some of the breathing techniques she learned in Yoga class. They helped a little.

But the underlying tension remained.

No matter what she did, she could not shake the feeling of dread.

Chapter 40

NIKOLIC LOWERED THE PISTOL AND ABSENTMINDEDLY returned it to his shoulder holster as he continued to drive. He took a deep breath and let it out slowly.

Paxton looked at Nikolic, waiting for an answer.

"Two years ago," Nikolic started, "my wife was diagnosed with IPF-- Idiopathic Pulmonary Fibrosis."

Paxton listened patiently.

"Have you ever heard of that?"

"No. I can't say I have."

"I hadn't heard of it either. It progressively damages the lungs. The doctors don't even know what causes it. All they could tell me was that the IPF would eventually kill her."

"That's terrible."

Nikolic looked at Paxton. "You don't understand. She won't just slip away in her sleep. What lies ahead for her is slow and painful suffocation. All we can do is sit and watch."

"There's no treatment?"

Nikolic had a far-away look in his eyes as he shook his head. Paxton didn't know what to say.

"She was given less than three years to live."

"I'm sorry." Paxton tried to imagine what Nikolic was going through—what his wife was going through. And what lay ahead for the both of them.

"There was nothing anybody could do." Nikolic blinked away a tear. "Then out of nowhere, I was approached in that tavern we just left by a Russian businessman."

"Grigori?"

"Yes, Grigori…McMurphy."

"What happened next?"

"Well, we talked quite a bit. We talked about everything under the sun. I talked to him about my wife's medical issues. He took great interest."

"And then?"

"And then he told me he could help."

"How so?"

"He said he could get her out of Yugoslavia and get her advanced medical treatment. Treatment that could very well save her life."

"What sort of treatment?"

"Lung transplant."

"That would work?"

"I checked with her doctors. They agreed that the only thing that could save her life would be a lung transplant. But they also told me that would take a very sophisticated medical network with skilled surgeons. Such a thing isn't an option here in Serbia."

"What was McMurphy's solution?"

"He said he could get her out of Serbia into a German hospital with a priority listing on the transplant list. He was like a godsend."

Paxton grunted at the thought of McMurphy being a godsend.

"It seemed a miracle that I happened by chance to meet a man who could help me."

"Only now you know it wasn't a miracle."

"No it wasn't."

"You were targeted as someone who could be turned."

"Yes. He knew just what to say to me. It was like he knew me my whole life."

"That is because he studied your dossier."

Nikolic nodded.

"How does that make you feel?" Paxton asked.

"I don't know. I don't care. All that's important to me is saving my wife's life. If he could do it, I didn't care what it took."

"And you believed he could make this happen?"

"Yes. He revealed to me that he really was an American intelligence officer."

Paxton was silent for a moment. Then he asked, "What did he want in return?"

"He said that if a Stealth fighter were to go down, he wanted me to arrange for Rugova to set up an exchange with the Chinese."

"Anything else?"

"Yes, he said he wanted to take the lead in extracting the device from the wreckage."

Paxton nodded in understanding.

"Anything else?"

"No. After the device was extracted, we were going to evacuate my wife to Germany."

Paxton was silent for a moment. Then he asked, "Tell me, Nikolic, how is your wife doing?"

"Not well. She is in hospital in Belgrade. The situation is grim and time is short."

Paxton glanced in the side mirror waiting for Smith to turn the corner. What was taking him so long?

Paxton agreed with Nikolic. "Time *is* short, and the situation is indeed grim."

• • •

Two miles higher than the plane Jill Paxton was flying in, the pair of B2 Stealth bombers crossed the Atlantic on their deadly mission. They were each equipped, just like the Stealth fighter, with the black box that defeated even the passive radar systems recently developed by the Chinese. The GPS coordinates of their targets were programmed into the autopilot, and the huge planes jetted toward Belgrade.

• • •

Smith turned the corner and accelerated toward the receding sedan carrying Paxton. The Yugo's engine was running rougher than ever as he wound it out. He was getting better at taking his hand off the wheel, quickly shifting and grabbing the wheel once again. But his car was no match for the powerful sedan in front of him.

He glanced in the mirror. Through the white smoke, he saw the police car turn the corner and follow him up the street. Smith's car was no match for that car either. He already had the accelerator to the floor, but he pressed it harder, as if that would somehow give him more speed.

In the mirror, Smith saw that the white smoke emanating from tailpipe was lessening. The clearer view allowed him to see three more police cars turn the corner and accelerate toward him. Every instinct in his body told him to turn down a side street and try to evade his pursuers. But that would mean losing Paxton. He wasn't willing to do that. He wasn't sure what he would do if he even were fortunate enough to catch up with the car carrying Paxton away. Nonetheless, the only acceptable option was to proceed forward.

Chapter 41

IN THE MIRROR, PAXTON FINALLY SAW SMITH'S CAR TURN the corner billowing smoke. Then he saw the disconcerting sight of the four police cars following Smith. Paxton's heart was in his throat. He tried to make conversation.

"Where exactly are we going?"

"My flat in the city. It is right around the next corner."

"Is that where McMurphy is waiting?"

"Yes." Nikolic turned at the next intersection and Paxton lost sight of Smith in the mirror.

Nikolic turned into a small parking garage and drove up the ramp. He swung the sedan into an empty parking spot and shut off the engine.

Paxton hoped and prayed Smith saw where they turned in.

Nikolic turned to Paxton and said, "Let's go up."

• • •

Smith leaned forward in the driver's seat as if that would make the car go faster. He was approaching the intersection where Nikolic's sedan had turned, and he needed to regain sight of the car.

He dialed the right turn into the steering wheel and downshifted. The engine revved and then fell silent.

Smith pressed the accelerator to the floor, but the car was coasting. He jiggled the gearshift around in neutral and pumped the clutch. The tachometer read zero and the speedometer was falling.

No more smoke emanated from the tailpipe.

Smith reached around the steering wheel and just then remembered that there was no ignition key. *Dammit!* He reached down further and clumsily mashed the two starter wires together.

Click.

He held the two wires together.

Click. Click. Click.

The oil-less engine had finally seized.

In the silence, Smith could hear his own heart thundering.

In front of him, there was no sign of the sedan. His eyes darted to the mirror.

The police cars were almost upon him. The roll of the Yugo slowed to a crawl.

If he ditched the car and bolted on foot, he might still have a chance. Besides, Paxton must be around here somewhere. The sedan didn't just disappear—it had to be parked somewhere. He hit the brakes and reached for the door handle.

Too late.

The police cars pulled up beside and in front of him. In an instant, officers dressed in all black swarmed him, and he was the aim-point of each of their guns.

Smith considered, just for an instant, opening fire with his machine gun. But he had no appetite for gunning down innocent police officers who were just doing their jobs. And he had even less appetite for the hail of return fire such a move would bring.

He did the only reasonable thing.

He raised his hands in surrender.

Chapter 42

PAXTON GOT OUT OF THE CAR AND STOOD FOR A MOMENT. He was still wondering about Smith's fate. He had visions of Smith driving right by the entrance to the parking garage. The vision got worse as he imagined the four police cars pursing the Yugo.

How can I signal Smith?

Nikolic broke his concentration by coming around the car and clapping Paxton on the shoulder.

"Come. I will show you some Serbian hospitality."

Nikolic extended his arm, palm up, out toward a metal door indicating for Paxton to lead the way.

Paxton walked over to the door and pushed on the bar. It swung open revealing a concrete stairwell.

"Fourth floor," Nikolic said.

Paxton began climbing with Nikolic right behind him. Their footsteps echoed off the stark walls. "Is that why you took Mc-

Murphy away? So you could salvage your deal?"

"Yes. My wife's life depends on that deal."

Paxton considered that for a moment as he continued to climb.

"But you left me to die."

"I knew Rugova was not ready to kill you. He still wanted information."

"Would you have let him kill me?"

Nikolic clapped Paxton's shoulder again as they climbed. "Of course not."

Paxton didn't believe him.

Each floor was numbered and featured a landing with four wooden doors. The fourth floor was no exception. Each of the doors had a letter.

"Over here." Nikolic led the way to the door labeled "B."

He pulled out a wad of keys and jiggled one in the door. It unlatched and he opened the door. Once again he held his arm out indicating for Paxton to enter.

Stale air confronted Paxton as he entered the apartment. The doorway led right into a kitchen area. All the appliances where white and appeared to be from the 1960s. Nikolic followed Paxton in and locked the door behind them. "Living room."

Paxton followed the directions and walked into the living room.

Sitting on the green couch was McMurphy. He was wearing a camouflage shirt and pants. Nothing sewn on the shirt. Scuffed boots. In other words, he was still wearing the same clothes that he had on the last time Paxton saw him. How many days had it been? Paxton wasn't quite sure.

McMurphy looked up, and his eyes locked on Paxton. The recognition was immediate.

"What the hell are you doing here, Paxton?" McMurphy questioned.

Paxton shook his head. *Same old McMurphy.*

"Time to go home," Paxton replied.

McMurphy snorted at the idea. "Everything is really fucked up now. You shouldn't have come here."

"Now listen here, McMurphy...." Paxton pointed a finger at McMurphy intending to read the riot act to the ungrateful bastard. Then Paxton noticed the handcuff on McMurphy's wrist. Paxton followed the chain with his eyes and saw the other end secured to a pipe that ran from floor to ceiling. "What the--?"

"He is right, you know," Nikolic said from behind Paxton. "You shouldn't have come here."

Nikolic punctuated the statement by pressing the barrel of his pistol into the back of Paxton's head.

Chapter 43

"I DEMAND TO SPEAK TO GENERAL REED THIS INSTANT!"
Colonel Ward was ready to come through the phone just to throttle the person at the other end.

"Sir, he is not available at the moment," Marshall responded.

"Make him available!"

"Sir, the general has given me strict orders that he is not to be disturbed for any reason."

Ward knew that Marshall was bound to follow the general's orders. He decided to change tactics. "Has Sergeant Paxton returned to Yugoslavia?"

"That is classified."

"Classified my ass…I've already seen the video."

"Video?"

"Yeah, the video," Ward replied. "Apparently Paxton has been captured by your jihadist friends."

Marshall went silent.

"What do you have to say about that?" Ward demanded.

"I haven't seen any video. All I know is we lost contact with Paxton and the others."

"He's trying to reestablish contact. The video is full of coded messages."

"Messages? What are the messages saying?" Marshall asked.

"Damned if I know."

• • •

The pararescuemen finally located the wreckage and respectfully retrieved the bodies from the downed Pave Hawk helicopter. First the bodies of the Navy SEALs were placed into body bags and carried to one of the Pave Hawks that had landed in a clearing fifty yards away. Then the bodies of the helicopter pilots—their comrades from the 255th Rescue Squadron—were loaded as well. This tragedy couldn't get any more personal.

They searched but found no sign of either Paxton or Smith. They placed explosives on the wreckage, retreated to a safe distance, and blew up the remains of the downed Pave Hawk. They then climbed aboard the other helicopter and headed back toward Italy.

Chapter 44

"**Captain Marshall, I want to know why you didn't** tell me that Sergeant Paxton had returned to Yugoslavia." Ward was furious.

"Colonel, as I told you, that information was strictly classified."

"I'm his commander. I have a right to know."

"Maybe…but you didn't have a *need* to know."

Ward switched the phone from one ear to the other. "How dare you order him back into a combat zone without first giving me the courtesy of a heads-up."

"We didn't order him."

"What?"

"We didn't order him. He volunteered."

"Bullshit. You all came up with another crazy scheme and convinced him to go."

"Sir, you have it all wrong. The crazy scheme, this time, was

Paxton's own idea. We told him not to do it. He had to convince *us* to let him go."

Now Ward was speechless.

"He didn't want anyone to know," Marshall continued. "He didn't want anyone to worry. And he didn't want anyone to try to stop him."

Ward could only shake his head. *Paxton!*

And then a thought occurred to him.

"Marshall, I sent Paxton's family over there."

"Yes, sir."

"You didn't stop me."

"As you recall, I told you it wasn't a good idea, but you insisted."

Unfortunately, Marshall was right.

"What the hell are we going to do when they arrive and Paxton isn't there?"

"I suppose I will make them comfortable, show them the sights, and keep them busy until Paxton comes back."

"Until Paxton comes back! He is in the hands of a bunch of terrorists. You say until he comes back! When will that be?"

Marshall didn't mention to Ward that Reed had blown up the headquarters of those very same terrorists.

"Your guess is as good as mine."

• • •

The Air Force passenger jet carrying John Paxton's family touched down on Brindisi's main runway. The installation had been closed as an active military base back in 1993. But because of operations in Bosnia and Serbia, NATO had set up limited operations at locations on the Mediterranean Sea. The base was currently being used mainly for staging rescue operations and for maintenance and repair of NATO aircraft. As a result, everything had a temporary feel to it.

Nonetheless, the facility was abuzz with activity. NATO officials traveling in and out, maintenance crews and their aircraft, plus the 255th Rescue Squadron that had taken up temporary residence in a large, dilapidated steel hangar.

Jill's plane taxied right past that hangar and past the site where the Pave Hawk took off taking Paxton back to Yugoslavia. Jill, however, was oblivious to that. She was busying herself getting her children ready to deplane. She fully expected to be greeted at the gate by John Paxton.

• • •

The Serbian police officers, clad in all black, yanked open the Yugo's door and grabbed Smith. They pulled him out and slammed him to the pavement. He landed painfully on the bullet wound in his arm. Smith felt like the outline of the machine pistol made a permanent indentation on his ribs.

Orders were screamed at him, and even though he didn't speak the language, he understood their meaning. He had no plans to move.

They gruffly relieved him of his machine gun. He was then dragged to his feet.

Evidently, they didn't care that his arm was in a sling. They removed the sling, yanked his arms back and cuffed him. Smith winced with the pain. Without so much as a discussion, they shoved him into the back of one of the police cars.

His arm started bleeding profusely again. Smith reflected once more that he should have stayed in the back of the police car back in the serenity of Italy.

The police cars all sped off, leaving the Yugo sitting there, lifeless with the driver's door still open.

Chapter 45

PAXTON STOOD COMPLETELY STILL EXCEPT FOR RAISING UP his hands until they were level with his ears. It felt like Nikolic was trying to burrow into his head with the barrel of the pistol.

"Can someone explain to me what the fuck is going on?" Paxton asked.

"Why don't you let your friend explain," Nikolic said.

Paxton looked at McMurphy, "Spill it, *buddy*. Why is the colonel acting so unappreciative of your efforts to save the life of his *wife?*"

McMurphy's ice blue eyes locked onto Paxton's. "Things have changed."

"Ya think?"

Paxton could hear Nikolic breathing heavily behind him.

"It was supposed to all go down smoothly." McMurphy explained. "We were supposed to make the exchange and then on our way out of the country, we were going to swing by here and take his wife with us."

Paxton thought about it for a moment. "So that is why Reed sent Pararescue along—to help evacuate a sick patient."

"Precisely."

"But it didn't go down smoothly," Paxton said.

"Once the Russians got involved for real, things went downhill quickly."

"Your cover was blown."

"Yes."

"It didn't help that I didn't speak Russian," Paxton added.

"It only accelerated the inevitable. Rugova had been tipped off. He knew we weren't who we said we were."

"Tipped off? By who?"

"Don't know. Damn leak at the Pentagon struck again."

"Shit."

"So why did they wait to arrest us?"

"They still needed me to extract the real device from the Stealth."

Paxton nodded his head ever so slightly. "Now that Nikolic has you, why not move forward with the plan?"

"Things have gotten complicated."

"Like they haven't been all along."

"Listen to me, Paxton! The Serbs suspect Nikolic was in on it, which, of course, he was."

"Shit."

"Exactly. Shit."

"Well, since he is still very much alive and armed, they must still trust him." The two Americans spoke as if Nikolic were not standing right there.

"Well, I blew that for him by calling General Reed about your family being in danger."

"How so?"

"I used *his* phone."

"So they think he let you do it."

"Which he didn't. In fact, he snatched it from me before I could finish my warning, and he locked me up." McMurphy emphasized the statement by lifting his iron-clad wrist.

"His phone was under surveillance?"

"We assume it is."

"Your wife?" Paxton asked Nikolic over his shoulder.

"She has taken a turn for the worst. As I told you, she is in hospital."

"Let's go get her," Paxton said.

"No can do," McMurphy said. "Since Nikolic has come under suspicion, her room is under 24-hour guard."

"You can't visit her?"

"Oh, I can go see her," Nikolic answered. "There is just no way I can leave with her."

"I see."

"I don't think you do," Nikolic said. "Tell him the best part."

"Yeah," McMurphy grunted. "The best part...the only way the colonel is going to find his way back into good graces is to bring my dead body to Rugova."

Paxton nodded again. He hoped Smith had seen where they went in and was going to burst through the door at any moment. Especially since he had already arrived at the logical conclusion: "And since everyone at the tavern saw me leave with Nikolic, obviously he is going to need to bring Rugova my body as well."

McMurphy scowled. "Paxton, you're smarter than I thought."

Chapter 46

CAPTAIN MARSHALL LEANED AGAINST THE WALL AT GATE 3A watching the passengers deplane, cross the tarmac, and enter the terminal. Officers and enlisted representing all five branches of the military. Civilians wearing suits and carrying briefcases. The last passengers to leave the plane were a long-legged blonde pushing a stroller with a small child clutching a teddy bear. A slightly larger child was walking beside her.

Marshall moved closer to the door. When they arrived, he opened it for them.

"Mrs. Paxton?"

Slightly surprised, she replied, "Yes."

"I'm Captain Marshall. I work with your husband, and I'm here to make sure you get to your quarters without any troubles."

"Where is John?"

"Work has him detained at the moment."

"We just flew thousands of miles to come see him, and he couldn't take five minutes out to greet his family?"

"I'm sorry."

"Don't be. He is the one who is going to be sorry. Let's go. We're exhausted. Take us to our room."

• • •

Paxton stood with his hands up, watching McMurphy and trying to gain some insight from his stoic expression. No help there. McMurphy was flat.

Delay.

Get Nikolic to talk.

I'm not sure what I'm delaying for. Smith has no idea where I am.

"So lemme get this straight, Nikolic. You don't even want to try to get your wife out of there?" Paxton asked.

"It is impossible," Nikolic replied. Paxton wished he could see the Serb's face.

"Nothing is impossible," Paxton stated.

"What do you think we should do? Shoot our way past the guards?" McMurphy said.

Paxton gave McMurphy a dirty look.

"Even if we killed the guards, we'd never get through the hall-ways and out the front door with his ailing wife before we were killed," McMurphy added in his typical unhelpful fashion.

"Guarding the door of the room? There must be another way in or out." Paxton stated.

"Paxton, her room is on the sixth floor of the hospital. No other doors. Just a window, and there is nothing below but the parking lot."

Paxton's mind raced. Maybe he could figure out a way to signal Smith his location in the apartment— if he was outside at all. His eyes darted around the room. Time was running out.

"So what are your options? What good will killing us do?"

"If I bring Rugova your bodies, maybe he will let me take my wife out of the country for treatment," Nikolic answered.

"You don't really believe that do you?" Paxton asked.

"Paxton! Stop antagonizing him!" McMurphy demanded.

"I'm just pointing out that he shouldn't trust Rugova— "

"Shut up, Paxton!"

"No, you shut up, McMurphy! Nikolic's way will result in all four of us winding up dead."

"You have a better idea?" Nikolic asked, pressing the pistol harder into the back of Paxton's head.

"Damn straight I do. You are forgetting one really important fact."

"Oh? What is that?" Nikolic asked.

As Nikolic finished his question, Paxton was already snapping around to his right, ducking his head down into his own right shoulder. Before the Serb could react, Paxton's move drove his right forearm into Nikolic's arm holding the gun, knocking it away from Paxton's body. In one continuous motion, Paxton smashed his left elbow into Nikolic's face. He then stepped with his left foot and continued twisting around. Paxton grabbed the pistol in both hands. His Krav Maga training kicked in as he wrenched Nikolic's arm out and twisted until he pulled the gun from his hands. He then drove his knee into the back of Nikolic's leg and smashed his elbow into his face again.

Nikolic went down hard.

Paxton backed up out of Nikolic's reach and pointed the pistol at the Serb who was doubled over on the ground.

"You forgot that I'm John Paxton, and I didn't come here to die."

Chapter 47

PAXTON WASTED NO TIME. HE QUICKLY RELEASED McMurphy and used the same set of handcuffs to lock up Nikolic.

Likewise, McMurphy wasted no time with thank-yous. "That was a dumbass thing you did coming back here, Paxton."

"My dumbass saved your smartass."

"We're not out of here yet," McMurphy replied.

Paxton didn't reply. He was busy looking in the freezer while holding a small towel. "Isn't there any ice?"

"Ice? Paxton, you are in Europe. You aren't going to find any ice in there."

Paxton sighed, wet the towel, and offered it to Nikolic. The Serb's nose and mouth were bleeding profusely. He had the look of a defeated man as he sat there on the couch, rumpled uniform, chained to a pipe in his own apartment. Nonetheless, Paxton kept the pistol in his hand, just in case.

McMurphy picked the keys up off the floor. Nikolic had lost them sometime during the brief struggle. "I've got the car keys. Let's get the fuck out of here."

"No!" Paxton barked.

McMurphy scowled at Paxton. "Excuse me?"

"We can't leave yet."

"Well, I'm sure as shit leaving…you either come with me now, Paxton, or your ass is walking."

Nikolic held the blood-soaked towel to his face.

"You're not going anywhere, McMurphy. You're going to stay and help me."

"Bullshit. Help you *what*?"

"Help me rescue Nikolic's wife…get her to Germany for her transplant."

Nikolic stopped what he was doing and looked up at Paxton.

McMurphy stood there looking at Paxton in disbelief. "You have got to be shitting me."

"I'm not shitting you."

McMurphy shook his head in an exaggerated manner, turned on his heel and headed toward the door. He was mumbling something about Paxton's evident lack of intelligence.

"I'm serious, McMurphy! Stop!"

McMurphy stopped in the doorway to the kitchen. Without turning to face Paxton he said, "What? Because you got that gun, you think you can keep me from leaving?"

McMurphy was genuinely surprised at the next sound he heard: it was the sound of the pistol hitting the floor.

Chapter 48

JILL PAXTON ARRANGED THINGS IN THE HOTEL ROOM TO make the kids feel more comfortable. She opened the suitcases and pulled out some toys. She then hung up some extra clothes she brought for John. Civilian clothes. He left in such a hurry, he had not even bothered to say goodbye to his family—let alone pack.

She took her clothes and carefully placed them in a drawer. It wasn't clear to her how long they were staying, but she didn't like to dig outfits out of a suitcase.

John, Jr. and Megan sat on the bed watching cartoons on the small television. She knew they couldn't understand a word said, but their giggles were proof that the language barrier didn't dampen their enjoyment. Megan clutched her "daddy bear."

After everything was emptied and the suitcases were put in the closet, Jill allowed herself to sit on the bed and lean back on the pillows.

It was a nice room. Right on base as Colonel Ward had promised. That gave her a sense of security. It was a room intended for officers, but strings had been pulled to allow them to stay in it even though John was an enlisted man.

Still it wasn't home.

In fact, it was a long way from home. In a strange country. No friends to comfort her. No vehicle to just hop in and drive around.

She was disconcerted to find that her cellphone didn't work here—there was apparently a different system in Europe. "No Service" even on roam.

The only truly comforting thought she had was, *at least we're closer to John.*

• • •

The two Pave Hawk helicopters carrying the PJs and the bodies from the downed copter continued their trek back toward Brindisi.

The pilot of the lead copter announced his plans to his crew over the intercom system. "We will land on the *Kersarge*, refuel, grab a bite to eat, then fly the rest of the way home."

One of the PJs replied, "Captain, that means we are going to have to eat Navy food."

"Either that," the pilot said, "or wait until I find a fly-through McDonald's. The choice is yours."

"Are we there yet?" pestered the smartass PJ.

Chapter 49

McMurphy spun around, fists up, ready for Paxton's assault.

He was almost disappointed to find that Paxton was standing still on the other side of the living room. Nikolic's pistol lay at Paxton's feet. No attack was coming.

"What?" McMurphy asked. "You're not going to try to stop me?"

"If you want to go, then go," Paxton said.

"I want to go." McMurphy started to turn toward the door.

"You want to go, but you know that isn't the right thing to do."

McMurphy stopped. Then he said, "If I stay, Rugova and his men are going to kill me, and you too, by the way. If I leave now, I've got a chance of staying alive. The choice is easy."

"The easy choice is the wrong choice."

"So says you."

"You know I'm right," Paxton replied.

"I know you're stupid."

"Since when does McMurphy run away from the mission? The McMurphy I know is always on task. The mission above all else. Safety be damned."

"You don't know shit about me." McMurphy took a step toward Paxton.

"I know that you don't let anything get in the way of completing the mission...the Stealth fighter being unexpectedly shot down before you were ready...being paired up with me—someone you call stupid...the C-17 being shot down with all of us onboard...you didn't let any of that stop you from pursuing the mission."

"Yeah, well now the mission is FUBAR."

"So what is new? It's been FUBAR from the start."

Nikolic sat silently, struggling to keep up with the conversation.

"The mission was to get the fake device into the hands of the Chinese," McMurphy said.

"True."

"But now they know it was a fake, the real device is gone, and our cover is blown. Game over, Paxton."

"I'll grant you that part of the mission has been compromised. But what about your promise to Nikolic?"

Nikolic was all ears.

"What of it?"

"Are you going to just walk away from it?"

"No. I'm going to run away from it, hop in the car, and drive away from it. If you were smart, you would do the same."

"You know I'm not going to do that. I'm dumb ole John Paxton."

McMurphy shook his head again. "Paxton, what the fuck do you care about a promise I made to some Serbian lieutenant colonel?"

"Because you didn't make that promise as McMurphy, asshole in chief. You made it as McMurphy, representative of the United States."

"The mission failed. No deal."

"Nikolic did everything he was supposed to do. He delivered a hungry Rugova to you. He made all the arrangements. He lived up to his end of the bargain." Paxton pointed at Nikolic. "It's not his fault some traitorous shithead at the Pentagon blew your cover."

"I don't get why you care," McMurphy said.

"Because if we don't make good on promises made to intelligence assets, if we back out every time the heat is on, then nobody is ever going to cooperate with us in the future. Come on McMurphy. You know this. You are in this business. I'm not."

"Damn right you are not. You wouldn't make it a day in intelligence. So stay the fuck out of it."

"I plan to stay out of it. I am, however, in the rescue business. I rescue people who are in bad situations, behind enemy lines. Mrs. Nikolic is in a bad situation, she is definitely behind enemy lines, and she damn sure needs rescuing. I'm going to do it with or without you. I would prefer that you help me. General Reed says you are well trained and might come in handy."

"Paxton, how the fuck are you going to waltz into a hospital in the middle of Belgrade, bombs falling all around, past the armed men guarding her door, sashay her right out the front door and all the way to Germany? Oh, and did I forget to mention that our cover is blown, and they are expecting us to try to take her? And how do you plan to do all this without getting yourself killed or killing the patient, who is very sick? How the fuck are you going to do all that?"

Paxton was silent for a moment. Both McMurphy and Nikolic were staring at Paxton. The pause was pregnant with triplets.

Paxton's arms fell to his side.

Finally he spoke. Three words: "I don't know."

Nikolic's chin fell to his chest. McMurphy shook his head again and turned toward the door.

"McMurphy," Paxton said. "I could use your help."

McMurphy took a step toward the door.

"McMurphy." This time it was Nikolic speaking. "Please help him. Please save my wife."

McMurphy stood there silently, his back to the other men.

"I've got to know, McMurphy," Paxton asked, "are you with me on this?"

Chapter 50

THE FIRST OF THE STEALTH BOMBERS FLEW INTO POSITION below the KC-135 tanker. The KC-135 Stratotanker is based on the Boeing 707 airliner. Instead of passengers, it carries 83,000 pounds of jet fuel that can be pumped through a telescoping boom that trails below the aircraft. The boom is controlled by an operator who lies prone in the rear of the plane.

The refueling port is on the top of the Stealth bomber, to the rear of the flight deck. The bomber flies as steady as possible and the boom operator extends the boom until both planes are connected. They have all practiced the maneuver countless times, but it still is a tense moment when you are lining up and connecting a plane carrying 83,000 pounds of jet fuel with a plane carrying 40,000 pounds of high explosives, miles high in turbulent air.

The connection was made, and the tanker began dumping the fuel into the bomber. In the process, the tanker became lighter and the bomber heavier, so the pilots had to continually adjust.

The first bomber was successfully refueled and detached from the Stratotanker. The next bomber flew into position and the process was repeated. Once that bomber was topped off, the Stratotanker veered away, headed to a rendezvous with other NATO aircraft.

The Stealth bombers, however, continued on toward the heart of Belgrade.

• • •

McMurphy turned toward Paxton. "Just exactly what the hell kind of help do you want from me, Paxton?"

"For one, I could use communications equipment. I'm thinking you might have access to some," Paxton said.

"What sort of communications equipment?" McMurphy asked.

"The kind that will get me in touch with General Reed. I can't very well use Nikolic's phone since that is presumed to be under surveillance."

"Shit. What else?"

"I'm going to need more weapons."

"Weapons might be a problem. But I know where there is a Sat phone."

"Good," Paxton said. He knew that the type of satellite phone McMurphy would be talking about could not be intercepted.

"Not good." McMurphy replied.

"Why?"

"It's not here. Somebody would have to go get it. That would be a dangerous trip. What else? You looking for some ruby slippers too?"

"I need you," Paxton said, "to watch my back."

"Forget it."

Paxton shifted gears, "Let's say you leave now, give me no help, and I stay to attempt the rescue."

"Your funeral."

"What will you say when you get back to Washington, and they ask why you left me behind?"

"I'll say I never saw you. You will be dead at that point, so no one will even know you came here, and no one can refute my story."

"That, my friend, is where you are wrong."

"What are you talking about?"

"This very moment, Sergeant Smith is outside." Paxton had visions of Smith driving around lost, followed by a parade of police cars. He didn't share that vision with the others. "I had him follow us here."

McMurphy's face reddened. "If Smith is here, they why the fuck do you need me? Why don't you just let him help you, and I can go home?"

"He will help me, but you know your way around here. We don't. So what do you say?"

Paxton and Nikolic both stared at McMurphy.

"I'll get you the Sat phone," McMurphy said. "But that is it. After that, I'm not sticking around. I'm not into suicide missions."

Chapter 51

PAXTON WALKED OVER TO NIKOLIC WITH THE HANDCUFF key in his hand. "Colonel, I'm going to release you now because we can't exactly move through the city with you in handcuffs without drawing attention to ourselves," Paxton explained. "But let me make something crystal clear to you. You do anything stupid, and McMurphy and I'll just leave. I won't even bother to shoot you. You'll be left to watch your wife die, and you'll have to explain to Rugova how you let us both get away. Understand?"

Nikolic nodded rapidly.

Paxton performed a quick search of Nikolic to make sure he didn't have any hidden weapons, then he unlocked the handcuffs and placed them in the cargo pocket of his pants. Nikolic shook his hands in front of him to restore circulation.

McMurphy was peering out the window.

"Do you have any more weapons?" Paxton asked Nikolic.

He shook his head.

"That's okay," Paxton said. "I have some weapons in the car with Smith."

McMurphy continued to scan the street from the window.

Paxton continued, "Do you have any hats, sunglasses? Jackets? Things McMurphy and I could wear to make us less recognizable? And some watches. We will need to coordinate times."

Paxton followed the Serb into the bedroom where he dug out some hats and jackets. He then opened a drawer and pulled out some old pairs of sunglasses and two watches.

Paxton and McMurphy donned the items. Nothing matched, but it wasn't like they were going to a fashion show. Paxton had Nikolic dig out a set for Smith.

Paxton looked over the group. Then he said, "Let's round up Smith and go get the Sat phone."

• • •

"What's that, Mommy?" John, Jr. asked excitedly. The windows of hotel room rattled to the sound of a jet engine revving up.

"That's an airplane honey," Jill answered.

"I wanna see."

"Come here, sweetie." Jill motioned for her son to come over to the window. They both peered out above the trees, looking for the source of the sound. Megan sat on the bed still engaged by the cartoons.

The engine screamed louder, but yet no plane took to the air.

Then the engine lowered in pitch and volume until it was no longer audible.

"I guess they changed their mind," Jill said as she patted her son on the head.

With the excitement done, the boy returned to watching television and Jill resumed reading a book.

But all she could think about was her husband's arrival. *Where are you, John?*

Chapter 52

PAXTON PUSHED THE LEVER AND REMOVED THE MAGAZINE from the pistol. He then racked the slide and ejected the one round that remained in the chamber. He pocketed the magazine and held the empty pistol out to Nikolic.

Nikolic hesitated.

"Take it," Paxton commanded. "Pretend we are your prisoners."

Nikolic looked at McMurphy.

"Do as Paxton says," McMurphy said. "In case your apartment is under surveillance. It will give the observers the impression you are still in charge."

"Sure…if you want to give up your only weapon." Nikolic held out his hand.

"I remind you, Colonel, we don't need a weapon," Paxton said. "Any funny business and McMurphy and I just leave. You and, more important, your wife will suffer the consequences.

On the other hand, if you stick with us, we will get you and your wife safely out of the country and get her the treatment she needs...Besides, if need be, McMurphy here can kill you with his bare hands."

McMurphy said nothing.

"What about you, Sergeant Paxton?" Nikolic asked. "Can you do the same?"

Paxton smiled. "Oh, I can do better than that. I'm a PJ. I can kill you with my bare hands...then I can bring you back to life and kill you again."

McMurphy rolled his eyes.

Nikolic didn't appear to completely understand, but he did get the message. "I am with you. Let us go then."

The men headed out the door and down the stairs to the parking garage. Paxton and McMurphy were out in front, Nikolic following with the raised empty pistol.

"Okay, Paxton, where is Smith?" McMurphy asked.

"I don't exactly know at this moment," Paxton answered.

"Then how the fuck are we supposed to find him?"

"That's easy...just look for the smoke."

• • •

"Sir," Marshall interrupted Reed as he sat in his room on Brindisi Air Base, "apparently Jashari's people have posted a video on the Internet of Paxton. Paxton appears to be a captive, and he is being made to denounce the United States—however...."

"However what?"

"I don't think the result was what Jashari had intended."

"No? How so?"

"Well….I guess you could say Paxton makes a fool of Jashari."

Reed smiled. "You don't say."

Marshall opened his laptop and played the video for the general.

"That Paxton has some moxie. You have to give him that," Reed said.

"Yes, sir."

"Any other communication from him or McMurphy?"

"No, sir."

"Any idea if either of them is still alive?"

"No, sir."

Reed took a long sip of his drink then added, "I'm guessing they are both still alive. Keep the phone handy. You never know…we might still hear from them."

Chapter 53

MᴄMᴜʀᴘʜʏ ᴄʟɪᴍʙᴇᴅ ʙᴇʜɪɴᴅ ᴛʜᴇ ᴡʜᴇᴇʟ ᴏꜰ Nɪᴋᴏʟɪᴄ's sedan. Paxton climbed into the passenger seat. Nikolic slid into the backseat, as if he were being driven around in some sort of official capacity.

"Try to act natural," Paxton said.

McMurphy maneuvered the big car out of the slot and down the ramp. They plunged out into the sunlight and turned left onto the street.

Paxton craned his neck around looking for Smith. It was then he saw the disconcerting sight of the Yugo sitting empty at the end of the block. The driver's door stood open. "What the...?"

McMurphy pulled up beside the car. There was no sign of Smith.

McMurphy rolled his window down and called out to some children playing on the sidewalk. He said something to them in Serbian.

They replied in an equally unintelligible manner. "Shit," was McMurphy's reaction.

"What did they say?" Paxton asked.

McMurphy turned to Paxton. "They said the black man in the car was arrested and taken away by the police."

"Fuck!"

"Exactly," McMurphy concurred.

Paxton jumped out of the sedan and ran over to the Yugo. He dove in through the open door and quickly searched inside the car.

"What are you looking for?" McMurphy asked.

"The weapons," Paxton answered as he stood up. "They are all gone, too. Shit."

"Now what do we do?" McMurphy asked.

"There is only one thing to do," Paxton said. "We go get Smith."

Chapter 54

"Paxton, you have got to be shitting me." McMurphy's jaw was tense and his fists were clenched.

"I'm serious," Paxton replied.

"What?" McMurphy asked. "Are we supposed to blast our way into a police station, unlock the cell and escape with Smith, guns blazing? Make that gun—we only have one pistol. Or do you think we are going to do it like in the Wild West and tie a rope to the bumper and yank the bars off the window with the car? It's bad enough you want to try to extract a sick woman from behind armed guards at a hospital…but this… this is insane."

"We don't need guns…or rope for that matter," Paxton said.

"Then how the fuck do you think we are going to get him out of police custody?"

"Walk in and ask for him," Paxton answered.

"You are going to walk in and ask for Smith?"

"No…Nikolic will."

"*I* will?" Nikolic said.

"I'm not sure that is a great idea," McMurphy added.

"I agree with McMurphy," Nickolic said.

"It will be fine," Paxton reassured.

"Why in the world would they just turn Smith over to Nikolic?" McMurphy asked.

"Simple," Paxton explained. "Sergeant Smith is technically a prisoner of war. Nikolic will demand custody on behalf of the Serbian Army. They shouldn't have a problem turning him over."

"Yeah, right. He walks in there and tells them we are waiting in the car, and you and I get arrested, too," McMurphy said.

"If he wants his wife to live, he won't do that. Besides, we have the goods on him. I doubt he wants us explaining to the interrogators how he was in on this from the beginning and that he was selling out his own country. You don't want that do you?"

Nikolic shook his head vigorously. "No…I don't even want to go in there at all."

"Well, Colonel. You don't have a choice. If you don't get Smith, then the deal is off. If you want me to rescue your wife, you deliver Smith. Understand?"

Nikolic nodded.

"Can you do that, Colonel, and not tell them about us?"

"Yes."

"I still think this is a bad idea," McMurphy said. "As you pointed out, he is a prisoner of war. Just let him stay there until the end of the conflict, and he will be returned home."

"No, that won't work. Once General Rugova realizes he has been tricked, and Mrs. Nikolic is safely out of the country, he will want revenge. Smith would be a sitting duck at that point. I didn't leave you behind, McMurphy, and I don't even like you. I sure as hell won't leave my man behind. "

Nikolic was taking several deep breaths. Sweat was pouring down his face.

"You okay?" Paxton asked.

"I think so…Sergeant Paxton…you want me to go in there, but you say you don't even know how you will rescue my wife."

"I've got an idea."

"Really? Please tell me. I need to know if it is really possible."

"Time is short," Paxton said. "McMurphy, take us to the police station while I tell Colonel Nikolic what I have in mind."

McMurphy started the engine, shifted into gear, and drove off.

Chapter 55

IT FELT TO PAXTON AS IF EVERYONE WAS LOOKING AT THE trio as they drove through Belgrade. People were out and about while things were quiet. For the people knew, when darkness came, so would the NATO bombers and cruise missiles.

It had been that way since the start of Operation Allied Force—the American-led operation with the goal of removing Slobodan Milosevic from power and removing Serbian troops, police, and paramilitary forces from Kosovo.

McMurphy maneuvered the sedan to a stop in front of a large stone building. Uniformed police officers and civilians were entering and leaving. All the activity made Paxton all the more uncomfortable. Somehow their disguises seemed utterly inadequate.

Paxton fished the handcuffs out of his pocket and handed them to Nikolic who appeared even whiter than he had before. Perhaps it was just the sunlight.

"No tricks?" Paxton asked.

"No tricks," Nikolic promised as he examined the cuffs.

Nikolic sat still for a moment—evidently contemplating his future and the embryonic plan Paxton had outlined for him. Then he asked McMurphy a question in Serbian.

McMurphy glanced at Paxton and answered in Nikolic's native language.

Nikolic nodded, opened the door, and got out.

Paxton and McMurphy watched Nikolic holster the empty pistol and walk through the front doors of the police station.

The two unarmed Americans sat quietly, staring at the front door of the station house. They both wondered if at any moment a barrage of heavily armed officers would burst out and arrest them.

Finally Paxton spoke up. "What did he ask you?"

McMurphy was silent. Then he said, "He asked if, after all he and I have been through together, if I would really kill him with my bare hands."

"What did you say?"

"I told him I would let you have the honor."

Paxton stared at McMurphy for a moment, trying to decide if he believed a word that came out of that man's mouth.

Finally Paxton asked, "Do you trust him?"

McMurphy didn't take his eyes off the front door as he said, "You haven't given me much choice in the matter."

Chapter 56

MORE THAN TWENTY MINUTES PASSED, AND THERE STILL was no sign of Nikolic. Paxton felt like sinking down in his seat so he wouldn't be so visible. McMurphy showed no emotion.

For the first time in awhile, Paxton allowed himself to visualize his family. At least they were safe behind the gates at Lackland. He knew it would a long time before Jill felt secure in their house—if ever again.

He wished he could hold her in his arms right now. His thoughts turned to his son and daughter. He was so used to seeing them every night—now it seemed like a lifetime since he had seen them. He wanted nothing more than to hold them and squeeze them and tell them how much he loved them.

His kids needed him.

Would going on this mission prevent him from raising his children? Was it going to rob them of their father?

Mission versus Family.

That was the choice he was trying to avoid by becoming an instructor.

That was a good plan until General Reed walked into his life. Reed and McMurphy!

Paxton examined McMurphy's face. He wondered what the man was thinking. What he was feeling—if he had any feelings at all?

He glanced again at the front of the police station. He wondered if they were amassing an assault team to come grab them.

A growing percentage of him wanted to tell McMurphy to just hit the gas and get the hell out of there.

But he couldn't leave Smith.

Besides, this was all his idea now. And he was the one to put Smith in this position.

Even if they succeed in freeing Smith, he still had to rescue Mrs. Nikolic. That was going to have its own host of problems.

He looked at McMurphy again. "Is there any way I can convince you to stay and help rescue Nikolic's wife?"

"Not just no—hell no."

"You ever think about— " Paxton was interrupted by Mc-Murphy.

"Here they come."

Paxton turned quickly to see which group of *they* McMurphy was referring to.

Paxton was pleased to see Smith, hands behind his back, being led out of the building by Nikolic. Nikolic had a large duffel bag over his shoulder. The confusion of Smith's face was obvious.

Both men climbed into the back of the sedan.

"Paxton? McMurphy? What the fuck is going on?" Smith asked.

"I've got a rescue to perform, and McMurphy here refuses to help me. So I sent Nikolic in to bail you out."

"Well, I'm glad to be out."

McMurphy started the engine and they drove off.

"What's in the bag, Colonel?" Paxton asked.

"You said you needed weapons," Nikolic answered. "So I had them turn over to me the weapons that were in the Yugo when Smith was arrested." He unzipped the bag. "One German-made M.P. 40 machine gun and one Italian-made Bennelli M1 shotgun."

Paxton was excited by that bonus. "How the hell did you do that?"

"They didn't want to turn him over to me. They said he was driving a stolen car...so I had to get a higher authority involved."

"Who?"

"General Rugova."

"Rugova? Please tell me you just dropped his name and went on."

"No. Sorry," Nikolic said. "I had to get Rugova on the phone. I told him that I had another American who I needed to question."

"So he knows that you have all of us?"

"Yes," Nikolic sighed. "But it worked. Rugova was able to get Smith released to me."

"At what cost?" McMurphy asked.

Nikolic sighed again. "I have to deliver all three of your bodies to Nikolic before midnight or he will have both myself and my wife killed."

Chapter 57

McMurphy DROVE AS QUICKLY AS HE DARED THROUGH THE streets of Belgrade. Paxton brought Smith up to date about the situation and the plan to rescue Nikolic's wife.

"So, McMurphy, where is the Sat phone?" Paxton asked.

"My place," McMurphy answered.

"Your place? You keep your spy equipment at your apartment? Weren't you worried it might get searched and you would be exposed?"

"My cover was as a Russian businessman. It wouldn't be unusual for a businessman to carry a Sat phone. Quite common, in fact. More convenient to call back to one's superiors without having to use unreliable land lines, etc."

"I assume yours is scrambled and secure?" Paxton asked.

"Very."

"Aren't you afraid they are watching your apartment?" Nikolic asked.

"It is a strong possibility," McMurphy said. "I told you it was going to be dangerous to get the Sat phone."

"So we keep up the cover," Paxton said. "We act like we are still Nikolic's prisoners and we are going to your apartment to gather evidence."

"Shit," Smith said. "I was hoping to get out of these handcuffs."

"Soon, Smith, soon," Paxton said.

"Here we are," McMurphy said. "I'm going to drive around the block to see what there is to see."

They circled the block and saw no obvious signs of surveillance. That didn't mean, however, that they were safe.

McMurphy parked the sedan and all four men got out. They entered the building and headed up the stairs. McMurphy led the way and Nikolic trailed behind, an unloaded gun leveled on them for show.

They arrived at a wooden door. McMurphy walked down the hall and reached up and unscrewed a tarnished vent cover. He reached in and fished out a key. He tightened the cover back, returned, and unlocked the door.

All four men filed into the apartment. Paxton shut and locked the door. It appeared even smaller than Nikolic's. Nikolic unlocked Smith's handcuffs.

McMurphy disappeared into the bedroom. He came out a few minutes later carrying in one hand what looked like an old-school cell phone sporting a fat antenna. McMurphy's Sat phone was definitely more advanced and more compact that the one Paxton saw in Jashari's possession. In his other hand was a small leather-covered box.

The men gathered around the dining table.

McMurphy opened a cabinet and pulled out a glass.

He crossed over to his small refrigerator, opened it, and pulled out an ice tray. He took out a few cubes and plunked them into the glass.

"I thought we were in Europe and wouldn't find any ice," Paxton said.

"I'm not going to drink my whiskey without ice—that would be uncivilized." He reached higher in the cabinet and pulled out a bottle of Seagram's Seven whiskey. McMurphy poured two fingers of the golden liquid over the ice.

"McMurphy, what the hell are you doing?" Paxton asked.

"I'm having a well-deserved drink," McMurphy replied. "You gotta problem with that?"

"Yes, I do," Paxton said. "With everything that has happened…with everything going on, . . ."

"Pax," Smith interrupted, touching Paxton's arm. "Let the man have a drink."

"No," Paxton continued, waving off Smith. "With everything going on…how the hell can you just sit there and have a drink…without offering us one too?"

Chapter 58

MᴄMᴜʀᴘʜʏ ꜱᴇᴛ ᴛʜʀᴇᴇ ᴍɪꜱᴍᴀᴛᴄʜᴇᴅ ɢʟᴀꜱꜱᴇꜱ ɪɴ ꜰʀᴏɴᴛ of the other men. His meager ice tray could only muster two cubes per glass. He eyed the bottle and said, "We might as well finish this off…I can't take it with me, and I'm never coming back." He poured.

"What are we drinking to?" Smith asked.

"The destruction of the Iraqi nerve gas before it could do any harm," Paxton replied. He held his glass out then he took a sip. The others followed suit.

The whiskey tasted good.

McMurphy sat in front of the leather-covered box that he had placed on the table. He lifted the Sat phone. "I'll call General Reed, but what are we going to tell him?"

"Do we have to worry about anyone else listening in?" Paxton asked.

"This phone is scrambled. Marshall carries a phone that looks ordinary, but can take regular calls or scrambled."

"What about call history?"

"There is none. This phone does not retain any numbers dialed—at least not in any format that the Serbs would be able to get."

"Then," Paxton said, "let's tell Reed our plan and ask for his help. If anyone can make this happen, he can."

McMurphy nodded and dialed the number from memory. All eyes were on him. He took another sip while he awaited the connection.

A voice could be heard answering the call. "Captain Marshall, this is McMurphy. Let me speak to General Reed."

The others were not breathing. McMurphy took another sip. Another voice filtered past McMurphy's ear.

"General Reed. I'm here with Nikolic. And Sergeant Smith. We are back in business...I have someone here who wants to talk to you."

With that, McMurphy handed the brick over to Paxton.

"General Reed, this is Sergeant Paxton....no sir...I am very much alive...yes sir...sir, I'll tell you about it later. Time is short and we need your help."

As Paxton spoke, McMurphy fiddled with the leather-covered box. Finally he opened it up and peered inside.

"General Reed," Paxton continued, "I'm going to rescue Nikolic's wife...I'm going to extract her so she can be transported out. I understand, sir...I'm volunteering. If we are going to be successful, this is what I need from you...."

Chapter 59

"Yes, sir…" Paxton continued on the Sat phone. "You have my word sir." With that, Paxton hit the call end button.

All eyes were on Paxton.

"Well? What'd he say?" McMurphy asked.

"He ordered me to not screw up," Paxton answered.

"What the hell does that mean?" Smith asked. "Is he going to give us what we need or not?"

"Yes. Everything we asked for."

"Just like that? That was easy." Smith said.

Paxton took a sip. "I think he feels guilty…and like he owes me one since we saved his ass by destroying the nerve gas."

"Word!" Smith exclaimed as he lifted his drink.

"When do we get my wife?" Nikolic asked.

"We have to wait for nightfall," Paxton explained.

"Well, since we have time," McMurphy said, "we should continue the celebration." He reached in the leather-covered wooden box and took out four cigars.

"Nice!" Smith said.

McMurphy presented them with flair. "Carlos Toraño Exodus Gold Churchills."

"Appropriately named," Paxton said as he reached for his.

"Enjoy them. It would be a pity for them to go to waste," McMurphy said.

Smith took his and asked, "Shouldn't we smoke the celebratory cigars *after* we complete the rescue?" He was seated between Paxton and McMurphy, and he looked at one and then the other.

Paxton chomped on the cigar. "Sergeant Smith, never pass up," he paused as he lit his cigar with the ritual it deserved, puffing heartily, "an opportunity to celebrate success." He removed the cigar from his mouth, turned it sideways and admired it. "You never know how much longer you have."

"Indeed." McMurphy added.

Nikolic was quiet and hesitant. He didn't appear ready to kick back and relax.

"Well, I'm not going to argue with you guys," Smith said. "Pass the lighter."

"That's the spirit," Paxton said.

Smith lit his stogie. "Hell, when this is all over, we can all get together and celebrate again."

"Well learned, young Jedi," Paxton said through a cloud of smoke.

"I'm afraid not," McMurphy said.

"What? Why not?" Smith asked.

"Because," McMurphy said, "you have your Sat phone. Nightfall will soon be upon us and then I am outta here…just like I told you…you will never see me again."

Paxton shook his head. "We can't convince you to stay and help?"

"'Fraid not."

"But you know your way around here," Smith said.

"You have Nikolic…he knows his way around way better than I do."

Nikolic looked even more worried.

"Fuck you, McMurphy," Paxton said.

"I share my whiskey and cigars with you, and that is how you speak to me, Paxton?"

"You weren't going to share until I said something."

McMurphy put his hands flat on the table and raised up off his chair.

Paxton jumped to his feet.

"Whoa, whoa, guys," Smith interjected as he extended his arms, one toward each man, hands up like stop signs.

The phone rang.

Everyone froze.

Paxton reached out for the Sat phone and hit the button to answer it. But the ringing didn't stop.

Smith and McMurphy looked at each other. Neither had a phone.

Then Nikolic dug into his pocket and pulled out the ringing phone. All eyes were on him as he opened it to look on the caller ID screen.

His eyes opened wide and he turned even whiter.

"What?" Smith asked.

"Who is it?" Paxton asked.

Nikolic looked at the others, a helpless look on his face. He held the phone out like he didn't want to answer it. "It's Rugova."

Chapter 60

NIKOLIC'S PHONE CONTINUED TO RING.

"Well, answer it, dammit!" McMurphy said.

"What am I going to say?" Nikolic asked.

"That depends entirely on what Rugova has to say. Now answer it before he gets any more suspicious."

Nikolic did as he was told. He carried out a conversation entirely in Serbian. McMurphy returned to his chair and listened to Nikolic's end. Paxton eased back down, and he and Smith sat and puffed their cigars, trying to discern what the looks on Nikolic's face indicated.

Nikolic continued his conversation. McMurphy was stoic. Finally, Nikolic hung up and put the phone away. He looked dejected.

"What did he want?" Paxton asked.

"He told me to hurry up with my interrogations. Now we won't be able to rescue my wife."

"Why not?" Paxton asked.

"He demanded that I deliver your bodies by eight o'clock tonight. Instead of rescuing my wife, I'm supposed to join him for the exchange."

"What exchange?" Paxton asked.

"Rugova is delivering the device from the plane to his buyer," Nikolic answered.

"Son of a bitch," McMurphy said.

"You mean to tell me Rugova still has the device from the Stealth fighter?" Paxton asked.

"Yes," Nikolic replied.

"I thought he would have gotten rid of it already," McMurphy said.

"Yeah, well, Rugova has been greedy. He has been pitting the Russians and the Chinese against each other in a bidding war."

"Who won?" McMurphy asked.

"He wouldn't tell me. I'm supposed to meet him at his office at 8 PM. If I don't have your dead bodies with me, he will kill me."

Paxton and McMurphy looked at each other.

Smith looked perplexed. "I'm confused. Is this the real device?"

"Yes!" Paxton and McMurphy answered simultaneously.

"What does this all mean?" Nikolic asked.

"It means," Paxton said, "that everything has changed."

Chapter 61

EVERYONE TRIED TO TALK AT ONCE AROUND THE TABLE IN the smoke-filled room. Everything truly had changed. It had just been assumed that the anti-radar device from the downed Stealth fighter had long since been transferred and had already left the country.

Paxton whistled sharply to quiet everyone down. "Listen here. We cannot allow Rugova to go forward with that transfer."

"No shit," McMurphy said, "but what can we do about it?"

"We stop it," Paxton answered.

"How?" Smith asked.

"We take out Rugova and the device."

"We don't even know where Rugova or the device is," McMurphy said.

"We don't…but Nikolic does."

All eyes turned to Nikolic.

"He told you were to meet him tonight?" McMurphy asked.

"Yes…it is the location where he is hiding the device. It is in a building on the other side of town."

"It's not on some military base?" Smith asked.

"No…he is keeping this secret from his superiors," Nikolic answered.

"Perfect," Paxton said, "he will feel safe making the exchange at his hideout. He won't be expecting trouble."

"I don't know about that," Nikolic said. "The place is guarded."

"I have an idea about how to deal with the guards…but I will need your assistance, Nikolic," Paxton said.

"What about my wife? Are you forgetting about her?"

"I haven't forgotten anyone!" Paxton snapped.

"Pax, what do you have in mind?" Smith asked.

"First things first…I have to call General Reed." Paxton reached for the Sat phone. He stared at the dial. "Where the hell is the redial?"

McMurphy reached his hand out for the phone. "There isn't one. I told you the phone does not store numbers…for security purposes….I'll dial Reed for you."

Paxton handed him the phone. "So when are you going to tell me Reed's number? I might need to call him after you leave."

"There will be no need," McMurphy said.

"Why?"

McMurphy started dialing. "Because I'm not going any-where."

Chapter 62

"WHAT THE HELL IS THAT SUPPOSED TO MEAN?" PAXTON asked.

"It means I'm not leaving," McMurphy said, stopping mid-dial. "I'm staying...to see the mission out."

"You're back in?" Smith asked.

"I'm back in," confirmed McMurphy.

"What changed your mind?" Paxton asked as he stuck his cigar back in his mouth.

"My original mission was to prevent anyone from getting the Stealth device...I have a chance to do that now...so I'm going to see this through."

"You in for all of it?" Paxton asked.

"What do you mean?" McMurphy asked.

"You in for the rescue, too?"

McMurphy nodded. "Yes, I'm in for that too."

Paxton reached out. "Welcome aboard."

McMurphy clasped his hand and they shook.

"You're still going to rescue my wife?" Nikolic asked.

"Of course, we are," Paxton said.

"Thank God! McMurphy said you were a good man, and that I could trust you!" Nikolic exclaimed.

"Is that so?" Paxton asked. He looked at McMurphy. "Just when did he say that?"

"Outside the police station," Nikolic said. "I wasn't sure if you would really do what you said you would do, so I asked him in my language if I could trust you."

"Is that so?" Paxton asked, smiling. "That's not how McMurphy relayed that conversation to me."

McMurphy gritted his teeth and resumed dialing.

"McMurphy thinks I'm a good man!" Paxton asked. "You hear that, Smith?"

"I sure did." Smith was enjoying the interaction.

"General Reed," McMurphy said into the phone with a little extra volume to cut off the line of discussion. "McMurphy again. Paxton wants to talk to you." He handed the phone out.

Paxton took it. "General, I have some good news."

• • •

After Reed finished his conversation with Paxton, he hung up and handed the phone to Marshall. "Get Operations on the line for me, Captain."

"What's up, sir?"

"The device is back in play."

"Sir?"

"Paxton has located the device, and he has a plan."

"Sir, haven't we gotten deep enough in this already? How many times are you going to let Paxton mess things up?"

"You know what, Marshall? I don't think Paxton has been our problem," Reed said. "In fact, I'm damn glad we picked him for this mission. I really think he is going to be able to save our bacon…now do as I say."

Chapter 63

ON BOARD THE KERSARGE, PARARESCUEMAN A1C JUSTIN Taylor expressed his disagreement with the plan. "It's bullshit." His mouth was full as he spoke.

"This one's purely volunteer," SrA Blake Maxwell explained. "If you feel that way, then don't go."

"I agree with Justin," A1C Travis Robertson chimed in. "Why would we risk our lives for a Serb?"

"Besides," Taylor added, "wasn't General Reed the prick that sent us on the goose chase to begin with? Why should we volunteer for that perfumed prince?"

The men continued to eat around the small galley table as they discussed the matter.

"Because," Maxwell said, "the request didn't originate with Reed."

"Who did it come from, the President? Yeah that makes me want to do it," Roberson said sarcastically.

"No, the request is from John Paxton," Maxwell said.

Robertson and Taylor glanced at each other.

"Why didn't you say so?" Taylor asked. "Count me in."

"Me, too," Robertson said.

"Then it's settled, we are going back."

• • •

"Colonel, is your wife in an open ward at the hospital?" Paxton asked.

"Originally she was, but once Rugova added the guards, they moved her over to a private room so they could isolate her and control access," Nikolic answered.

"That is both good and bad for us," Paxton said. "I need for you to draw an exact layout." Paxton pushed a pen and paper over to the Serb.

Paxton and the others spent the rest of the time until sundown planning and coordinating with General Reed via the Sat phone.

Soon it would be show time.

Chapter 64

TWO FUEL-LADEN AIR FORCE PAVE HAWK HELICOPTERS took off from the *Kersarge* and headed toward Serbia. The pararescuemen on board, all former students of Paxton's, were loaded down with weapons and medical supplies.

Bullets and bandages.

Such is the stock in trade of the PJ.

Flying well ahead of the helicopters and substantially higher was a flight of Navy F/A-18 fighter jets. They headed toward Belgrade with some specialized weapons.

Still higher flew the two B-2 Spirits. They carried even more specialized weapons, including some never-before used in combat "soft" bombs.

Chapter 65

AS NIGHT FELL, PAXTON AND THE OTHERS LOADED THEIR weapons and equipment into Nikolic's car. The men climbed in with McMurphy at the wheel. He started the engine, and they pulled away from the curb.

Just as most residents were scurrying home in fear of the anticipated night of NATO bombing, the men were leaving shelter and headed toward the heart of Belgrade.

They were not the only ones on the move. A black sedan pulled from the curb a block away and followed them downtown.

• • •

The AGM-88 is known as the HARM missile. HARM stands for High-speed Anti-Radiation Missile. It was developed by Texas Instruments, and production was eventually taken over by Raytheon. The HARM is designed to find and destroy enemy radar. In the nose of the missile is an antenna that detects the microwaves emitted by a radar antenna. Once it detects enemy radar—it is sophisticated enough to distinguish the signal generated from allied radar—it locks in and its electronic guidance system automatically directs the missile directly into the source of the signal, destroying the radar installation with 150 pounds of explosives.

The F/A-18 Hornets were still over the horizon when they lit the Thiokol dual-thrust rocket engines on the HARMs they were carrying. The barrage of HARMs rocketed at twice the speed of sound toward the air-defense radars protecting the southwestern approach of Belgrade. The pilots omitted the normal radio call of "Magnum" to announce the launch of the missiles. They were aware that the Serbs monitored radio transmissions, and they did not want to give them any warning the Serbs could exploit by turning off their radar. Instead the Hornet pilots turned around and headed back to their aircraft carrier. Their part of the mission was complete. Momentarily, Serbian defense radar covering the southwest portion of the city would be rendered blind.

Chapter 66

THE EXPLOSIONS SOUNDED LIKE THUNDER TO PAXTON AS HE rode in Nikolic's car. Paxton instinctively tightened his grip on the shotgun lying across his lap.

"Those must be the HARM missiles," Paxton said.

McMurphy nodded as he maneuvered the car through the nearly empty city streets. Air-raid sirens wailed, and the few people outside scurried into buildings.

Smith and Nikolic scanned the surroundings from the back seat. No one seemed to be paying any attention to their car. Taking cover was the order of the hour.

Another series of explosions rang out, this time more forceful. And a hell of a lot closer.

"Shit!" Smith exclaimed.

"Cruise missiles," Paxton explained as everyone raised up from their duck.

Traffic laws no longer applied as cars sped through red lights and around traffic circles. McMurphy would slow as he approached an intersection and then plow through.

Nikolic kept telling him to watch out. While Nikolic was right that they couldn't afford a collision at this critical moment, McMurphy appeared annoyed at his backseat driving.

And then the unthinkable happened, McMurphy accelerated through an intersection and some idiot, probably in fear for his life, zoomed through the intersection from the sedan's right.

McMurphy locked up the brakes and steered sharply to the left, but there was nothing he could do. The car smashed violently into the right front quarter panel of Nikolic's sedan.

• • •

Approximately fifty miles outside of Belgrade the two Spirit bombers separated to go their own ways. The first one turned and arrowed directly toward its intended target.

The bomber was right on schedule.

The second one settled into a wide circle— a sort of holding pattern. Its pilots awaited further orders regarding its target.

The residents of Belgrade were in for a big surprise tonight.

Chapter 67

"MOTHER FUCKER!" MCMURPHY EXCLAIMED.

The car had struck their sedan, careened off of it and now sat in the middle of the intersection. Its impact had spun the sedan about ninety degrees to the left so that they sat looking down the side street.

McMurphy shifted into reverse and floored the accelerator.

The sedan squealed and rattled as McMurphy turned the wheel to get the car pointed in the right direction again.

"Go! Go!" Paxton shouted.

The stunned driver of the other car watched McMurphy.

Another cruise missile struck only a few blocks away, jarring everyone back to reality.

The other driver floored it and sped off.

No one was going to be exchanging driver information today.

McMurphy burned rubber. The sedan sounded as if it were held together by springs as he sped toward the hospital.

The sedan that followed them slowed for the intersection and then passed through without incident.

• • •

The first Spirit bomber aligned itself on a path that would take it directly over the transformer and switching yards for the Obrenovac thermoelectric plant outside of Belgrade. The bomb bay doors spread open, and a cluster of BLU-114/B carbon-graphite bombs was released. The highly-classified munitions are known unofficially as "soft" bombs.

The bombs continued down a glide path and, at the appointed time, burst— showering bomblets over the intended target. The bomblets detonated in mid-air, spreading a cloud of specially-coated carbon-fiber filaments.

The cloud of tiny carbon-fiber floated down gently. When the filaments came into contact with the power transformers at the switching station, the highly conductive graphite caused great arcs of electricity.

Man-made lightning.

With a terrible sound, the vital component of Belgrade's power grid short-circuited. No one was killed or injured. And Serbian engineers would be able to repair the damage relatively quickly.

But the desired result was achieved: In an instant, it was lights out all over Belgrade.

• • •

The city lights winked out, leaving only the sedan's one working headlight to lead the way.

"The Spirits just struck," Paxton said. Everything was coming together just as they had planned.

The car continued to rattle along, the fender rubbing on the right front wheel.

"The hospital will be that much easier to find," McMurphy said.

"How do you figure?"

A large ten-story building lay up ahead. McMurphy voiced the thought that just crossed everyone's mind as they looked at the hospital.

"It's the only place in town with its lights still on."

Chapter 68

INDEED THE LIGHTS WERE STILL ON IN THE HOSPITAL. THE auxiliary generators had kicked in soon after the power grid went down.

The garish light on the sixth-floor ward illuminated miserable patients. Their iron beds lined the walls in an open ward. Privacy was non-existent. Stern nurses dressed in smocks robotically attended to their duties.

The elevator doors lurched open unevenly. From inside, Nikolic could see past the nurses' station all the way across the ward to the little alcove on the left-hand side. In the alcove, he saw the closed door of his wife's private room. Outside, hovered two of Rugova's special policemen. They wore black trousers tucked sharply into shiny leather boots. Equally shiny leather holsters held their pistols.

Her room might as well have been a million kilometers from the elevator. Nikolic steeled himself for crossing the distance.

His wife's life depended upon everything going flawlessly.

The plan they were about to execute seemed impossible. Failure would mean his wife's death in addition to his own. But she was already dying. A feeling of resignation welled up inside him. He wanted to give up. It seemed easier to just confess to the policemen and plead with Rugova for his wife's life.

Nikolic knew, however, that Rugova wouldn't help her. She would die if he didn't go through with the American's plan.

The only person who could save her life now was SMSgt John Paxton.

He is a good man and you can trust him.

McMurphy had said so.

A shiver pulsed through Nikolic's body as the special policemen looked over at him standing in the elevator.

He had to do this. There really was no turning back at this point.

Deep breath.

The time for action had arrived.

The elevator doors started to close. Nikolic's hand shot out and caught them.

He gave one door a push and they opened again.

Nikolic tuned out everything else and stepped forward onto the sixth floor ward.

• • •

Downstairs, the black sedan that had followed Nikolic's car had parked near the front entrance of the hospital. The driver flipped his cell phone shut and gave orders to the passengers.

All four men got out simultaneously. They were dressed identically to the special police guarding Nikolic's wife. These men were, however, more heavily armed. Each carried an AK-74 selective-fire assault rifle. The Soviet-made rifles were the more advanced version of Kalashnikov's AK-47 design.

The men filed in the front doors of the hospital. There could be no doubt that they meant business.

Chapter 69

THE AMERICANS HAD USED THE CONFUSION THAT REIGNED at the busy hospital to make the necessary preparations. Paxton glanced at the watch he had borrowed from Nikolic and then looked at McMurphy. Quick nod.

Both men followed Nikolic off the elevator.

The two Americans were dressed in stolen hospital scrubs, tucked in like doctors. Surgical hats covered their hair and surgical masks hid their faces. They looked ready for the operating room.

McMurphy carried a black medical bag and a clipboard. Paxton dragged a cylinder of oxygen on wheels. It was metallic gray with a green top.

Nikolic paused as the doors closed behind the group. Paxton gave him a gentle shove to start him walking again.

McMurphy carried on a one-way conversation with Nikolic in Serbian. Nikolic merely nodded. Paxton pretended he was interested even though he didn't understand a word. He knew they were carrying on a fake medical dialog.

Paxton kept his eyes on the guards. They made no move toward their weapons. Evidently, he and McMurphy were convincing so far.

The nurses seemed too busy taking care of patients to pay attention to the men. Paxton's eyes moved back and forth. His mask diverted his warm breath back along his cheeks.

The trio passed the charge nurse desk and continued toward the private room.

The smell of body fluids and cleaning solutions was overwhelming.

Paxton prayed that the guards would not look at his feet. When they changed clothes, they didn't have any different shoes to wear. The scrubs looked funny combined with their combat boots. To hide them, McMurphy and Paxton covered the boots with paper booties, but Paxton could tell the paper was ripping off with each step.

Walk faster!

But McMurphy and Nikolic seemed to be taking their sweet time crossing the ward. Their window of opportunity was closing.

Three more steps and they arrived at the small alcove. The door was right up against the corner. McMurphy looked at his clipboard and then said something in an authoritative voice to the guards.

One guard replied.

McMurphy said something else and then the guard opened

the door.

With that, Paxton, Nikolic, and McMurphy walked into Nikolic's wife's hospital room.

• • •

The Serbs with the assault rifles piled into the elevator. One of them mashed the button for the sixth floor, and the doors squeaked shut. The electric motor engaged and the elevator began to rise.

Chapter 70

PAXTON PULLED THE DOOR SHUT BEHIND THEM. THE hospital room was small. Much smaller than a typical American hospital room. The walls were covered in tacky wallpaper. Nikolic's sketch accurately depicted the layout. On the far wall, drab curtains partially covered a dirty window. Below the window sat an ancient radiator just like Nikolic had drawn. The room was L-shaped with a bathroom and shower immediately to the right. Past that, the room opened to the right. In the center of the right-hand side of the room was an iron bed.

A frail woman lay on the bed. An IV dripped medicine into her right arm, and an oxygen mask covered her nose and mouth. The plastic tubing from the mask led back to a valve that protruded from the wall. Her eyes were wide with surprise. Her left hand lifted off the bed toward her husband.

Across from the foot of the bed on the left side of the room was a large wooden chest of drawers. Medical supplies and equipment were probably housed in there. A dying bouquet of flowers sat in a vase atop the dresser. A metal tray with a half-eaten meal sat on the nightstand. A carton of milk with a bent straw had been placed within the woman's reach.

More important, on the other side of the bed next to the IV bag stood a wide-eyed nurse. She faced the patient with her back to the curtains.

McMurphy said something to her in her language.

She snapped back at him. This was not good. They couldn't accomplish the mission with her in the room.

McMurphy crossed over to the nurse in two steps, wrapped his arms around her waist and hefted her up off the floor. She yelped. McMurphy carried the nurse past Paxton, opened the door, and deposited her in the hallway.

McMurphy slammed the door, turned the lock and spun around.

"What are you looking at?" McMurphy asked. "Get to work!"

With that, Paxton and Nikolic got busy.

• • •

Jill Paxton bolted up in bed to the screech of a jet engine.

Where am I?

Then it came back to her. She was on some air base in Italy waiting to spend time with her husband.

What time is it?

It wasn't that late—she had dozed off reading to the kids. Megan and John, Jr. were sprawled out asleep on the bed. Their schedules were all messed up from travel.

The sound of the jet increased dramatically and then died off.

What's up with that?

This is a crazy place. It seems planes get ready to take off, rev up their motors and then change their mind.

Weird.

She changed into her nightgown as she tried to sort out her feelings. She was mad at John for not being there, but she was also starting to worry.

Where was he?

What was he doing?

Was he in danger again?

• • •

Paxton crossed to the side of the bed where the nurse had stood, his back to the radiator. He pulled the oxygen tank with him. Nikolic leaned over his wife, holding her left hand and explaining to her what was going on. Nikolic's wife was shaking her head at what he was telling her. He whispered calming words as tears rolled down her cheeks.

Her ashen face was a mask of fear.

The door handle jiggled, then someone in the hallway knocked on the door. McMurphy replied loudly in Serbian. He walked to the chest of drawers as he spoke.

The knocking turned into pounding. Someone was shouting on the other side. A male voice.

McMurphy leaned his back against the chest of drawers and began shoving it toward the door. Every so often the paper covering his boots would cause one of his feet to slip. The room seemed very crowded with them all working feverishly.

The pounding and shouting became more insistent.

Nikolic's wife looked at Paxton, unsure what to think of him.

Paxton yanked off his surgical mask and hat so she could better see his face. "Everything is going to be okay," Paxton said as he gently brushed the hair off of her forehead. He knew she couldn't understand him but hoped she would understand the tone of his voice.

The doorknob rattled back and forth, and the door shook with the pounding. McMurphy continued to heave the chest toward the door. The vase with the flowers fell and shattered on the floor.

Paxton grabbed the IV bag off the stand and placed it on Mrs. Nikolic's stomach.

McMurphy shoved the chest against the door with all his might. He then reached over and hit the switch turning the lights off.

He then switched them back on. He turned them off and on a couple more times as he watched the window. A flashlight beam flickered on the glass.

Message received.

Bang!

"Shit!" Splinters showered McMurphy.

Evidently, the guards in the hallway didn't have a key and decided to shoot off the lock with a pistol.

McMurphy yanked his mask and hat off, reached into the medical bag he had been carrying and produced Nikolic's Makarov pistol. He held it at the ready, pointed at the ceiling.

The light from outside flashed back and forth on the window urgently.

"Paxton, we are running out of time!" McMurphy urged.

"I've got a patient to deal with, McMurphy," Paxton replied.

Another bullet chopped through the door. McMurphy spun away to the side. He didn't want to blindly fire back through the door and risk hitting a patient or nurse.

Nikolic was lying across his wife to shield her from the bullets. In reality, his body wouldn't prevent a bullet from passing through both their bodies.

Bang!

More splinters from the door flew, and the doorknob fell off and clattered on the floor.

• • •

The elevator doors lurched opened on the sixth floor ward, and Rugova's men with the rifles fanned out. It only took them an instant to see where the action was. Nurses and patients huddled in fear as the two special policemen fired with their pistols at the door of the private room. The men carrying rifles raced over to help their comrades break into the room.

Chapter 71

Even with the doorknob gone, the latch seemed to somehow hold the door closed.

Thud!

Something hit the outside of the door hard.

Thud!

The guards were apparently trying to kick the door in. The latch, combined with the large wooden chest resisted their attempts.

"Shit." Paxton was looking around and opening drawers on the side table.

"What?" Nikolic asked.

"Tank key…I need a tank key to turn on the O2." Paxton slapped the top of the portable oxygen tank as he spoke.

Nikolic looked to his left and right but did not find the small wrench known as a tank key. The wrench fits over the tank's valve and is used to open and close the oxygen supply.

"McMurphy!" Paxton said, "let me see the gun for a sec."

McMurphy passed the semi-automatic pistol to Paxton. Paxton pulled the slide back, then eased it closed on the oxygen tank's valve. He then rotated the pistol like a large wrench. The tank started hissing.

"Cool." Paxton passed the pistol back to McMurphy.

Thud!

The chest of drawers bounced away from the door slightly.

Thud!

The door would not hold much longer. Rugova's men were coming.

But the next sound Paxton heard changed everything.

• • •

Rugova's men outside the door heard it as well. It took them a moment to understand what was happening. Once they figured it out, they sprung into action. The leader shouted some orders as he ran over to one of the windows on the ward. Two of the men with rifles turned and ran toward the emergency stairwell. They burst through that door and thundered down the stairs.

The leader yelled an order to the others. The pistol wasn't getting the job done. So the one remaining man with a rifle raised it, pointed it toward the door to the private room and switched off the safety.

• • •

Chapter 72

PAXTON YANKED THE OXYGEN TUBING OFF THE VALVE protruding from the wall and quickly connected it to the hissing oxygen bottle on the floor next to the bed. The bag on the patient's non-rebreather mask re-inflated. He then checked the flow of oxygen. It was good. The patient was ready to transport.

A hail of bullets ripped through the door, straight through the chest of drawers, and stitched a pattern in the wall. Plaster dust and pieces of wallpaper flew everywhere. Clearly the Serbs had switched to a more powerful weapon.

"Ready yet?" McMurphy asked. He was leaning against the wall to the patient's left. From time to time, he would peer around the corner to check the condition of the quickly deteriorating door.

"We're good to go," Paxton replied.

Bullets tore more gaping holes in the door. McMurphy recoiled. A hand reached in through one of the holes. McMurphy raised his pistol and shot right through the back of the probing hand. The person attached to the hand screamed in the hallway as the hand jerked back out of the room leaving blood splattered on the wall.

McMurphy took the opportunity to cross to the window. A flashlight continued to flick back and forth through the glass. McMurphy grabbed the latch and wrenched it upward, unlocking the window. He then pounded on the window against the layers of paint. The window worked its way up on its track until it was all the way open. A cool breeze made the curtains dance.

The deep sound outside became markedly louder. It was the unmistakable sound of a United States Air Force Pave Hawk helicopter. Paxton stuck his head outside and looked up. The helicopter hovered off to the side of the building above the window. It was higher than the roof of the hospital. Paxton waved to the PJ looking out of the open sliding door. A litter began lowering from the winch attached to the side of the copter. The down draft from the rotor blades caused the basket to spin and sway.

Another fusillade of bullets ripped through the door striking the wall right next to the window. Everyone instinctively ducked whenever the shots came.

McMurphy evidently figured that by now all the patients and nurses had moved to a safe location because he let loose with his pistol. He fired straight back through the door in the direction the bullets came from. There was another scream in the hallway. A blind hit.

The geometry was such that Rugova's men had to stand in the alcove to shoot into the room. They couldn't get a good angle without putting themselves in McMurphy's line of fire. Inside the room, one had the advantage of staying near the head of the bed, around the corner of the L, out of Rugova's men's line of fire.

Paxton looked up. The litter was coming down rapidly, but now it was careening into the side of the building.

"Almost time to go," Paxton said back into the room. Under her oxygen mask, Nikolic's wife was crying. Nikolic was cradling her head in his hands as he lay across her.

The litter was almost at the sixth floor, but it would bounce off the side of the building and swing out over the parking lot, then crash back into the building.

Paxton reached out when it went spinning past, but it was just beyond his grasp.

Dammit!

PJ Justin Taylor was hanging partially out of the sliding door of the helicopter trying to guide the basket to Paxton, but the crosswind combined with the downwash was making it difficult to control. Pushing and pulling on the cable up at the level of the helicopter had little effect seventy feet below.

Paxton leaned out as far as he could, and the litter smacked the back of his hand as it passed by. He grabbed the night air.

Paxton came back in and looked around. He grabbed the IV tree and stretched back out the window, extending his reach. This time when the litter spun by, he snagged it with the metal hook. He pulled the litter in through the window just as more bullets pierced the door.

Inside the litter were three harnesses and a canvas bag. Paxton tossed those on the nightstand spilling the milk and meal. He guided the litter to the floor and said, "Let's go!"

The three men lifted the woman off the iron bed and placed her gently on the wire mesh litter. The IV bag was still on her abdomen. There was plenty room for her to lie flat, and the sides of the basket would help hold her in place. She was shaking her head no but was not putting up much of a fight. Nikolic tried to calm her.

McMurphy tightened the straps on the patient as Paxton carefully laid the oxygen bottle next to her on the stretcher. Not exactly a comfortable place for her to have it, but a lot more comfortable than trying to make the trip up to the helicopter with no oxygen. Her lungs were so damaged that she had to have a constant supply of 100% oxygen.

Nikolic gave her a kiss as more bullets shattered the door. McMurphy returned fire.

"Now!" Paxton shouted.

Nikolic wouldn't let go of his wife's hands as Paxton and McMurphy heaved the litter up onto the window ledge. Paxton leaned out and signaled the PJ. The winch took up the slack on the line.

Nikolic still would not let go of his wife so McMurphy grabbed him and pulled him back, breaking his grip. As he did that, Paxton shoved the litter containing Mrs. Nikolic and it swung free of the window ledge out into the night.

Chapter 73

THE TWO MEN WITH RIFLES WHO HAD GONE DOWNSTAIRS ran from the stairwell through the front doors and onto the driveway. They looked up at the sound of the helicopter. The unlit black copter was nearly impossible to see as it hovered over the side of the building. The lights from the hospital ruined their night vision. What was clear was the litter suspended by a cable and careening off the side of the building. It spun in the wind as it was winched slowly upward. They could see a person in the basket.

It took a moment for the men to process what they were seeing. Then one tapped the other on the shoulder and pointed upward.

Both men simultaneously raised their rifles toward the sky. They clicked the safeties off and aimed toward the sound of the copter.

They both commenced firing. The brass from the rounds bounced on the driveway at their feet.

• • •

Airman Taylor was leaning out on his harness trying to control the litter containing the Serbian woman when he saw the muzzle flashes below.

"Shit, they're shooting at us!"

Senior Airman Maxwell peered out of the helicopter door and aimed his M4 rifle but then thought better of it. With the copter pitching and shuddering as it was and the litter spinning and swaying, there was too much chance of accidentally hitting the patient. The good news was that the constant movement of the copter made it that much more difficult for the riflemen to target. Maxwell pulled his rifle back and turned his attention to helping Taylor reel in the woman.

• • •

Smith was standing next to Nikolic's car and saw Rugova's men about fifty yards away. They were outside the hospital entrance firing at the helicopter. He tossed aside the flashlight he had used to mark Nikolic's wife's window for the helicopter crew. He shifted to a position behind Nikolic's car and painfully raised his MP-40 machine pistol up to eye level. He leaned on the side of the car and used the roof to steady his weapon. His ribs burned. The wound in his arm ached, and his sling hindered his movements. But he managed to line up one of

Rugova's men in the iron sights and pull the trigger.

The fifty-plus-year-old weapon jumped in his hands as it stuttered out a string of rounds.

The MP-40 was not the most accurate weapon the Germans ever made, but it did an effective job. One of Rugova's men crumpled to the concrete. The other man spun and dashed behind their sedan. He peered over the hood and fired at Smith from his protected position.

Smith was tempted to fire back, but he wanted a clear shot. This was not the time to waste ammo, for when his magazine ran empty, that was it. He looked around trying to figure out how to maneuver to a better firing position without making himself an easy target.

The man behind the car turned to his right, raised his rifle, and fired at the helicopter again. Smith didn't wait for a better shot but instead blasted out the windows of the car the man was hiding behind.

Maybe the flying glass will throw off his aim.

Smith saw the rifle come up again and fire at the vulnerable copter. He couldn't tell from here, but for all he knew, the patient hanging from the cable might already be riddled with bullet holes. Rugova's man had to be stopped. Smith stepped out from the cover Nikolic's car provided and circled around to approach the Serb from behind.

Chapter 74

INSIDE THE HOSPITAL ROOM, MCMURPHY BUSIED HIMSELF returning fire through the door. The sound of the helicopter above and gunfire below could be heard through the open window. The gunfire in the room and in the hallway, however, was much louder.

After the last shot, the slide on McMurphy's pistol locked back indicating he was out of ammo. McMurphy tossed the Makarov onto the bed and grabbed a harness off the side table. "Now or never."

Paxton nodded and helped Nikolic step into his harness and tightened it around his waist. Then he put on his own. McMurphy had already put on his harness. Paxton reached into the canvas bag and produced a coil of climbing rope.

Paxton clipped a Figure Eight Ring onto his harness using a locking carabiner. He fed the rope through the ring in such a manner that it would act as a friction multiplier and through the carabiner to prevent it from slipping around the ring and forming a knot. He then fed the rope through Nikolic's harness. He tied off one end to the radiator under the window and tossed the other end out the window.

• • •

The end of the coil of rope landed next to Rugova's man hiding behind the car in front of the hospital entrance. He followed the rope up with his rifle and aimed at the open window. His finger rested on the trigger. He was ready to take out anyone foolish enough to climb out the window onto that rope.

• • •

"Okay, Colonel," Paxton said, "you are going to go down with me."

Nikolic nodded.

"Just hold on to me, and I will control our descent."

Paxton put one boot on the radiator, one hand on the window ledge, and pulled himself up. He then sat down on the ledge and swung one leg outside, right into the line of sight of the man with the rifle down below.

• • •

The man with the rifle carefully aimed at Paxton's leg. He didn't pull the trigger yet because he wanted to wait until his target was all the way out the window and committed so he could get a nice shot at the center of mass.

Paxton's head and shoulders emerged next. He was still clad in hospital scrubs. The man with the rifle began to take the slack out of the trigger.

Click!

He spun around toward the sound. Smith stood about ten yards away, struggling with his jammed machine gun. The World War II era weapon's age and an unknown maintenance history combined disastrously, leaving Smith exposed and unable to fire a shot.

The man swung his rifle around toward Smith. Smith dove behind the car in which Rugova's men had arrived. The man fired two rounds just as the American disappeared from sight.

Chapter 75

PARARESCUEMAN TAYLOR STRUGGLED WITH THE CABLE raising the litter. He had tuned out all the shooting below. He focused on the task at hand and was glad that in another few feet the patient would clear the side of the building.

Once the basket cleared the roofline, the litter continued to rotate, but it no longer smacked into the brick face of the hospital. He was about to breathe a sigh of relief when a gust of wind caused the copter to suddenly dip ten feet. At the end of the cable below the litter with the patient dipped correspondingly. Half the litter struck the edge of the building's roof, causing the head end to pitch upward and the leg end to drop down. The patient was securely strapped in, so she remained on the litter.

The same could not be said for the oxygen tank.

The tank slid right off the litter. The plastic tubing supplying oxygen to the patient popped off the tank's valve with a tug and remained attached to the patient's mask.

Taylor watched helplessly as the heavy tank tumbled in what seemed like slow motion right to the spot where Paxton was climbing out of the window.

• • •

Paxton gripped the rope tightly, climbed completely outside and reached out for Nikolic to climb out on the rope with him. He looked up to see how they were doing recovering the patient just in time to see the tank falling toward his head.

Paxton lurched to the right, just out of the path of the tank. He felt the breeze as it sped past on its way down.

• • •

The Serb with the rifle took a step toward the back of the sedan. He held his rifle at the ready. He could see part of a bandaged arm moving in and out of his view around the corner of the car. It looked like an elbow going back and forth. He took one more large step and lined up the rifle on the man who was crouching down trying to clear the jam in his machine gun.

• • •

Smith looked up and saw the barrel of the rifle pointing right at him. Instinct told him to jump out of the way, but he knew it was too late. The Serb was less than ten feet away. He had come this far only for the odds to catch up to him. Smith wasn't sure, but he thought he saw the hint of a smile on the man's face.

Chapter 76

SMITH SAW A FLASH, HEARD AN INCREDIBLY LOUD BOOM, and was instantly sprayed by a warm sticky liquid.

But he didn't feel any pain.

That's funny. Last time I was shot it hurt like hell.

He could still hear the sound of the helicopter, but the sound was muffled. He was surprised to find that his arms still moved. He wiped the liquid off his eyes and looked at it.

Blood.

He raised his head to see if the gunman was still smiling, but he was gone. No sign of him.

Smith pushed himself to his feet. He was definitely still alive. Where did the Serb go?

That question was instantly answered when Smith took one step toward the back of the car. Lying on the pavement in a pool of blood was the mangled body of the Serb. It didn't look human.

What the fuck?

It wasn't until Smith's hearing started to come back that he realized that it had been impaired by an explosion. He saw a bloody metal cylinder lying on the street rocking back and forth about twenty yards from the body. Its gray and green walls were peeled back like a banana.

He connected the dots. That cylinder used to be an oxygen tank. He glanced up. Evidently, an oxygen tank had fallen from the litter. That was over a hundred-foot drop. The flash he had seen was the tank slamming to the ground. Oxygen tanks are pressurized to 2,200 pounds-per-square-inch. The top valve probably sheared off on impact. Once the integrity of the cylinder was compromised, the pressure could no longer be contained. The bottle detonated and launched itself like a rocket. The Serb was standing in the wrong place at the wrong time, right in the cylinder's path. Had Smith not been behind the car, he probably would have been struck as well.

A shiver went down his spine. What a way to go.

Shit, Smith, pull yourself together.

He shook it off and mentally switched gears. He busied himself retrieving the rifles from both dead Serbs. They were going to need the additional weapons. The night wasn't anywhere near over yet.

• • •

Taylor pulled the wire basket carrying Nikolic's wife into the Pave Hawk. Her eyes were closed, her skin was gray, and she wasn't moving. She looked dead. Taylor knew that her oxygen levels had probably dropped as fast as the tank had fallen. The loss of her source of oxygen, combined with her damaged lungs had caused her to lose consciousness.

"You okay?" Taylor tried to shout above the sounds of the hovering copter as he shook her. He couldn't tell if she was merely unconscious or already dead.

Pararescueman Robertson was ready with a new non-re-breather mask attached to a fresh bottle of oxygen. He pulled the old one off and placed the new one over the patient's nose and mouth. The bag fully inflated as a high flow of pure oxygen gushed into the mask.

She still didn't respond.

He checked and found a faint pulse. She was still alive, although barely. She was in respiratory arrest.

Robertson had to quickly establish and protect an airway. He reached for the medical kit and realized it had two bullet holes in it. Clearly some of the Serbian gunfire had penetrated into the Pave Hawk.

He reached into the kit and fished out an endotracheal tube and a packet of lubricant. He ripped open the packet and coated the tube with the lubricant. He then reached back into the kit and pulled out the laryngoscope. It felt odd in his hand for some reason. He extended the blade that is used to depress the tongue to enable the intubation process, but the light at the end of the blade did not come on.

Robertson examined the device and realized why it had felt strange. The back portion had been shattered by a bullet. With no light on the end of the blade, the scope was useless. He tossed it aside. Using a laryngoscope to get an endotracheal tube down to the patient's lungs while flying in a helicopter was an incredibly difficult task. Now Robertson didn't even have the benefit of the scope. He couldn't just insert the tube down her throat blindly, because it would travel down her esophagus and deliver oxygen uselessly into her stomach.

If Mrs. Nikolic was ever going to breathe again, Robertson was going to have to fall back on a procedure the PJs are trained in called Tactile Intubation.

As the name of the procedure suggests, Robertson was going to have to use his fingers to feel his way. He inserted his gloved left hand into her mouth. He was grateful that she was unconscious, because it made it somewhat less likely that she would bite down on his fingers. The copter pitched and rolled as he worked. He pushed his fingers down Mrs. Nikolic's throat, felt around, and found her epiglottis. He then used his gloved right hand to insert the tube over the top of his left index and middle fingers and into the glottis. He pushed the tube past her vocal chords, deep down until it hit the spot where her airway split into the left and right lungs. He then removed his left hand from her mouth. He held the tube in place with his left hand as he removed with his right hand the stylet—the bendable wire that is used to make the tube firm for insertion--from inside the tube.

He inflated the small balloon at the other end of the tube so it would stay in place inside her airway. Then he attached an Artificial Mechanical Breathing Unit (AMBU) bag to the tube. He also attached the oxygen supply to the unit.

Robertson rhythmically squeezed the AMBU bag forcing oxygen into Mrs. Nikolic's starved lungs. He prayed he wasn't too late.

A tense moment passed until she stirred. She was alive.

Taylor took the opportunity to assess her from head to foot. A deep red stain was growing on the part of the hospital gown covering her left leg. He snatched the hem back and saw a bullet wound just above the knee. He could see blood pooling under the back of her knee. Those bastards shot the patient as she was being evacuated. An innocent woman—one of their fellow countrymen. Taylor shook his head and went to work to stem the bleeding as the helicopter nosed down and broke from its hover.

• • •

Paxton had rappelled halfway down the rope carrying Nikolic when McMurphy stepped out on the rope. McMurphy wished he could fire a few more rounds into the room to keep the Serbs at bay, but he had already abandoned the empty Makarov pistol. The men had to hurry down because they knew that once the Serbs entered the room, they would cut the rope.

The two remaining special policemen burst into the hospital room and raced for the window. Seeing the rope secured to the radiator, the first one produced a knife, bent over and proceeded to saw on the fibers. The second one popped out of the window and swept his rifle down and took dead aim on McMurphy.

Chapter 77

MAXWELL LINED UP THE SHOT AS THE PAVE HAWK SWOOPED past the open hospital window. He pulled the trigger twice. The Serb aiming at McMurphy slumped on the windowsill, and his rifle slipped from his hands.

Paxton looked up when he saw the rifle fall past him and clatter onto the sidewalk. McMurphy was rappelling down above him. Paxton's hands were burning. He wished he had a pair of gloves. Fatigue was setting in as he was supporting Nikolic's weight as well as his own. At any moment he feared the Serb upstairs would cut through the rope and they would fall the rest of the way. He loosened his grip and the rope burned through his hand as he slid down the rope as fast as he dared.

Paxton touched the sidewalk and helped Nikolic unclip himself from the rope. McMurphy was still ten feet off the ground when the rope went slack. The Serb above had managed to cut all the way through it.

McMurphy plummeted to the ground and rolled onto his side, grabbing his ankle. He was almost immediately followed to the ground by the frayed end of the rope.

The three men were met by Smith. Paxton checked on McMurphy.

"You okay?"

"Yeah, I think I twisted my ankle."

Paxton helped McMurphy to his feet. Smith handed Paxton one of the rifles he had collected, and he used the other to scan their surroundings. From the time he cut the climbing rope, everyone was waiting for the last Serb guard to pop his head out of the window, but evidently after seeing what happened to his colleague he thought better of it. No other threat appeared at the moment, but it was time to get out of there.

Paxton, who was illuminated by the lights from the hospital, waved to the pilot of the Pave Hawk, and the unlit helicopter flew off into the dark sky.

Paxton had to help McMurphy to the car. He looked at Nikolic. The man appeared completely spent. Paxton was not about to show him any mercy.

"Come on, Nikolic. We upheld our end of the bargain…now it is time for you to step up to the plate."

Nikolic looked confused. And scared.

"Get in," Paxton commanded. "Drive us to General Rugova."

Chapter 78

NIKOLIC CLIMBED BEHIND THE WHEEL OF HIS BEAT-UP sedan. McMurphy and Smith got into the back seat and shut the doors. Paxton walked around the back of the car and stopped when he reached the trunk. He bashed the left taillight in with the butt of his rifle. He did the same with the right one.

"What the hell did you do that for?" Smith asked when Paxton climbed into the passenger seat. Nikolic seemed too resigned to care about the further damage Paxton inflicted upon his car.

"I want us to be able to roll up on Rugova's hideout with our lights off. I don't want any brake lights giving us away," Paxton explained.

Nikolic cranked the engine and drove off before any more of Rugova's men could come after them.

The car shuddered and squeaked as the front tire rubbed against the dented fender. The dark, deserted streets were lit only by the car's left headlight. Occasionally a large explosion could be heard in the distance as cruise missiles struck various military targets. Anti-Aircraft Artillery (Triple – A) was the constant response from the Serbs on the ground.

Nikolic expertly maneuvered through the dark streets. After numerous turns, Nikolic slowed down and turned off the car's one remaining headlight. He pulled along the curb and stopped.

He pointed toward a three-story brick building a block and a half away. "There. Rugova wanted me to meet him in that building." It was easy enough to see because it evidently had its own generator. Lights shone through the windows.

An army staff car was parked on the street in front of the entrance. Three other cars were parked on the street as well. A group of a dozen or so special policemen were milling about outside the building. They each carried a rifle. Light from the building glinted off their shiny boots.

"Any way to tell if he has made the exchange yet?" Paxton asked.

"No," Nikolic answered. "But I believe he is in there because that is his staff car outside."

"Shit. Look at all those guards," Smith said.

"Rugova is probably waiting for you right now," McMurphy added.

"He's here on time," Paxton said, "and he has all of us with him, just like Rugova asked—only we're not dead."

"You got that right," Smith added.

"What now?" Nikolic asked.

"I need to know if the device is still inside that building," Paxton said.

"How do you plan to do that?" Smith asked.

Paxton sighed. "That's what I'm trying to figure out."

• • •

The PJs stabilized Mrs. Nikolic and gave her a sedative as the Pave Hawk helicopter made its way in the dark. It followed generally the same path it had used to come into the city because the HARM missiles had taken out all of the Serbian radar installations along that path. The pilots kept the copter at a low level to make it more difficult for any long-distance radar or missiles to lock in on it. The unlit black helicopter was almost impossible to see with all of the city's lights out.

The pilots wore Night Vision Goggles (NVGs). The goggles enabled them to see obstructions in the dark, but they also took away any peripheral vision. As a result the pilot and co-pilot had to constantly look around for danger.

It was an exhausting task, but one they were well practiced at.

Eventually the copter left the city and continued on for a rendezvous with the *Kersarge*.

Chapter 79

"I SAY WE SEND NIKOLIC IN THERE," MCMURPHY suggested.

"That could work," Paxton said. "He's one of them. He takes his cell with him, and if he sees the device, he calls us. Give him the Sat phone number."

Nikolic's eyes were wide, and all the color had drained from his face.

"I got one better than that," McMurphy said. "We switch phones. He takes the Sat phone in. He calls us when he sees the device. Then he moves over right next to the device and stands there."

"Why?" Smith asked.

"The GPS unit in the Sat phone is always pinging the satellite," McMurphy explained. "The boys in blue can pick those coordinates, dial them into a GPS-guided smart bomb, and take the damn thing out with an air strike."

"Damn," Smith said.

"What?" Nikolic said. "I can't do that…no way…I…I…it's suicide."

"Maybe not," Paxton said. "You might be able to hide it near the device and then high-tail it out of there."

"No." Nikolic was shaking his head. "I can't. I won't…I won't be able to get within ten meters of the device. "

"Ten meters works for me," McMurphy said. "The bombs we use are pretty big."

"No, you don't understand. Rugova *knows*. He may have only suspected before, but after what we did at the hospital…. If I show my face, I'm a dead man."

"We rescued your wife. If you want to see her again, do what we ask." Paxton said.

"I won't. You cannot make me."

"Like hell," Paxton said. "Do it, or one call on the Sat phone and that helicopter sets down and drops your wife off in the middle of nowhere."

"Damn, that's cold," Smith said.

"You wouldn't do that!" Nikolic protested.

"Maybe he wouldn't, but I would." McMurphy raised the Sat phone for emphasis.

Tears welled up in Nikolic's eyes.

"Um, how do we call in an air strike if he has the Sat phone?" Smith asked.

"I don't need a Sat phone. I've got numbers I can call from any phone. Pay phone…Nikolic's cell…you name it." McMurphy explained. "At this point, who cares if it is scrambled or not?"

Nikolic was frozen except for the big gulp he took.

"Better hurry up and get moving, Colonel," Paxton said. "Soon the copter will be out over the Adriatic. Is your wife a good swimmer?"

"You bastards!"

"Don't talk about my mother that way!" McMurphy said. He started dialing the Sat phone.

"Wait! Wait!" Nikolic was looking out the window.

"Time's up."

"No! Wait! It won't work!" Nikolic was frantic.

"Sure it will," Paxton added.

"No! We can't do it," Nikolic said as he pointed. "Look!"

All eyes turned toward the building. Outside it was a hubbub of activity. A group of men exited the front door. Among them a large, older man carrying a bag.

"There's Rugova," Nikolic said.

The man climbed into the back of the staff car.

"They're leaving," Smith said.

"What the hell?" Paxton said.

"I bet your device is in that bag he is carrying," Nikolic said.

"I thought you said the exchange was happening at this building," McMurphy said.

"No. I said he wanted to *meet* me at this building. He never said where the exchange was going to happen."

"Fuck!" Paxton exclaimed.

The lights on the staff car winked on, and it pulled away from the curb. Two other cars full of troops pulled out after it.

"There they go," Smith said.

"What do we do now?" Nikolic asked.

"Follow them," Paxton commanded. "And for God's sake, keep your lights off."

Chapter 80

NIKOLIC STARTED THE ENGINE AND HAD TO FIGHT THE instinct to turn on the headlights. Or headlight as the case was. He pulled out and followed the caravan of cars down the dark city street.

"Maybe we can attack Rugova's car," Smith said.

Paxton shook his head. "Nah. We've got, what, two rifles and a shotgun? Hardly any ammo. We're outgunned."

"What are we going to do then?"

"Let's see where they go." Paxton said. "Give me that Sat phone. I want to update Reed."

McMurphy dialed the number and handed him the phone. Paxton explained to Reed what was happening and then hung up. He then turned to Nikolic and said, "Stay far enough back that they don't see us."

Nikolic slowed but stayed where he could see the taillights of Rugova's caravan.

They continued to follow Rugova through the city. The streets were empty because it was getting late, and the American bombs would hit from time to time.

Rugova's brake lights lit as his car approached a complex of buildings surrounded by a tall iron fence. Guards standing in the driveway opened the gates, and the general's car turned in. The two other cars full of guards followed his car in. The large gates closed behind them.

"Pull over," Paxton commanded. Nikolic pulled to the curb.

"Shit, we lost 'em," Smith said.

"At least we now know where the exchange is going to take place…and who the buyers are," McMurphy said.

"We tried to stop it," Smith added. "Just missed the shot at the buzzer."

"The situation is hopeless," Nikolic said.

"No it is not," Paxton said.

Nikolic scoffed. "Yes it is…there is no way I can get through those gates…I can't plant any phone for you."

"You don't have to," Paxton said.

"What do you mean? We calling it off?" Smith asked.

"I'm not calling anything off."

"You're not still thinking of an air strike, are you? That's nuts!" Smith said.

"Well, as Nikolic said…none of us can get through those gates. An air strike is our only option."

Smith shook his head.

"How do you plan to call in an air strike with any accuracy?" McMurphy asked. "We can't get GPS coordinates."

"We don't need 'em," Paxton replied as his eyes scanned up the side of the largest building in the complex to the flagpole on top of the roof. "I'm pretty sure our war planners have the exact coordinates already."

The power was still on at that building. On the pole flew the brightly lit red flag of the People's Republic of China.

Chapter 81

"SERGEANT PAXTON, WE ARE NOT GOING TO BOMB THE Chinese Embassy!" General Reed said into the phone.

"Sir, this is our only chance," Paxton replied in the Sat phone. "If we don't attack now, we will never see the device again."

"Do you have any idea what sort of international incident that would be? You are talking about an act of war!"

"Sir, we have them red-handed with a piece of stolen American technology. Our entire stealth program will be vulnerable if they are allowed to get away with this."

"I'm sorry, but I'm not going to risk starting a war."

"So that's it? You're giving up?" Paxton asked.

"Yes, if that is what you want to call it," Reed replied. "Head to the evacuation chopper and come home…that's an order."

"Sir, I can't hear you…the connection is bad…I'll have to call you back," Paxton said as he hung up.

"Reed wouldn't go for it, huh?" McMurphy asked.

Paxton shook his head. "After everything he has done, we get so close and he pulls the plug…everything, everything we have done to this point was in vain."

McMurphy pursed his lips and nodded.

Smith started breathing again. "Pax, you did everything you could. Don't you think it is time to go home?"

"No," Paxton said. "I never quit. There has to be another way,"

No one said anything for a full minute.

McMurphy put his hand out and said, "Give me the phone."

Paxton looked at McMurphy. "Why?"

"I need to make a call."

Paxton handed him the phone. "What?"

"Reed won't give the order to drop the bombs, but I have people who will."

Chapter 82

THE NINE-LINE BRIEF FLASHED ON THE INFORMATION SCREEN onboard the second Stealth bomber. "Here we go," the mission commander said as he sat in the right seat and examined the information. The nine-liner contains all the information the flight crew needs to strike a target, including target description, location, and elevation. They entered the new coordinates into the navigation system.

"Took 'em long enough to get the info to us," the pilot said.

"There are friendlies nearby the target, so I'm guessing this info came from Company men," the pilot said, referring to the Central Intelligence Agency.

"What's the target?"

"Some sort of hardened compound. The buildings are down-town, so we have to be careful of collateral." Collateral damage to non-combatants was always a fear when strategic bombing is carried out.

The GPS coordinates were fed into the targeting system of the guided bombs onboard. Each contained 500 pounds of high explosives. No soft bombs this time. The Stealth bomber broke from its orbit and headed toward its newly designated target.

• • •

Paxton and the others sat quietly in Nikolic's car for what seemed like an eternity. They had moved the car back a prudent distance from the embassy compound. Everyone's unspoken thought was: Would the bomber arrive before the device moved again?

"What's taking so damn long?" Smith asked.

"Channels," McMurphy replied. Bombing a foreign embassy was going to be a huge international incident, regardless of whether it was justified.

Paxton thought about his family and the threat Rugova had dispatched against them. He could still see Rugova's face as he told Paxton that he had given the order for their murder. How many other people had he ordered murdered? His special police were international war criminals. And now he was selling stolen secret technology to the Chinese. How many American airmen would lose their lives once that technology was exploited by the Chinese? But that would all end tonight. Paxton would see to it.

A bright orange flash interrupted the thoughts. The shockwave could be felt in their guts as windows all around shattered. The Chinese flag disappeared in the fireball and column of black smoke.

"Daaaaamn!" Smith expressed the consensus.

"Now can we get out of here?" Nikolic asked as he reached for the ignition.

"No!" Paxton grabbed his hand.

"What? Why not? Let's get the hell out of here," McMurphy said.

Sirens wailed in the background.

"Not yet," Paxton said. "I have to be sure."

"Sure of what?"

"That this is over."

Chapter 83

"**WHAT THE HELL IS THAT SUPPOSED TO MEAN?**" SMITH ASKED.

"I have to get a closer look," Paxton answered.

"Okay, so we'll drive by," McMurphy said.

"Not good enough…I've got to get inside."

"How you plan to do that?" Smith asked.

Just then a fire truck sped by, red lights flashing and siren wailing.

"Just wait here," Paxton said. "If I'm not back in twenty minutes, assume I'm not coming back."

Paxton slammed the door before anyone could talk him out of it. He ran down the sidewalk, his scrubs flapping in the breeze. Three more fire trucks passed by.

The embassy guards had opened the gates for the fire trucks. The three men in the car watched as Paxton reached the open gates, turned in, and disappeared.

• • •

Paxton did his best to blend in with the rescue crews. His hospital uniform gave him the color of authority. He hoped that no one tried to talk to him.

He ran up the driveway as he surveyed the damage. The building was engulfed in flames. Thick black smoke billowed out of the windows. The roof partially collapsed. Gaping holes fractured the concrete siding. A direct hit. Just as planned.

Firemen unrolled hoses as others sprayed the flames licking out of windows.

Paxton ran toward one of the newly-created gaping holes in the side of the concrete structure. He could hear someone urgently shouting at him. Probably telling him to stop. Paxton pretended he couldn't hear him and climbed through the opening.

Inside the building, the smell of burning wood, insulation, and plastic was overwhelming. The power was now off to the building, so it took a moment for Paxton's eyes to adjust. Red flashes reflected off the inside walls from emergency vehicles parked outside. He could no longer see the fire, but he could hear its rumble.

He stayed low to avoid toxic fumes as he picked his way over smashed furniture. He could hear the diesel engines rev as the fire trucks' pumps engaged. He had no idea which way to go, so he just worked his way deeper into the building.

He paused. His ears picked up the sound of a person calling out. He turned his head slowly to ascertain the direction the sound was coming from. Once he was sure, he set out toward the voice.

A thought surfaced way in the back of his mind that he better mark his path so he could find his way back out. Not seeing anyway to readily mark his path, he just continued toward the building's center.

The red flashing from the fire engine lights was replaced by the orange glow of fire. He still could not see the fire, but its roar grew louder. The roar and the shouting were coming from the same place. Paxton headed toward the sound.

His throat burned. He coughed. It felt like it was scraping the back of his throat with a fork. He pulled the scrub top up to cover his nose and mouth. It didn't really help.

Down a hallway the flickering orange light was particularly bright. Paxton headed toward that light.

He moved as quickly as possible with his crouched posture. Every so often he would encounter a door off to the side. He would swing the door open and peer inside. Nothing but empty rooms so far.

The roof creaked and buckled. He wondered if he should proceed.

I have to know this is over.

He put his hand up over his head, as if he could deflect the roof should it decide to collapse.

Paxton reached the end of hallway. Not only was the orange light bright, but he could feel heat from the flames. There was a doorway to the left, through which all the light and heat escaped. The doorway was partially blocked by a fallen beam. Paxton braced himself, then he thrust himself under the beam, through the doorway into the burning room.

Chapter 84

A BLAST FURNACE OF HEAT MET PAXTON ON THE OTHER side of the doorway. He surveyed the room as he coughed and hacked mercilessly. He saw the wood paneling burning across the room. Furniture was strewn about. A desk was overturned off to the right.

On the floor near the burning wall lay a crumpled body. It was not moving.

He heard an agonized cry and turned to his left. Paxton's eyes followed the length of a concrete pillar that lay on its side, starting on the floor and extending halfway up the burning wall. Under the pillar, was a gray-haired man. He was flopping side-to-side and moaning. His legs were pinned under the fallen pillar. Near the man's head was a leather bag. The one they had seen Rugova carry to the car earlier.

Paxton crossed over to the injured man. One look at his face confirmed what Paxton already suspected: Rugova.

Rugova looked startled—as if he never expected anyone to respond to his cries for help. His expression turned to relief. He said something in Serbian that sounded thankful.

Paxton pulled the scrub top down off his nose and mouth. "I don't understand you."

Rugova recognized the face. He appeared confused. "Paxton?" He coughed.

"Yes, General Rugova. I'm so glad you remember me."

"You've come for me?" Rugova was now speaking English.

"Hardly." Paxton stepped over Rugova and retrieved the leather bag. He opened it and saw the device from the Stealth fighter inside. "I came for this."

"But you are going to save me?" Rugova asked. "Right?"

Paxton looked down at Rugova as he crouched over him. He didn't say anything. The fire cracked and popped relentlessly.

"Right?" Rugova asked again.

The fire roared louder. Paxton turned toward another body. He moved next to it. It was a man wearing a green military uniform cinched in the middle by a leather belt. Red shoulder boards with gold stitching adorned the Asian man's coat. Paxton couldn't find a pulse. The air was so hot it felt as if he were breathing in the flames. Paxton grabbed the identification badge hanging from the dead man's neck. He threw it in the bag with the high tech device.

"Paxton, you have to rescue me!"

Paxton turned back toward Rugova. "Why do you say that?"

Rugova coughed. "Because you're pararescue." It sounded like he spit the word pararescue.

"So?"

"You save lives…Not just American lives…I know what you did for Nikolic's wife."

"What does she have to do with anything?"

"She is the wife of your enemy…yet you saved her. You will save me next."

"She deserved to be saved," Paxton said. "She is innocent."

The carpet caught on fire and the flames began to spill toward Paxton.

"I am innocent too," Rugova croaked out.

Paxton chuckled. "Bullshit."

"Please save me, Sergeant Paxton."

Images of Rugova's telling Paxton that he had sent assassins after Paxton's family flashed through his mind. He would never forget that feeling. The anguish. The helplessness. The anger.

"Give me one good reason."

"A second chance."

"What?"

"Give me a second chance."

"Did you ever give your victims a second chance? You're a war criminal. You released your animals against innocent people. Civilians. Rape. Murder. Driving people from their homes. Why should you get something you were unwilling to give?"

Rugova shook his head. His cheeks were wet. Paxton wasn't sure if it was tears or sweat.

"Save me! You will be richly rewarded. I have money."

"I don't want your money. My family being safe and making sure you know you failed in your plans is all the reward I need."

Paxton closed the leather bag and stepped over Rugova. Rugova grabbed his ankle.

"Save me Paxton!"

Paxton didn't say anything.

"If you don't save me, and the firemen do, I will spend the rest of my life sending men after your family. You will have no peace."

Paxton smiled. "I've got news for you, General. No one else is coming. I'm your only hope…and you just convinced me."

"You can't leave me here to die. You have to rescue me. It is in your creed."

The flames roared within a few yards of the men. Paxton looked at them and then back down at Rugova.

"I'm United States Pararescueman John Paxton. These things I do, that others may live."

Paxton pulled the scrub top back up over his nose and mouth, turned, and headed back toward the doorway. Paxton never looked back as Rugova's cursing turned into screams of agony.

Chapter 85

PAXTON DUCKED UNDER THE BEAM AND THROUGH THE doorway. He had no way to tell if he had used up the twenty minutes he had asked the others to wait. The sound of Rugova's screams stopped abruptly. He no longer kept low to avoid the toxic fumes but instead ran as fast as he could down the dark hallway. He headed toward the flashing red lights and the sound of the revving pumps.

He climbed over the scattered furniture and reached the hole in the wall that he had used to enter the building. He stepped through the opening with his left foot. He then ducked and maneuvered his body through the opening. Then he stepped outside with his right foot and pulled the leather bag through behind him.

He spun around and ran toward the driveway. One of the firemen stepped out into his path, his arms out to catch Paxton.

Paxton plowed through him like he was channeling Emmitt

Smith and continued to run toward the open gate.

No one was manning the entrance, and Paxton ran through the gate out onto the sidewalk. He turned left and headed back toward the car.

As he ran, his lungs filled with the cool, fresh night air. The smell of the smoke would not go away.

At first he thought his eyes had not adjusted, but as he got closer he realized his eyes were not playing tricks on him. He slowed to a jog and then a walk. Breathless, he stopped at the empty spot where the car had been parked. He looked around. The car was nowhere in sight.

I guess my twenty minutes were up.

Chapter 86

PAXTON STOOD THERE ALL ALONE, COVERED IN SOOT, holding the leather bag. He had to get the hell out of there. The burning embassy complex was sure to become the focus of international attention, and if he had any chance of getting away, he had better not be anywhere near it when the crowds arrived.

He jogged along the sidewalk in the direction from which they had arrived. He had no idea where in the city he was or how to find his way out. He knew there was a second Pave Hawk helicopter out there somewhere waiting to evacuate them, but he didn't have any idea how to locate the rendezvous point from here. Besides, they were probably already gone.

No matter. He was alive and Rugova was dead. Jashari too. McMurphy, Smith, Nikolic and Nikolic's wife were all free and probably safe. The chemical weapons were destroyed, and he was holding the real device from the Stealth fighter. His own family was safe. Mission just about accomplished.

Maybe I should destroy the device.

He didn't want it to fall back into the wrong hands if he were captured or killed. But part of him didn't want to destroy it. It seemed like he might still need it. Although he was too tired to figure out why.

The squeal of tires broke him free from his thoughts. Paxton spun around toward the sound of a vehicle accelerating toward him. He heard it but didn't see it. He instinctively sought cover.

Shit!

Now he wished had destroyed the device. Too late now. He pressed himself into a dark alcove. He wondered if he had been spotted.

He got the answer when a dark sedan with no headlights on slid to a stop in front of his hiding spot. The rear window behind the driver rolled down.

"Get the fuck in the car, Paxton!" Smith's voice was unmistakable.

• • •

Once Paxton slammed the door shut, Nikolic floored it. He switched on the one remaining headlight so he could see where he was going.

"Shit, I thought you guys had left," Paxton said.

"We should have," McMurphy said. "Your twenty minutes were up some time ago."

"So why didn't you leave?"

"Nikolic and Smith insisted we wait for you."

"Where did you go then?"

"We felt a little exposed," Smith explained, "sitting there as all the emergency vehicles drove by. So we thought it best if we kept on the move and watched to see if you came out."

Paxton nodded.

Then he turned to McMurphy. "Where are we on the evac plans?"

"The Pave Hawk had to pull back to refuel," McMurphy said. "But we have a new rendezvous point. Nikolic knows the way. We head there and wait for them."

"So what happened in there?" Smith asked.

"Rugova is dead. So is a member of the Chinese military. I've got his ID badge, so we can see if he pops up on any lists. And I've got the device."

"Let's get to the helicopter so we can get the hell out of here," McMurphy said.

"Amen, brother," Smith agreed.

Chapter 87

NIKOLIC DROVE THEM OUT OF BELGRADE, AND WHEN THEY arrived at the rendezvous spot he pulled off the road and parked behind a clump of trees. He turned the headlight off, and they sat in the dark. The sedan was not visible from the road.

Paxton called Reed using the Sat phone and updated him. Reed sounded relieved that Paxton had retrieved the real device.

It would have been a good time to get some sleep, but the men were so keyed up they just sat there in silence waiting for the first sounds of the helicopter. They were still waiting as the sun rose in the sky.

• • •

The knock on the door startled Jill. *John?*
She bolted to the door and opened it only to be disappointed. "Captain Marshall! I didn't expect you."

"I figured you probably felt trapped here in your room, so I thought I'd take you and the kids out for breakfast and maybe a tour of the base."

"Wow. That is very kind of you."

"It is the least we can do. I realize what a hardship it has been on you and your family, and I feel that the general and I are the cause."

Jill didn't disagree.

"Well, why don't you get ready? I will wait for you down in the lobby. Also, if you need to do any shopping, I'll show you where the commissary is."

"Thank you, Captain. We will be out in a few minutes."

• • •

After she got herself and her children ready, Jill met Marshall in the lobby. He helped her with the car seat. He strapped it into the back seat of the Air Force sedan he had checked out.

He drove them over to the chow hall and bought them breakfast. Jill picked at her fruit cup.

"I hope you have been comfortable so far," Marshall said.

"It certainly is not home," Jill replied. "Then again, no place feels like home anymore."

"I'm so sorry for what happened to you and your children."

"Thank you."

"I'm sure you have questions. I'll answer what I can."

"When can I see John?"

"Soon. He is almost done with his duties. Maybe as soon as

this evening."

"Really?"

"I can't say for sure, but that is how it looks now."

Jill visibly relaxed. She reached over and wiped Megan's face with a paper napkin.

"So where would you like to go next?"

"I'd like to hit the BX. Pick up a couple items." BX was short for Base Exchange, which was sort of like a department store on base.

"No problem."

"Captain?"

"Yes."

"Why do planes on this base keep revving up their engines and then not taking off?"

Marshall chuckled. "I can show you why."

• • •

After breakfast, Marshall drove Jill and her kids over to the other side of the base. They parked in front of a large metal hangar. The sound of a jet engine shrieked inside the building. A red warning light flashed.

"Your son is going to enjoy this."

"Airplane, mommy!" John, Jr. exclaimed.

They walked in the door that boasted to be the "Control Entrance."

Inside, they encountered a second door. Marshall spoke into an intercom, and the door unlocked. Jill carried her daughter and followed Marshall inside.

A couple of airmen were seated at a large control panel. Marshall said something to them, and they nodded. In front of them was a large window that allowed them to see inside the rest of the hangar. Beyond the glass was a high-ceiling bay with a concrete floor. Across the bay was a large jet engine mounted on a test rack. The engine screeched and blasted blue flame out of the back. The flames traveled down a tunnel that led, presumably, outside.

Jill held Megan tightly in her arms. The little girl seemed apprehensive. John, Jr. stood on his tiptoes to see the action taking place on the other side of the window. Jill could see airmen wearing headphones working on the engine in the bay.

"What is this place?" Jill asked.

"Engine repair shop," Marshall explained. "That is an engine from…sergeant, what is that from?"

The sergeant said something to Marshall that Jill couldn't hear. Marshall continued. "It is from an F-15 Eagle fighter plane."

"What, do they work on them here?"

"Exactly. They take the engine out of the plane and place it on the test stand using that crane." Marshall pointed to an overhead crane in the rafters of the bay. "They then can make repairs and test it."

"I see."

"And when they test it, they rev it up to full throttle. That is why you kept hearing planes rev up but not take off."

"Very interesting," Jill said. "What are those yellow lines on the floor?"

"Safety lines. They spread out like a cone from the front of the engine. The suction from the engine is so strong, the men must make sure they don't place anything like a tool or something within that zone. Otherwise it could get sucked into the engine."

"It is that strong?"

"It could suck a person in if they are not careful."

"Goodness."

"But it is okay. See that screen in front of the mouth of the engine? It is placed there for safety when the engine is fired up to keep anything from getting sucked in."

"Are we safe here?"

Marshall laughed. "Of course, we are. The glass in that window is bulletproof. We are completely safe on this side."

"This place makes me nervous. Can we go shopping now?"

"Of course. Now John, Jr. can tell his dad what he saw. But let's go. The BX is calling."

Chapter 88

PAXTON HEARD THE HELICOPTER FIRST. "HERE IT COMES."

The others listened, and they, too, heard the distinctive sound of the rotor blades. They opened the doors and climbed out of the beat-up sedan. Paxton grabbed one of the AK-74 rifles and the leather bag containing the device. He also grabbed the Benelli shotgun. Sort of a trophy. A very useful trophy.

Smith grabbed the other AK rifle. McMurphy and Nikolic were unarmed.

The sound of the copter grew louder. The men scanned the clearing from their position in the trees. No one was out there.

They then scanned the sky. Once the Pave Hawk was visible, the men moved out into the opening. They waved to the chopper.

The Pave Hawk descended toward the opening. Paxton and Smith swept the perimeter with their rifles, making sure no one waited in ambush. The airman manning the mini-gun on the side was visible as the Pave Hawk settled onto the grass.

The four men climbed aboard and quickly put on headphones to enable communication.

"Let's go home!" Smith exclaimed as the helicopter took off. He high-fived the airman on board.

"Not quite yet," Paxton said.

"What'd you mean, not quite yet?"

"Before we leave Yugoslavia," Paxton explained, "we have to make one more stop."

• • •

Marshall pushed the cart for Jill as she took various items from the shelves. Megan rode in the basket's seat and John, Jr. rode in the basket along with her selections. She grabbed some toiletries, snacks and some books and magazines.

When they arrived at the checkout counter, Marshall pulled out his wallet.

"What are you doing?" Jill asked.

"I'm paying. It's the least I can do."

"No, I can't accept."

"Please, Mrs. Paxton. You have small children. I'm sure you are on a tight budget. Besides, I've got an expense account. Use it or lose it."

"I just don't feel right."

"I don't have a wife or children. Please let me spend it so they don't cut my travel budget next time." Marshall laughed.

Jill laughed, too, and let him pay.

Chapter 89

PAXTON HAD INSTRUCTED THE PAVE HAWK PILOTS ON where he wanted them to fly. He also told them that it was critical that they not tell General Reed where they were going.

Smith wasn't happy that they were not headed home, and he didn't care who knew. Nikolic looked very worried. Paxton could not tell if he worried about his wife, or worried about where they were headed. McMurphy's face told no story.

After a long flight, the Pave Hawk circled its destination, looking for a landing spot. From the air, Smith immediately recognized where they were.

"Aw man, why'd we come back here?"

"So we have the right place?" Paxton asked.

"Yeah...I have bad memories from this place."

Paxton surveyed the destruction from the air. Destroyed vehicles. Bodies. Fortunately, there were no signs of life. It was safe to land.

The Pave Hawk set down, and Paxton climbed out. He tried to imagine the firefight that had taken place here. Smith followed him off the helicopter.

"You caused a lot of damage," Paxton said to Smith.

"We wanted to get out of here, and this SAM site stood between us and our ride home," Smith said, referring to the Surface to Air Missile site.

"See, those missiles were going to shoot down the helicopters, so I shot up the control panel in there," Smith pointed to the command truck. Smith then pointed toward the charred missile launcher. "Then we blew up the missiles so they couldn't be used anymore." Then he pointed to the ground beyond them. "And the copters picked us all up here."

"Did you take anything away from this site?"

"We got out just with our lives."

"Okay."

"Pax?"

"Yes?"

"Why are we here?"

"Because I'm hoping to God something doesn't exist, but I have a real bad feeling I'm going to find it here."

• • •

Marshall helped Jill bring the shopping bags into her temporary quarters. He placed Megan's car seat in the corner. The kids jumped on the bed, giggling.

"Is there anything else I can do for you?" Marshall asked.

"Just send John over as soon as you can."

"Yes, ma'am, we're working on it. You and the kids have a great rest of the day."

"Thank you," Jill said as she closed the door.

Chapter 90

PAXTON CLIMBED THE STAIRS TO THE COMMAND TRUCK AND opened the door. Inside it was dark and cold. Smith held the door open to allow more light to enter the command center.

Paxton saw the launch control and radar screen. Bullet holes in the control panel were a lasting tribute to Smith's handiwork. He was relieved there were no dead men in the confined space. For that matter, he was grateful that there were no live ones either.

He crossed over to the table right next to the radar screen. It was littered with binders, papers, drinks, ashes, and cigarette butts. He rifled through the items.

"Want to tell me what the hell you are looking for?" Smith asked.

"I'm not sure exactly," Paxton said.

"Then how are you going to find it?"

"I'll know it when I see it."

McMurphy pushed past Smith and entered the command room. "Come on, Paxton. It's time to go."

"Not yet."

"The helicopter attracted attention. Soon there will be Serbian Army troops showing up."

"Hmm-hmm."

Paxton picked up a piece of yellow NCR paper. It was the type used to make multiple copies in a dot matrix printer. Sort of like some banks and credit unions use to print out receipts. The tractor-feed holes were still attached on either side of the paper. He examined it in the limited light.

"Son of a bitch."

"What?"

"This is what I was looking for." Paxton continued to examine it. "And it is very bad news."

• • •

Medics rushed Ms. Nikolic onto a waiting medical jet. The Pave Hawk had worked its way all the way back to Brindisi. The plane took off and headed for Germany where a highly specialized team awaited to give her the best care available.

Chapter 91

"I DON'T CARE WHAT IT IS, WE NEED TO GET OUT OF HERE," McMurphy said.

"Oh, I think you will be very, very interested in what this is," Paxton said.

"If you tell me what it is, can we then get the hell out of here?" McMurphy asked.

"That depends."

"On what?"

Smith stood in the doorway and watched the two men. He kept peering over his shoulder as if he was expecting someone to show up at any moment, which, of course, he was.

"It depends on what it says."

"Paxton!" McMurphy boomed. "You are holding us up, and you don't even know what the paper says?"

"Not really," Paxton explained. "I can't read the Serbo-Croat, or whatever, but I can tell what it is."

"Which is…"

"It is clearly a printout of an email," Paxton began. "I cannot read what it says, but there is a chart with it that contains the flight paths and times for all the Stealth fighters from the night the Stealth was shot down."

The room was silent for a moment as that sunk in.

"So that's how they shot down the Stealth," Smith said. "How the hell did that info get to an anti-aircraft missile battery here?"

"Obviously, it was sent to them by someone with access to such things," McMurphy answered.

"Oh, not just any such someone," Paxton added.

"What do you mean?" McMurphy asked.

"That someone happened to include a name," Paxton said. "I can't read the rest, but I can clearly read the name…the name typed on here is yours, McMurphy."

Chapter 92

BEFORE MCMURPHY COULD PROTEST, PAXTON HAD RAISED the barrel of his Benelli shotgun and pointed it at McMurphy's face.

"Bullshit," McMurphy said as he raised his hands.

"No bullshit," Paxton said. "It is right here on the printout. Smith, come verify."

Smith stepped past McMurphy and looked on the yellow page where Paxton was pointing. "Son of a…it definitely says 'McMurphy.'"

McMurphy was shaking his head. "That's crazy! Why would I feed the Serbs info that they could use to shoot down one of our planes?"

"Not so crazy," Paxton said. "Obviously you and General Reed were so anxious to pull off your little scheme to swap devices that you couldn't just wait around to see if a Stealth got shot down…You had to make it happen."

"How could I pull that off?"

"Very easily," Paxton said. "You are a man with lots of contacts in both governments. You were able to blend in here in Serbia for over five years, and yet, you can pick up the phone and call in an air strike on an embassy. You're very resourceful, McMurphy."

"I wouldn't endanger the life of a pilot to accomplish the mission," McMurphy countered.

"Frankly, McMurphy, I don't know what you would stop at."

"And you think I'm dumb enough to sign my own name to the transmittal?"

"That does give me pause," Paxton admitted. "Smith, bring Nikolic here."

"Why?" Smith asked.

"Because," Paxton answered, "I need to get this thing translated."

• • •

Once Smith returned with a puzzled Nikolic, Paxton commanded him to stand apart from McMurphy. Paxton's shotgun continued to point at McMurphy.

"We don't have time for this shit, Paxton," McMurphy said. "The Serbs are coming."

"Maybe he is right. Maybe we should do this later," Smith said.

"I'm getting to the bottom of this now," Paxton said. "Colonel Nikolic, I need you to translate this for me."

"Oh, so you are going to just believe him?" McMurphy asked.

"No, you are going to translate it for me, too." Paxton pulled the two carbon copies apart. He handed one to Nikolic and the other to McMurphy. He then picked up two pens and some blank paper from the table. "Each of you is going to translate it into English. Then I'm going to compare the translations. If one word differs, I'll kill both of you right here."

Nikolic's eyes were wide. McMurphy just looked angry.

Paxton handed them the pens and paper and told them to get to work.

"Oh, and any attempt to destroy the document I handed you will be considered by me a confession of guilt. I don't think I have to tell you what the penalty will be."

• • •

Chapter 93

Nikolic nervously scribbled the translation onto a blank piece of paper. McMurphy did the same, only he didn't seem nervous. Smith kept peeking out the door, waiting for the Serbian Army to arrive.

McMurphy finished first. He handed the yellow paper and the paper with the translation to Paxton. Nikolic seemed more concerned with getting every word correct. Sweat was pouring down his face.

Paxton busied himself reading McMurphy's translation. He did not say a word.

Finally, Nikolic finished and handed his papers to Paxton. Paxton scanned it. He seemed to know exactly what he was looking for. When he found it he said, "Very interesting."

"What?" Smith asked, trying to read Paxton's face.

Paxton said, "I think I now have the answer about McMurphy."

"Which is?"

"The first part of the document relates to the Stealth fighters. It is not directly from an American, but it is clearly detailed information provided by some American who was in the know and committing treason." Paxton examined the paper more. "There is some middleman, probably to hide the identity of the American, who then conveyed this message to the Serbs, who obviously transmitted copies of this to all the SAM sites in hopes of shooting down a Stealth. This being one of the SAM sites, and Smith and his team being kind enough to kill or run off its crew, we were lucky to find a copy of this smoking gun."

"So what's the bottom line?" Smith asked.

"The money phrase says, and I quote, 'U.S. source says the name is McMurphy. Unknown cover.' Unquote."

"What is that supposed to mean?"

"I checked both translations, and they are exactly the same. It says, *the name* is McMurphy. Not *my name* is McMurphy."

"So?"

"So, McMurphy is not the source of this information."

"But McMurphy could have sent the message."

"Not likely. It continues to say, 'Unknown cover.' In other words, whoever sent this did not know that McMurphy was operating in Serbia under the cover name of Grigori."

"He could be lying."

"Lying is always a possibility, but why would McMurphy blow his own cover? If he was behind this message, why would he give them his real name? He would have said the name is Grigori."

"So what are you saying?" Smith asked. "That McMurphy isn't the one who committed treason?"

"Not only am I saying that, but I'm also saying that whoever is behind this had a reckless disregard for McMurphy's life." Paxton lowered the shotgun as he spoke.

Nikolic looked relieved.

"Since you now know that I wasn't behind this, who do you think is?" McMurphy asked.

Paxton looked at McMurphy. "The person who revealed this had access to the Stealth mission plans and also knew who you were. Our little escapade was so secretive, so cut off from the rest of the command structure that only a very limited universe of people knew both those things. In fact, the evidence points to only one place."

Chapter 94

PAXTON REMAINED SILENT FOR MOST OF THE FLIGHT BACK.
The Pave Hawk stopped only to refuel aboard the *Kersage* before continuing all the way to Brindisi. Just before landing, Paxton handed McMurphy the identification badge he had taken from the dead man in the Chinese embassy.

"Maybe your sources can find out who that man was and how far this goes."

McMurphy nodded.

Paxton stared out at the airfield below.

"Pax," McMurphy interrupted, "you sure you want to do this alone?"

"I'm sure."

McMurphy wrote something on a piece of paper. "Here."

Paxton looked at him, puzzled.

"I still have the Sat phone. If you need anything…."

Paxton nodded as he turned to look out again.

The Pave Hawk landed in front of the pararescue hangar, and Paxton climbed out first. He squinted in the sunlight as he surveyed the welcome committee of two: General Reed and Captain Marshall.

"Sirs, let's do this inside," Paxton said as he walked right past them.

The three men went into the hangar and straight into Colonel Hicks's empty office. Reed walked to the other side of the desk and sat down. Marshall stood to the side of the desk. Paxton stood holding the leather bag across the desk from Reed.

"Welcome back, Sergeant Paxton," Reed said. "What do you have for us?"

"I have the genuine device from the downed Stealth fighter… plus a little surprise."

"Surprise?" Reed said. "What sort of surprise?"

Paxton reached into his pocket and produced the yellow piece of paper he had taken from the SAM site. He unfolded it and dropped in on the desk in front of Reed.

Reed picked it up and examined it. Marshall leaned over to get a better look.

"What is this?" Reed asked.

"Like you don't know," Paxton replied.

"I don't."

"You should know…you sent it."

Reed stared at Paxton, his face red. "I did no such thing!"

"Come on, General, quit pretending."

"I can't even read it…how the hell would I have sent it?"

"Then you caused it to be sent. All I know is when we get

to the bottom of this, it'll be discovered that you're behind it."

"I still don't know what it is," Reed said.

"All the information necessary to shoot down a Stealth fighter."

"Do you know what you are accusing the general of?" Marshall asked angrily.

"I know exactly what I'm accusing him of, and I have the proof."

"Some email written in a language I don't speak with flight information is proof? That could have come from lots of places. I'm not the only person with access to mission plans."

"Yeah? Well read on. How many people have access to mission plans *and* know of McMurphy? That entire population of suspects is sitting in this room."

Reed shook his head in disbelief.

"Paxton, you are nuts," Marshall said.

"Maybe, but the facts speak for themselves. And don't think about getting cute and tearing up the evidence. I have another copy."

"Sergeant, why would I purposely try to get a Stealth fighter shot down? I have spent the latter part of my career overseeing improvements to the Stealth fighter to ensure just the opposite."

"I wondered that myself at first, but then I realized that you were so anxious to pull off your scheme to switch the real device for a fake one that you couldn't sit around and wait for the Serbs to get lucky. You gave them what they needed. You don't need a radar to see and shoot down the slow-flying Stealth if you know exactly when and where to look."

"So you really think I sent mission plans to the Serbs so I could carry out my plan to trick the Chinese?"

"That's how it looks to me...and that is how it is going to look to a jury at your court martial."

"I can't believe my ears," Reed said as he leaned back in his chair.

"You damn near got away with it, too," Paxton added. "Whose idea was it to send me on the mission?"

"Well, it was obvious that pararescue was a perfect fit to extract Mrs. Nikolic so we could get Colonel Nikolic's cooperation," Reed explained. "But Marshall here picked you to lead the team...based on your experience and language abilities."

"You should fire him," Paxton said. "I was the wrong man to pick if you wanted to get away with this. Not only because my language abilities suck but because it got personal once my family was threatened. Had that not happened, I probably would not have looked deeper and figured out that you were behind this."

"Damn it, man! I'm not behind this!"

"You said it yourself. This mission doesn't exist. It was off the books. Who else had the information included in that email?"

"I don't know...maybe it was compiled from multiple sources. We already know that there is a leak at the Pentagon...that is why the first attempts failed, and two CIA officers lost their lives. I thought we had kept the Pentagon in the dark, but evidently not."

"Multiple sources?" Paxton shook his head. "That's a stretch. You had the information, the opportunity, and the motive."

"I may have had the information and the opportunity," Reed said, "but I certainly didn't have the motive."

"Of course you did. Maybe your intentions were ultimately good. Maybe you felt that the Chinese were too close to defeating the device, and it was imperative that you proceed with your plan to pull off the switch at once. Perhaps you made some sort of crazy judgment call that it was worth risking one pilot's life in exchange for all the future pilots who would be saved. People died, General. You're going to face the death penalty."

"It is obvious that once again the fatigue of the mission has set in and you are unable to think clearly," Reed said.

"What the hell is *that* supposed to mean?"

"You are so wrong, Sergeant. Paxton. If you would just think about it, you would realize what I'm saying is true. I had nothing to do with this email."

"Prove it."

"I told you from the beginning that the plan to switch the devices was a contingency plan. It was only to be implemented in the event a Stealth fighter got shot down. We were worried that if that happened, the Chinese would get their hands on the real device. So I hatched the plan to have McMurphy trick the Serbs into taking the fake device and selling it to the Chinese."

"Except that you turned the contingency into reality," Paxton said.

Reed shook his head. "Think about it, Paxton." Reed leaned forward. His eyes burrowed into Paxton's. "If my whole plan was based on McMurphy's ability to trick the Serbs, why in the hell would I blow his cover by giving them his real name?"

"I don't know…I just know McMurphy would not have given you his cover name, so maybe you were grasping at straws."

Reed continued, "You think I wanted to force the action by causing a Stealth fighter to be shot down on purpose so McMurphy could pull off the switch, right?"

"Yes," Paxton said. "That is exactly what I think."

"McMurphy was still in D.C. with me when this email was sent. That is why we had to rush to get him—and you—inserted into Serbia. If what you say was true, why would I send such an email *before* I had McMurphy trained and in place?"

Chapter 95

PAXTON STOOD IN STUNNED SILENCE. HE WAS STILL wearing the sooty hospital scrubs. He didn't know what to think. Everything General Reed said made sense. The timing was all wrong. He could see it now. That email didn't further Reed's plans—it screwed them up. Reed obviously wasn't the one who sent it.

But who sent it, then?

Why would someone purposely screw up Reed's plans? Who would even know about them to do it?

There were too many questions. Reed was right. Paxton was exhausted. He was having trouble focusing.

"Sergeant Paxton, I truly appreciate your bringing this to our attention," Reed said. "You have done outstanding work. I can see why you are so well respected. As a thank-you for what you have done in recovering the device and uncovering the plot, I'm going to forget that you have accused me of treason, not once but twice, and I'm going to personally see to it that all the charges against you are dropped."

The charges!

Paxton had forgotten all about those. The memories flooded back.

"And what about the charges against Sergeant Smith?" Paxton asked.

"Those will all be dropped as well," Reed assured. "It is clear to me that you both were doing what you thought was right."

"This is not over," Paxton said.

"No it is not," Reed replied. "Captain Marshall and I are going to open an investigation into who sent this email."

"I'm going to make sure it gets investigated by the proper authorities," Paxton said.

"We welcome that," Reed said as he pushed the yellow paper across the table to Paxton. "As a sign of my good faith, I'm returning this evidence to you for safekeeping, for I have no doubt that you will pursue this."

"Damn straight I will."

"You need to get cleaned up and get some well-deserved rest. Captain Marshall has arranged a room for you over in the airman dorms. You will be staying on the same wing as the other PJs."

"When do I get to go home?"

"We will arrange a flight home as soon as possible…perhaps as early as tomorrow."

"Thank you."

Reed produced a large black bag. It was the same bag that

was on the flight from Texas to Florida. "Here is your regular uniform." Paxton took all of the items, including the yellow paper. He folded the paper and placed it back in his pocket.

Reed reached into his coat pocket and produced more of Paxton's belongings. "Here are your wallet and dog tags. So you can return to being John Paxton."

Paxton accepted the last of the items and said, "I've got news for you, General: I never stopped being John Paxton."

Chapter 96

THERE WAS A KNOCK AT THE DOOR. JILL PUT HER BOOK down and got up.

"Who is it, Mommy?" John, Jr. asked.

"I don't know, honey. Lemme see." Jill crossed the room and unlocked the door. She opened it up.

Her eyes widened as she saw who it was. Her voice was filled with surprise as she said, "I didn't think I'd see you again."

• • •

Paxton took a long hot shower in the dorm room in the Airmen's dorms. He could not scrub hard enough to remove the feeling from the mission. He looked at the wound on his knee. All but one of the stitches had pulled out. It was going to leave a nasty scar.

His mind reeled. Who was the guilty party? Who set this all in motion? Who could he trust?

He toweled off and shaved. He had laid out his uniform on the bed. Next to it were both copies of the yellow paper, his wallet, and the piece of paper that McMurphy had given him. He dressed and placed the items in his pockets. Also on the bed were the black bag and the Benelli shotgun. He wouldn't truly feel safe until he was home.

Home.

Time to call Jill and the kids. He got dressed and dug through the bag. No cell phone. Then he remembered that Colonel Ward had taken that from him. It was probably sitting in a drawer in his office back at Lackland.

No worries. He would just use the room phone and reverse the charges. He picked up the receiver and dialed zero. He gave instructions to the international operator and waited while the phone rang. It continued to ring until he heard his own voice on the answering machine.

"Hey, honey, I'm safe. Just trying to reach you. I'll try your cell."

He gave the cell number to the operator, but that call went directly to voice mail.

Paxton sighed.

I suppose it is karma…I haven't exactly been available.

Paxton lay back on the bed trying to take everything in. He had come so far, but it still seemed to be a dead end.

He needed to hear a familiar voice.

He dialed the number for Colonel Ward.

"Paxton! How the hell are you?"

"I'm okay, sir. I'm still trying to work out a few things here, but I should be returning to work there tomorrow."

"Nonsense," Ward said. "Take some time off to enjoy your family."

"Oh, I plan to, sir. I've got some things I want to run by you, and it would be better in person. So I figure I'll stop by the office tomorrow, we can touch base, and then maybe I'll take the rest of the week off."

"Why don't you take advantage of seeing the sights for a few days over there in Italy? You deserve it. Then you can come home and brief me."

"That is awfully nice of you, sir, but I want to come home and spend time with my family."

"What's wrong with spending time with your family in Italy"

"What are you talking about? My family isn't in Italy."

"Yes they are. I sent them."

"You sent my family to Italy? They are here now?"

"Yes. I wanted to surprise you."

"I had no idea. When did they get here?"

"Yesterday. Didn't Captain Marshall tell you? I set it all up with him."

Ward's words hit Paxton like a bucket of ice water.

"Paxton, you there?"

Paxton slammed the phone down as he bolted to his feet. He grabbed the shotgun, shoved it into the black bag, hoisted it onto his shoulder and ran out the door.

Chapter 97

PAXTON RAN OUT INTO THE FADING LIGHT OF THE afternoon. He swiveled his head to the left and right. He saw a tall, thin young man dressed in blues walking toward the dorm entrance.

"Airman! Which way to the enlisted temporary quarters?"

The young man pointed to Paxton's left. "They're down the street that way, Sergeant. About five blocks."

Paxton thanked him and began running. His stomach was in a knot. His rational mind was still in denial, but his instincts were certain.

He could feel the shotgun bounce around in the bag with each stride. It felt like he was running in slow motion, as if this were a dream. Or a nightmare.

There was little traffic on base. Paxton examined every car he saw. And the occupants of the cars stared at the sergeant running with the gym bag slung on his back. Late for a workout?

He ran past several administrative buildings and supply depots. Then he saw the small wooden sign with wooden letters affixed. Quaint like a summer camp, they read "Airman Temporary Quarters."

Paxton burst through the front doors and up to the front desk. Behind the desk was a civilian woman. Startled, she looked up at the broad-shouldered sweating man who just arrived.

"What room are the Paxtons in?" He asked before she could even offer to help him.

She looked at her computer screen. "I don't have any Paxtons registered."

"How about under Marshall or Reed?"

The clerk scowled at her computer screen. "Nope. No one here by that name."

"A woman and two small kids. Boy and a girl."

She shook her head. "Nobody here that fits that description. Just a group of crew chiefs out of Moffitt and some personnel folks from Keesler."

"You sure?"

Insulted the woman huffed, "Yes, I'm sure."

Paxton thought about it for a moment. "Officers' Quarters. Where are they?"

The woman pointed over the counter. "Three blocks that way, then take a left. Second building over. Can't miss it."

Paxton was out the door before the woman finished. He ran as fast as possible. He tried to quell the panic. Would he get there in time? Was he overreacting?

He counted the blocks out loud as he ran. He turned left and headed toward the second building. It was much nicer than the Airman's Quarters. In the distance Paxton heard a jet engine start up.

He pushed his way through the glass double doors. This desk was also manned by a civilian. A man in his late sixties or early seventies.

"I'm looking for the Paxtons. What room?" Paxton had his hands on his knees and panting as he spoke.

The man swiveled the screen slightly and typed with his two index fingers. His eyebrows raised. Then he pursed his lips, scowled and hunted a pecked some more on the keyboard.

"Well?"

"I'm afraid we don't have anyone here by that name."

"Reed. Try Reed."

The man pressed some more buttons. Paxton had just about caught his breath at this point.

"Nope."

"How about Marshall?"

The man considered Paxton for a moment, and then typed some more. "Which one?"

"What do you mean?"

"We have three rooms registered to Marshall."

Paxton thought about it for a moment. "The one that arrived yesterday. What room?"

"We have one booked yesterday, but I can't give you the room number…I can call…."

Before the man could finish his statement Paxton had leaned

over the counter and spun the computer screen toward him.

Marshall, Room 224.

"Hey!" The clerk shouted, but Paxton was already gone.

Paxton bounded up the steps two at a time. He plowed through the door and down the second floor hallway. He reached room 224 and pounded on the door.

No response.

He pounded some more. "Jill! It's me. Open up!"

He tried the door. It was unlocked. He shoved into the room.

No one was there.

He looked around. He saw bags from the BX and a couple juice boxes on the table. On the bed, were a book and a teddy bear dressed in camouflage. Megan's bear!

Paxton grabbed the bear to be sure. There was no doubt about it. He turned, looking around the room. The dresser had a mirror with a piece of paper taped to it.

In big red letters on the paper were the words *Sergeant Paxton*.

Chapter 98

PAXTON SNATCHED THE NOTE OFF THE MIRROR. THE window rattled with the sound of the jet revving its engine. He turned the note over.

> SENIOR MASTER SERGEANT PAXTON:
>
> IF YOU EVER WANT TO SEE YOUR FAMILY AGAIN, MEET ME AT HANGAR #4. COME ALONE AND BRING THE YELLOW PAPERS.
>
> SINCERELY,
> YOUR WORST NIGHTMARE

Paxton took a piece of paper out of his pocket and stepped over to the phone.

Paxton hung up after a very brief conversation and ran back out the door. He practically jumped the two flights down the stairs and bolted out into the early evening. With the black bag still slung over his shoulder, he ran toward the flight line.

• • •

The hangars were adorned with large black numbers painted on them. Parts of the numbers were missing, as if a stencil were used.

One. Two. Three.

Paxton passed hangars until he arrived at the one with the large four painted on it. This one had a red light flashing.

It also had the incredibly loud sound of a jet engine emanating from behind its walls.

Paxton ran up to the door that said Control Entrance and yanked on it. It was locked. There was a note taped to the door. It had the same handwriting as the note in the room.

PLEASE USE OTHER DOOR.
YWN

Paxton turned to the right and ran to the other door. He tried it. It was unlocked. He shrugged the bag off his shoulder and fished out the Benelli shotgun. He aimed it low as he turned the doorknob and burst through. It was a small room before the main hangar door. No one was there.

In the way of the next door was a chair. On the chair sat a walkie-talkie radio attached to a set of headphones. A note was taped to the radio.

USE THESE TO HEAR ME.
YWN

Paxton picked up the radio and clipped it to his pants. He put the headphones on and raised the microphone to his mouth.

"Where is my family?" Paxton said into the microphone.

"Come on in and see," was the reply.

Paxton raised the shotgun and kicked the chair out of the way. He then felt the next doorknob. It turned freely. He steadied himself and slowly pushed on the door with his shoulder, opening it slightly. His shotgun leading the way.

Chapter 99

THE SCREAM OF THE JET ENGINE BECAME INSTANTLY louder with the door cracked open. Paxton pushed the shotgun through the small opening. Over the barrel of his shotgun, Paxton scanned the scene in front of him. The hangar was large with a very high ceiling. About forty meters away off to his right was a large test stand. Attached to the stand was a gray-metallic jet engine. The first thing that caught his attention was the blue flame that shot out of the exhaust and down a dark tunnel. He opened the door more. He scanned left, followed the outline of the engine and the various pipes and tubing that fed it. Its turbine blades were a blur.

Paxton noticed that someone had removed the safety screen from the mouth of the engine. A small tornado of condensation swooped constantly into the front of the spinning turbine.

Paxton continued turning to his left, opening the door with the motion, his finger on the outside of the trigger guard. The danger zone was painted in bright yellow on the floor of the hangar in front of the jet's mouth. It spread wider as it got farther from the engine. On the far side of the danger zone, Paxton saw a flat cart. On the cart looking at him with terror in their eyes were Jill, John, Jr. and Megan. They were tied up and gagged.

Paxton lowered the shotgun and started for his family. He stopped abruptly when he realized that he would never make it across to the other side of the danger zone. The screaming engine appeared to be from a jet fighter. He had seen videos of humans sucked into less powerful engines. Anything not bolted down would be immediately sucked into the engine.

What was worse, if he tried to cross and failed, the engine couldn't gobble him up without additional consequences. The engine would likely explode and kill his family. He considered running around the back of the engine, but with the after-burner blazing, he didn't stand a chance. He would be roasted alive. In short, he was not going to make it across to where his family was while that engine was at full throttle.

His thoughts were interrupted when he realized that the cart was rolling toward the danger zone. Upon closer examination, he saw the steel cable attached to the cart's handle. He followed the cable as it snaked along the ground and then up to the overhead crane. The winch on the crane slowly wound in the cable like a deep-sea fisherman hauling in a marlin.

"That's right, Sergeant Paxton," the headphones crackled. "Your family will be pulled right into the death zone unless you do exactly as I say."

Paxton turned further to the left. Behind the glass of the control booth stood Captain Marshall.

Chapter 100

"**What the fuck do you want, Marshall?**" **Paxton** spit the words into the microphone.

"I want the evidence. I want the yellow paper."

"Fuck you!" Paxton raised the shotgun and pulled the trigger.

The control booth glass instantly spidered around the shotgun slug as it embedded itself and stopped in the high-tech polymers.

Marshall laughed over the air. "Sergeant Paxton, don't you know I'm completely safe behind this glass? It is designed to survive in the event of an engine explosion."

Son of a bitch.

"Now show me the yellow paper."

Paxton stood there defiantly.

"So be it. I'll speed up the process." Marshall touched a control and Paxton's family jerked as the cart speed increased.

"Okay, okay," Paxton said as he fished the yellow page out of his pocket.

"Hold it up so I can see it."

Paxton did as he was told.

"Very good. Now take it over and toss it into the engine."

Paxton hesitated for a moment and then stepped closer to the danger zone. The wind rushed by, causing his uniform to snap back and forth.

He held the paper out at arms length. The paper flapped rapidly, just about tearing around his fingers. He let go. The paper was immediately swept into a spiral, racing along the ground and then up. There was a huff as the paper disappeared into spinning turbine blades. The blue flame of the afterburner flashed white and then back to blue.

"Now the other copy."

"I don't have it with me."

"Bullshit, Paxton. You would never let that out of your sight." Marshall reached down for the winch control again.

"Okay, here it is," Paxton says, holding the other copy out.

"You know what to do."

Paxton extended his arm into the danger zone. The paper flapped so quickly it was a blur. It was the last piece of physical evidence of Marshall's treason. Paxton opened his fingers, and the paper was swept into the engine.

The jet coughed white flame and then back to blue.

"There you go," Paxton said. "Now let my family go."

"Not yet."

"What more do you want?"

"You're next."

Paxton cocked his head sideways.

"You heard me. Follow the paper into the jet."

"Why?"

"You know too much. Now do it!"

"Fuck you, Marshall."

"Either follow the paper, or you will follow your family into the jet. Your choice." Marshall reached for the control panel.

Chapter 101

THIS FUCKER'S INSANE.

Paxton knew he had to buy some time. Get him talking.

"Why did you do it, Marshall?"

"I'm not admitting to anything."

"I'm going to die. Can you at least have the decency to let me know why?"

There was no reply. The cart continued to inch toward the yellow paint.

"Okay," Paxton said. "How about I give you my theory, and you let me know if I'm right or not." Paxton's mind was racing. He had one remaining slug loaded in the shotgun. He could try to fire it at the jet engine, but that would probably cause it to disintegrate, throwing steel turbine blades all around the hangar like shrapnel. Jill and the kids were too close to the mouth of the engine to risk that.

"I think you are working for the Red Chinese," Paxton said.

"You were probably approached because you work in the office of technology in the Pentagon. You don't have to admit anything, just correct me if I'm wrong."

Marshall was silent.

Maybe he could shoot out the fuel line. That would kill the engine. Paxton looked at the pipes and tubing feeding the engine. Even if he knew which one was the fuel line, which he didn't, shooting a pipe carrying pressurized jet fuel didn't seem like the best idea. Especially next to a red-hot jet engine—the explosion and fire would probably kill them all.

Besides, there might be a duplicate fuel line on the other side that would continue feeding the engine. Paxton had no idea—he wasn't a crew chief.

"The Chinese wanted the device so they could reverse engineer it," Paxton continued. "You were the one who warned them that Reed tried to pass them a fake one."

Marshall was silent.

"Two CIA officers were killed."

Paxton spun around. He thought he had sensed someone behind him. No one was there. He continued. "Then Operation Allied Force began, and a great opportunity opened up for everyone."

The cart edged closer to the yellow. Paxton looked at the cable. It would be a challenging shot. The cable was narrow and a shotgun does not impart the same level of accuracy on a slug that a rifle does on a bullet. For one thing, the barrel of a shotgun is not rifled. The rifling grooves cut into the barrel of a rifle impart a twist on a bullet. That rotation increases the accuracy and range just as the spiral does on a football thrown by a quarterback.

Worse yet, the cable was not stationary. It was whipping around in the wash of air being sucked into the jet. The other unknown was what that air, moving at the speed of a tornado, would do to the trajectory of the slug. Being that he would be shooting in the direction of his family, the risk was too great.

He would have to find another way.

"The Chinese saw it as a chance to get their hands on a real Stealth fighter device…if one got shot down. Reed equally saw it as an opportunity to pass a fake device off and hatched the plot to pull off a switch."

Marshall remained silent. He didn't cut Paxton off, but the cart edged closer. Paxton could see the terror in his family's eyes. They were close enough now that he could also see the tears.

The cable was out as an option. With his eyes, Paxton followed the cable up to the crane. If he shot the winch mechanism, that could stop the progress of the cart. And it would be a shot toward the ceiling, so his family would not be in the line of fire.

But the cable disappeared into a maze of steel beams and solid plates. There was no way he could take out the winch with his one remaining shot. Keep talking and thinking.

"Reed's plan was going to mess up the Chinese. So you warned them. A new urgency came over them. If they were going to get their device, a Stealth would have to get shot down before McMurphy arrived back in Serbia."

Marshall remained silent. Jill was trying to position herself to shield her children.

"So you made that happen by giving the Chinese the flight plans for the Stealth. They transmitted it to their counterparts in Serbia, who disseminated the information to all of their SAM sites. That is why I found a copy at the one site I visited. The copy that is now destroyed."

The cart was only a few feet from the yellow. Paxton watched helplessly as his wife's hair whipped around in the man-made hurricane.

"You also warned them about McMurphy. Only you didn't know what cover McMurphy was operating under, and he sure as hell wasn't going to tell you."

Jill was shaking her head. The gag prevented any screams. Her eyes said "help me."

"Anyway, the Stealth got nailed. It was a lucky shot by the Serbs, but your flight info improved their odds. It still looked like McMurphy would get there in time to screw up your plan, so you tried to delay things by suggesting that Reed come pick me up in Texas to lead the mission. You came up with some lame excuses as to why I was vital, but the real reason was delay."

Marshall was silent.

"How are you going to get away with this? People don't just disappear."

Marshall's voice crackled through the radio. "Accidents happen…I'll make it look like you and your family were killed by accident after wandering into the wrong hangar."

The cart continued to move. The front wheels crossed the yellow line.

"What about the others?" Paxton's voice was frantic. "There are a lot of people dead because of you. The two CIA officers. The pilots of the Pave Hawk. The SEALs, Ketterman and Spaulding. That is blood on your hands."

"I've heard enough!" Marshall said. "You have until the count of three to throw yourself into the jet. One!" Marshall reached for the winch speed control.

"What guarantee do I have that you won't kill my family after I'm gone?"

"You don't have any. Two!"

"So why the fuck would I do it then?"

The jet engine seemed to scream even louder as Marshall's hand was on the winch control as he said, "so you don't have to watch them die. Three!"

Chapter 102

THE CART HOLDING PAXTON'S FAMILY JERKED FURTHER into the yellow death zone just as all the lights went out.

Paxton was stunned. It took a moment for him to realize what had happened. And it took another moment for his eyes to adjust to the blue glow provided by the jet's afterburner.

All the electric power to the hangar had been cut at once. In the blue glow, Paxton could see that the cart had stopped with the front two wheels in the yellow death zone, and his family still sat on top. The electric motor of the crane was stopped.

The jet engine continued to scream because it operated on its own internal power.

Marshall could no longer control the crane or the engine. He also could no longer communicate with Paxton. Once Marshall realized that he could no longer remotely control the action, he yanked his headphones off, tossed them next to his pistol, and headed for the door into the hangar on the side of

Paxton's family.

Paxton saw Marshall burst into the hangar and head toward the cart.

Son of a bitch is going to push them in!

Caution was no longer an option. Paxton swung the shotgun up and aimed at the blue-framed dark silhouette of pipes feeding the engine.

Blam!

Paxton nicked the fuel line.

Whoosh!

Flames sprayed outward and onto the engine.

The explosion knocked Paxton over and caused Marshall to lose his footing. He skidded on the concrete floor.

With the fuel line damaged but still intact, the engine continued to be fed fuel, but at an inconsistent rate. Instead of a smooth whine, it starting going *Wump Wump Wump.*

Paxton could feel the wind become choppy and slightly less powerful. The severed fuel line continued to feed the fire, which spilt out onto the concrete floor.

Marshall pushed to his feet and steadied himself. He shook his head to clear it, then he again moved toward the cart.

Paxton dropped his empty shotgun and ran to his left, toward the control booth.

Wump Wump Wump

The engine sounded bad—like it was going to destroy itself.

Marshall extended his arms as he approached the cart. Paxton was almost to the far wall where the control booth glass was when he suddenly turned right. He leapt across the yellow line into the danger zone.

Paxton took a few strides before the suction really grabbed hold of him. It felt like it was pulling his uniform off. The suction was jerky, in time with the engine's *Wump Wump*. Paxton continued to plow forward toward the other side at the same time the suction was pulling him toward the mouth of the engine. The combined forces set him on an angular path toward the cart, which was closer to the engine than he was.

Paxton could see in the light of the raging fire the evil look on Marshall's face as he bent over to push the back of the low cart. Paxton pushed with all his might with each stride. But it was like trying to run in a swimming pool. Or like trying to run across a raging river. The current was winning out. Paxton lost his footing. He saw Jill's face as he slid by the cart.

Paxton stabbed a hand out and caught the leeward corner of the cart. He didn't hang on, but it was enough to spin the cart counterclockwise ninety degrees.

The sudden rotation caught Marshall off guard, and he lost his balance as he tried to push the cart. The cart rolled toward the engine, instead of into the danger zone. The angled danger zone paint receded from it. The steel cable stopped it from rolling any further. Marshall stumbled and fell forward right into the danger zone.

Paxton slid along the yellow-painted concrete floor as the powerful engine sucked him toward its mouth. The test stand held the engine about five feet off the floor. As he got close to the mouth, the wheezing engine pulled Paxton off the floor.

Paxton reached out and grabbed onto one of the test stand

supports. He was upside down, with his feet level with the mouth of the engine, hanging on with everything he could, so he wouldn't be pulled in.

The smell of jet fuel was sickening and the hellish light from the fire reminded him of the inside of the Chinese embassy.

Wump Wump Wump.

What would happen first? Would he lose his grip and be sucked in? Or would the engine disintegrate and shred them all with flying steel? Or would they all simply roast in jet fuel-fed fire?

Paxton wasn't about to let any of that happen. He strained to pull himself down, out of the stream of the suction. If he could break the suction, he could get away and save his family.

His hands were sweating, and he feared they would simply slip off the metal handhold. His arms were trembling with the strain. The suction pulled the headphones right off, and the sound of the high-pitched scream of the engine was unbearable.

He reached down further with his other hand, grabbed another piece of metal and pulled.

Please God, give me strength.

Slowly, he moved down slightly. He was doing it. He was starting to pull himself out of the vortex. A little more and he might break free.

Just then something slammed into him like a truck.

Chapter 103

P**AXTON DIDN'T UNDERSTAND WHAT HAD HAPPENED AT** first. He was trying to pull himself free of the jet engine's suction, and he now found himself upside down pinned against the test stand by something. A body. Someone else.

He felt the other person paw at him and grab on. Paxton turned his head and saw in the orange glow of the fire that it was Marshall.

The man had lost his footing and had been sucked toward the engine just as he had. And now he was hanging onto Paxton for dear life.

Not only was he hanging on, he was trying to climb down Paxton. Down out of the pull of the suction. This strained Paxton's grip even more. Just as a drowning man will climb up on top of his rescuer, drowning the rescuer in the process, Marshall was climbing away from the mouth of the engine, pushing Paxton toward the mouth with each movement.

I've got to get him off me!

Paxton couldn't hold on for both of them. Marshall was not holding onto the test stand at all. He was just holding on to Paxton. Marshall was acting like a sail in the wind, and he was pulling Paxton off the test stand in the process.

Fuck fuck fuck.

Paxton tried to twist left and right to free himself from Marshall's grip. He almost succeeded, but it caused Marshall to wrap his arm around Paxton's neck so he could hang on better.

Now Paxton was being choked, too. He knew it wouldn't be long before he lost consciousness. And once that happened, they both would be sucked in.

Paxton's heart was beating out of his chest. He was trapped in this hellish reality. Not only was he about to suffer a gruesome death, but he would do so right in front of his family. Plus, without help, they would not be able to get away before the fire consumed them.

Paxton tried to reverse head-butt Marshall, but that only gave Marshall the opportunity to grip Paxton's neck tighter.

A little part of him just wanted to let go.

Wouldn't that be easier?

Just stop fighting and relax. Let whatever happens happen?

Fuck no,

Get a grip, Paxton! Never quit!

With new resolve, Paxton pulled down. His arms were burning as he pulled even harder.

He felt the grip of the suction loosening. That spurred him on. He reached out again and grabbed a handhold even closer to the ground. He pulled. Now only his feet and ankles were directly over the opening of the engine.

Reach, pull. Reach, pull.

His feet were now completely out of mouth of the engine.

Marshall tried to climb down even faster by grabbing Paxton's head. Paxton couldn't get a breath.

Reach, pull.

The suction became less and less. Plus Marshall was shielding him from it.

Paxton then realized Marshall wasn't trying to climb on top of him. He was trying to break Paxton's neck.

Son of a bitch.

Marshall adjusted his grip tighter and tried to twist Paxton's head.

Reach, pull.

Paxton wrapped his right arm around a steel bar as tight as he could. He reached up with his left hand and grabbed at Marshall's face. Paxton could feel Marshall's teeth chomping at his hand. Paxton pushed a thumb into Marshall's eye.

Marshall recoiled back, naturally loosening his grip on Paxton's neck. Then Paxton brought his knees up under him.

Wump Wump Wump.

The engine continued to gulp the smoke-filled air.

In one explosive move, Paxton flung Marshall up and off of him. Marshall tried to catch himself by reaching out to Paxton, but he was caught in the grip of the engine's suction. Marshall disappeared in a flash into the mouth of the jet.

The jet made a terrible sound as Paxton was sprayed with blood.

In an instant there was silence. The jet engine had choked on Marshall's body. Flames flared as the fuel that the engine had been burning was now burning up the engine.

Paxton collapsed to the floor. He pushed himself to his feet. He turned and ran over to his wife and children. He quickly untied them, and they climbed off the cart.

"Let's go!"

He picked up John, Jr., and Jill grabbed Megan. The four of them ran across the yellow paint toward the door Paxton had come in. They blasted through that door and the one behind it. They fell to the ground outside in the cool night air.

Chapter 104

PAXTON'S HEAD WAS POUNDING, AND THE RINGING IN HIS ears seemed to be inside his skull. But they were all outside the hangar and alive.

Paxton squeezed Jill. He could feel her tears on his neck.

He then picked up his daughter and held her close. She hugged her daddy. He picked up his son in his other arm, and all four of them hugged each other. Words would not come, but tears flowed.

They all stood there together outside Hangar #4. They didn't seem to know what to do next. Emotions had already been drained.

A shadow moved across Jill as a figure stepped in front of the streetlight. She was startled.

Paxton spun around, ready for action.

Upon seeing who it was, he relaxed. "Oh, it's you. Where the hell have you been?"

"What do you mean?" McMurphy asked.

"I called you on your Sat phone from the hotel room. I said for you to meet me over here right away. You took your sweet time getting here."

"I've been here, Pax."

Paxton looked at him in disbelief. He thought he could hear sirens in the background, but his ears hurt so bad he couldn't be sure.

"The control door was locked," McMurphy explained, "so I peeked in the other door. I was behind you and saw what was happening, so I immediately ran out and cut the power to the building."

"You…you did that?" Paxton asked.

"Yes, I did that."

"Thank you."

"And then I called the security police and the fire department. Not much else I could do under the circumstances."

Paxton nodded. "You did good."

"I wish I could have done more. Are you all okay?"

"I…I think so. Physically anyway…Jill meet McMurphy."

Jill stepped forward and hugged McMurphy. He didn't know what to do. So he hugged her back. "Thank you," Jill said through tears.

"And this is my son John and daughter Megan."

"You have a beautiful family."

"Thank you." Paxton extended his hand, and he and McMurphy shook.

"It's true," McMurphy said.

"No, I mean, thank you for everything."

McMurphy nodded. "Just doin' my job."

The sirens got closer.

"You know, Pax, I was wrong about you."

"How so?"

"You were the exact right person for this mission."

"And the irony is that Marshall was the one who picked me."

"Ironic indeed. Oh, and Pax, one more thing."

"What?"

"I'm sorry I caused you to lose your Kimber pistol at the start of this mission. That was one sweet gun."

Paxton shrugged. "No worries. I lost the pistol, but I gained a sweet Italian made shotgun."

McMurphy scowled.

"What?" Paxton asked.

McMurphy didn't say a word. He just pointed. Paxton turned to follow his point to watch flames pour out of the roof of Hangar #4. Then flames and smoke burst out of the door they had just exited.

"Shit," Paxton said. "I guess I lost the shotgun too."

Chapter 105

Paxton raised the wine glass, "To us."

"To us," Jill clinked glasses with Paxton and took a sip.

John could see the moon reflect in Jill's blue eyes. The red dress she wore brought out the strawberry in her hair.

"Mi Scusi, are you ready to order?" The waiter asked.

Paxton laughed. "No, sorry. We haven't even looked at the menu." He reached out and touched Jill's hand as he talked.

"More time? Si?"

"Grazie," Paxton replied. He was wearing the suit Jill had packed for him.

"I didn't know you spoke Italian," Jill laughed.

"I didn't know either." Paxton laughed. "Jill, look at this place." He indicated the port. Lights on boats and from the town reflected off the water.

"It's beautiful," Jill agreed.

"Nah, it's acceptable," Paxton said. "*You* are beautiful."

"Aw, thank you," Jill said smiling as she leaned in. Paxton's lips met hers.

They then both took another sip of wine. "This is just about perfect," Paxton said.

"Just about," Jill agreed. "I just wish the kids could be right here with us."

Paxton laughed. "I agree. But it's not like they are far away."

Jill and Paxton turned and looked at the next table over. John, Jr. sat in a booster seat and Megan in a high chair. Smith was attempting to entertain them. Smith was also wearing a suit. One purchased on base earlier that day.

"How are things, Octavious?" Paxton asked.

"Man, I'm so not ready for kids!"

The Paxtons laughed. And so did the rest of the PJs at the next table over.

Jill looked around. Even though she was at an Italian restaurant in Italy, she felt safe. Not only were all the PJs there to provide security, but John was there.

And that made all the difference.

Chapter 106

A MAN WITH A DARK COMPLEXION, WEARING GREEN fatigues sat behind a large desk in Takrit, Iraq. He fiddled with a solid gold pen. Two guards dragged a man in to the large room. The man's hands were bound behind him. He was wearing a tan shirt and blue jeans. His eyes were fixed on the floor.

"Your Excellency, here he is," one of the guards said.

"Yes," the man behind the desk said. "Look at me!"

The bound man looked up briefly, then his eyes dropped to the floor.

"What do you have to say for yourself?"

"I am sorry, Your Excellency."

"That is not good enough. Did you know that the device you brought me was a *fake*!"

"I did not know that, Your Excellency."

"How could you fail me like that?"

"I am not worthy, Your Excellency."

"No, you are not!" The man got up and paced around the room. "What am I to do now? Did you know I entrusted to you the last of my nerve gas, and you traded it for a fake device!"

"I am so sorry, Your Excellency."

"Now I don't have any nerve gas! What am I supposed to do? Lie? Pretend to the world that I still have it?"

"I don't know, Your Excellency."

"Enough with you. I should have never trusted you!" Then to the guards, "Execute him!"

"No!" The bound man cried.

The guards started dragging the man toward the door. "Stop!" His Excellency said, "One more question."

"Yes, Your Excellency."

"Who was it that tricked you into taking the fake device in exchange for my nerve gas?"

The bound man's eyes rolled around, as if he were thinking. "His name is John Paxton."

The man behind the desk screamed, "Not again! Allah save me from John Paxton!"

Chapter 107

SIX MONTHS LATER

Things had returned to normal, more or less, at the Paxton household. The kids were in bed. Paxton took a shower after a five-mile run. He toweled off and then secured the towel around his waist as he stepped into the bedroom.

Jill lay in bed wearing a nightgown and reading a magazine. Paxton leaned in and kissed her on the lips. It was so good to be home.

"Got good news today," Paxton said.

"Really? What?"

"I heard from Nikolic. His wife received a lung transplant last week and is doing great. She is expected to fully recover."

"That is great news."

Jill then grew silent.

"What?" Paxton asked.

"What makes people do evil things?"

"That, my dear, is a complex question."

"Like Marshall. What made him turn on his own country?"

"We probably will never know. The investigation revealed he was working for the Chinese. Reed was cleared."

"Why would he work for them?"

"The Chinese have a way of controlling people. They will plant something that will ruin someone. Then threaten to reveal that thing."

"Does that work?"

"More than you would think. People fear embarrassment sometimes more than death."

"Unbelievable."

"Agreed." Paxton continued, "This was quite a big deal. The president had to apologize to the Chinese for bombing their embassy. Can you believe that? They were stealing our technology, and we had to apologize to them. The official story is that the CIA used old maps when it ordered the bombing. Isn't that nuts?"

"It's all nuts."

"But at least it is over and we are together," Paxton said caressing her arm.

Before Jill could say anything else, the phone rang. Jill sat up and grabbed it off the nightstand.

Paxton leaned in and gently kissed the side of her neck as she spoke on the phone.

"Who, may I ask, is calling for him?" Jill asked. She sounded annoyed. She was silent for a moment, listening, then she covered the mouthpiece and said, "It's for you, John. It's General

Reed." Paxton didn't seem to be paying any attention to what she was saying. "He says he needs your help right away."

He climbed onto the bed next to her and kept giving her tiny kisses.

"What do I tell him?" Jill asked, still covering the mouthpiece.

Paxton allowed the towel to drop to the floor, turned his lips to her ear and whispered, "Tell him I'm not available."

Photo by AponteStudios.com

About the Author

Award-winning author Robert Capko lives in Central Florida. His pararescue thrillers Say Goodbye and The Long Road Home give a glimpse into the lives of and honor those Air Force special operators who save others and live by the creed, "These things we do, that others may live."

Robert is a college professor and a decorated veteran of the United States Air Force. He is a graduate of the University of Florida and Nova Southeastern University. He enjoys whitewater rafting, football and auto racing. He is currently working on his next thriller, which will feature an unconventional action hero.

He invites you to:
Write a review
Check out his website at: www.robertcapko.com
Join his fan page at: www.facebook.com/robertjcapkofanpage
Follow him on Twitter at: twitter.com/robertcapko